ESCAPEMENT

TIMOTHY POWELL

ESCAPEMENT

For Mom

CHAPTER
ONE

A S HE SAT and waited for his section to be called, Dalton Mallet continued to get lost in the letter that was held firmly in his hands. He
read every line, word by word, over and over, still not believing what he
was seeing. He had read these lines at least a hundred times but still
couldn't believe it was him that was selected. Right before he began to
read it again, an announcement came over the speaker.

"Now boarding, First Class."

Dalton neatly folded the letter, put it in an envelope, and placed it in
his jacket pocket. He grabbed his carry-on bag and proceeded to the desk,
where two attendants who were obviously faking their smiles were waiting.

"Excuse me?" Dalton asked. "Does this announcement mean anyone
flying First Class can board?"

"Yes, honey," the cute blonde one answered. "Go right in through the
terminal there and take your seat."

"Sorry, first time flying. I didn't know," Dalton exclaimed as he
presented his ticket and hung his head down. Dalton shuffled his feet
moving through the terminal, still not believing he was here. True, he
had never flown before. He hadn't even been to the airport in his
life. But the time had come to do so. Who turns down an all-expense-
paid trip?

When Dalton stepped onto the plane and presented his ticket, he was
directed to his seat, which looked nothing like what he saw in the movies.
What was I expecting? Dalton thought as he placed his carry-on bag into
the overhead compartment. After doing this, he sat down on the

plush, pleather seat and sighed heavily. Was he really here? Was he really going to go through with this? *Too late to turn back now,* Dalton thought to himself as he closed his eyes to relax.

"First time flying?" he heard off to his left, so he squinted his eyes and turned his head a bit to see if the question was meant for him.

An older woman, Dalton guessed to be in her 50's or 60's, was staring right at him. She was looking at him with a wry smile while sitting up in her seat as if she had known him from somewhere.

"Yes, ma'am," Dalton said. "Is it that obvious?"

"Yes, dear," the stranger said while patting his hand. "You see, you seem to have a death clutch on that armrest there and the business section hasn't even boarded yet. Relax, honey, planes fly all the time. Nice to meet you. I'm Susan."

"Dalton, Dalton Mallet," he said as he extended his hand to her. "This is all so new to me."

"Really? You've never flown before? How old are you, young man?" Susan asked as she shook his hand.

"I'm 29, well, 30 actually. I'll be 30 at the end of the month," Dalton said.

"And you've never flown?" Susan asked while shaking her head back and forth.

"No, ma'am," Dalton said. "Never really needed to 'til now I suppose. And to be honest, I would've driven. But this trip was already paid for."

"Well, there's nothing to it. Trips this length usually have a movie and a pretty decent meal to pass the time. I also heard if you talk sweet to the attendants, they'll make sure you don't run out of the good stuff," Susan said as she held up two airplane bottles of tequila.

As Dalton began to laugh, business class began to board. He was a bit more relaxed now and thankful that Susan was sitting close to him. Dalton always got along with older people and kids. He knew the flight was going to be about five-plus hours, so it was good that she was around to keep him company.

"So, you said this trip was paid for?" Susan started back again. "I don't mean to get in your business or nothin', but are you what they call a high-roller?"

"No, ma'am, not at all," Dalton said as he was still laughing a bit from the alcohol remark. "I actually won a contest, so to speak."

"A contest? To Las Vegas? They're always giving free trips to good people so they can take their money from 'em. Don't you get off this plane and give 'em all your money," Susan said.

"I'm not going to gamble, ma'am. It's more of a once in a lifetime opportunity," Dalton replied, still smiling.

"Well, now I'm a bit curious, young man. Once in a lifetime opportunity? In Las Vegas? I'm 62, getting older by the day, and I'm not sure I'd even approach that one," Susan said as she unscrewed her first of many tiny airplane bottles and took a sip.

"I'm not too sure I believe it either, Susan, but I've done what research I could and it checks out so far. Have you ever heard of Riker Industries?" Dalton asked.

Susan shook her head, not wanting to put down her liquor bottle for a response.

"Riker Industries is a company out of Las Vegas," Dalton said.

"No shit, son, that's where we're headed. I figured out that much," she said laughingly.

"Yes, ma'am. Apparently, they're a lot like Google. They have a big presence online and such. Basically, they ran a contest a year ago. Maybe you saw the commercials. They've been on all the time," Dalton said.

Susan finished up her tiny bottle and placed it beside her on her seat. She looked right at Dalton and asked, "The 'change your life' commercials?"

"Yes, ma'am," Dalton replied. "Those are the ones. Anyway, you see, all the commercials, ads, and stuff stated that someone could receive a life-changing event. They guaranteed your life would change as you knew it, forever, and that's it. No other information. Nothing.

Anyone that had bought and registered one of their televisions, computers, watches, or anything they sold would automatically be registered and entered into their life-changing event. They call it the Escapement."

"I do remember hearing about that. I watch a lot of court shows on television in the afternoons and those commercials are always on. Always saying they will change your life. I thought it was just a big conspiracy to buy everything they sold," Susan said as she twisted open another bottle.

"I did too until I received this letter ten days ago," Dalton said as he pulled the envelope out of his coat pocket.

Dalton pulled the letter out of the envelope and handed it to Susan. Before she took the letter from him, she twisted the top back on her drink and placed it beside the empty one. As she grabbed the letter, the attendants started their safety lecture for the passengers to hear before the captain was to tell everyone their destination and how high he would be flying.

"Pay attention to those ladies so you'll know what to do if we have an emergency, young man," Susan said. "I'll read this after they're done. I'd hate to be trying to explain to everyone how a seatbelt works and some old ass woman ruined it for me. How the hell would we ever get buckled in?"

When the attendants finished their little show and the captain addressed the masses, the plane began its trip down the runway and ulti-mately into the air.

"You are now leaving Raleigh, next stop, Las Vegas!" the captain said over the loudspeaker, which drew applause from the rear section of the plane.

Dalton grabbed onto the armrests as tight as he could when the plane took off. He was pretty certain he closed his eyes as well, but he couldn't know for sure.

"Dalton, son," he heard Susan say to him as the plane began to level off. "I sure hope you don't fart."

"What?" Dalton asked.

"The way you're clinching that armrest again. Your butthole is probably clenched so tight that if you pass gas, everyone will think you're whistlin' dixie!" Susan said.

Immediately, Dalton began to laugh and the tenseness was relieved. He thanked Susan for the laugh. She in turn thanked him and said she would read his letter after she put on her glasses.

While Susan was looking for her glasses, Dalton got the attention of one of the flight attendants and asked for a drink. She smiled and asked if he wanted a glass of wine or something a little stronger. He opted for stronger. Whiskey, neat.

The time it took to get his drink was about the same amount of time it took Susan to find her glasses.

"I can never find anything in this damn bag," Susan exclaimed as she scurried through the bag relentlessly in pursuit of her spectacles.

Dalton smiled at her as the flight attendant placed his drink on his seat-back tray. He thanked her and took a sip. It was exactly what he needed.

"Sweet shit on a Cheez-It, here they are," Susan exclaimed as she took out her glasses. "Now, let's read this letter."

Pin #4812

Dalton Mallet,

Congratulations are in order. You have won the opportunity to take place in our life-changing event, the Escapement. We cannot divulge what the aptly titled Escapement is at this moment, for you see, some legal matters have to be tended to first. However, trust me when I say this is well worth your time and effort. THIS WILL CHANGE YOUR LIFE FOREVER!

Keep in mind we are not forcing you to accept our offer. It's only that, an offer.

Enclosed is a first-class ticket with your name on it and your *flight information. Once you arrive at McCarran International Airport in Las Vegas on Monday, November 26, our driver will greet you and provide you with transportation to the Bellagio, where you will be staying in the Penthouse Suite. If you would like to gamble, take in some sites, or maybe enjoy the fountains at the Bellagio, please do so because I would like you to enjoy yourself before we talk business. As a matter of fact, a cashier's check for $500 is also enclosed for you to spend as you wish. Please consider this a gift for your stay. And no, you do not have to pay it back.*

Tuesday, November 27, we will have our driver pick you up at 9:30 a.m., Pacific Standard Time, and he will drive you to our offices so we can discuss the Escapement. Keep in mind, you can turn down this offer at any time. No questions asked. Tell us you aren't interested and we will fly you back, First Class, and act like this never happened. No harm, no foul. One thing though. You were chosen out of 3.6 billion people in the world. That's half of the world's population. We will not be holding another contest like this one, for reasons you will understand once we have our discussion. Therefore, if you turn this down, you nor anyone else will ever get this chance again. It's you, or no one. Take it or leave it.

You have a lot to think about, so I will leave you to it. Use the tickets. Let's talk. If you do not like what I have to say, no hard feelings. You can fly back home and resume your life just as you left it. But...this is Las Vegas. I'm betting what we have to say will make you think about things you have never thought about before. I'm betting you will need more time than what we give you to decide exactly how you want your life to change. I'm betting that your life WILL change forever.

I can't wait to meet you, Dalton.

Sincerely,

Jeffrey Riker
CEO Riker Industries

P.S. I'm also betting that you read this letter over and over, trying to figure out exactly what we are offering. You will never guess it, so you may as well come hear me out. See you soon!

Underneath the writing on the letter, Susan also noticed a note handwritten in blue ink. All it said was, 'I hope you are able to find what it is you've been missing...Love, B'

"That man, Mr. Riker, had some interesting things to say. And what in the world is an Escapement?" Susan asked as she folded the letter and handed it back to Dalton, who was watching her read every word.

"Yes, ma'am, he did, and I have no idea what an Escapement is," Dalton said, taking another sip of his drink.

"Well, young man, congratulations. Looks like you have a big decision ahead of you. A word of advice?" Susan asked.

"Absolutely," Dalton said.

"I know you've probably heard this so many times before, and perhaps from many people before you got on this flight, but I'm going to say it too. If it sounds too good to be true, it usually is," Susan said.

"Yes, ma'am, I've heard that so many times in the past couple of days, I probably say it in my sleep," Dalton said.

Susan shook her head at him and started again. "You didn't let me finish. If it sounds too good to be true, it usually is. However, that isn't always correct. Suspicion, cynicism and doubt that are inherent in this belief can and does keep people from taking advantage of excellent opportunities. Richard Carlson said that. I sat in one of his seminars one time and it opened my eyes. Why do you think I'm 60 and on a plane headed to Las Vegas?"

9

"Maybe you have family? Perhaps even a contest that you've won as well?" Dalton responded.

"Hell, no!" Susan exclaimed. "I'm going to Vegas to watch the Chippendales muscle men in their underwear. You only live once!"

As Dalton shook his head in laughter, Susan asked, "Dalton, I don't mean to pry, but if you don't mind, who's B?"

Dalton stopped laughing almost immediately and turned his head to look out the window. He picked up his glass and finished his whiskey. As he sat the glass down, he attempted to collect his thoughts before speaking, knowing that the words wouldn't come out the exact way he intended. Dalton tried anyway.

"She's the reason I didn't want to take this trip or this offer, but she's also the reason I'm here," Dalton said.

Susan sat back and let out a sigh before she spoke. "Oh," she said. "Well, if you would like to talk about it, I do believe we have the time. We also have alcohol available if we need it," she said, holding up two more tiny bottles of alcohol in-between her fingers.

"No, ma'am, I'm sure you wouldn't want to be bored to tears with the intricacies of my so-called disaster of a life," Dalton answered back politely.

"We all have a story, dear," Susan said. "Some stories have their good and bad parts, but it's what we do to get to the ending that matters. Every chapter of the story can change based on the choices that are made. I'm sure it isn't nearly as bad as you think it is."

"Perhaps it isn't," Dalton said, as he turned his head to stare back out the window.

Susan caught sight of this and realized it was a touchy subject.

"Dalton," she said. "Since you don't want to talk about it, can I talk to you about how excited I am to see chiseled gods of men with tuxedos around their penises?"

Susan began to ramble on about shirtless men and her excitement to see them; Dalton continued to listen and laugh along with her. This went on for several more minutes until the attendants decided it was time to begin the in-flight movie.

"I hope it's Magic Mike," Susan said, giggling.

"I hope not," Dalton replied. "You're going to see enough of that if and when we ever get to Las Vegas!"

"It will never be enough," Susan said.

The movie turned out to be a superhero movie, one Dalton had seen many times over. He was fairly certain Susan had never seen this type of movie before.

"Well, this isn't what I was in the mood for, but I'm sure someone's happy about it," Susan said. "I believe I'm going to try and sleep a bit. I probably need the rest. Never been a fan of the comic movies anyway. Maybe when I wake up, we can continue our conversation?"

"Of course," Dalton said. "Sleep well."

"Oh, I will," Susan responded. "Especially if that Channing Tatum character shows up in my dreams!"

Dalton shook his head and laughed. Susan was a nice person to talk to. He figured she was just as nice as anyone to enjoy his first plane ride with.

As an attendant walked by, Dalton asked for another drink. Once it was poured, he relaxed a bit in his seat. He grabbed the glass and began to look out of the window and sip. He reached for the letter and read it again, still not believing he was in a plane, headed toward Las Vegas to do who knows what. As he got to the end of the letter, he focused on the handwritten note written in blue. He rubbed over the note with his thumb as he sipped his drink. He read the words on paper again out loud, but not above a whisper.

"I hope you are able to find what it is you've been missing...Love, B," Dalton read.

"I hope I do too...God, I miss you," he said to himself as he lowered his head and decided to finish his drink.

CHAPTER
TWO

D ALTON DECIDED TO watch the movie again like he had done many times before. He always enjoyed these types of movies. He liked comic books and watching what he read as a boy come to life on the big screen. Dalton didn't care if the movies weren't liked by the masses, he enjoyed them all for what they were, an escape from reality. He could be a kid again and see his heroes come to life.

As the movie was coming to a close, one of the attendants came by with the in-flight meals. Dalton removed his headphones and thanked the attendant as she placed the meal on his seat-back tray. It looked like chicken on the plate, but a very tiny portion. There were also some green beans and a small serving of potatoes with a roll. The attendant asked Dalton if he would like another drink. He declined and requested a bottle of water. She quickly removed one from the side compartment of her little device she was using to distribute the food, smiled, and moved on to the next person.

As Dalton began to cut into what looked like chicken, he heard a familiar voice beside him.

"I bet they serve better meals in prison," Susan said.

Dalton laughed and welcomed Susan back from her sleep.

"If I knew this is what we were being served, I would've kept sleeping. This is First Class; I think I deserve a steak!" Susan said.

"A steak would've been nice. I guess this is an attempt to hold us over 'til we get to Vegas," Dalton said.

"Tastes like shit," Susan said, still eating it nonetheless.

Dalton began to eat and realized that Susan wasn't that far off, but anything was better than nothing.

While eating their meals, Dalton and Susan spoke a little more.

"So, Mr. Mallet," Susan said. "What is it you do for a living? I figure if we're going to break this hard-ass bread together, we may as well get to know each other a little better."

"Well," Dalton said. "I guess you could say I'm a handyman of sorts. I do a little bit of everything. Plumbing, electrical, small construction; a jack of all trades, but a master of none, so to speak."

"Is that right?" Susan asked. "It's good to be skilled in many different areas. Always marketable."

"Yes, ma'am," Dalton said. "I do what I can to make a little bit of money. It doesn't make me rich by any means, but I can make my own schedule. If I need more money, I can help a contractor or something. It's not too bad, I guess."

"No, it really isn't," Susan said. "Could actually be a lot worse!"

"Yes, ma'am, it could," Dalton replied. "At least I have a job and I'm pretty good at what I do. I try to make an honest living."

"That is truly good, young man. Many people today don't believe in working, or working hard for that matter," Susan said. "Back when I was younger, I worked hard for everything I got. I earned what little I had, but it was worth it."

"I worked on a tobacco farm when I was younger," Dalton responded. "From when I was 14 until I was 18. Hard work."

"I'm sure it was," Susan said. "I never worked on a farm or anything, but I was never given a handout. I would babysit every once in a while but stayed focused on school mostly. Loved learning new things. Worked all kinds of odd jobs paying my way through school when I got older. My father passed when I was 13 and mom did all she could to help, but it was tough on her being a single parent of two kids."

"I'm sure it was," Dalton said. "I'm sorry you lost your father at such a tough age."

"Oh, it's okay, son," Susan said. "After dad passed, I kept myself busy as much as possible. Without boring you too much, life happened. Had some ups and downs, but I'm happy where I am right now."

"Well, that's a good thing," Dalton said.

"Yes, it is," Susan said. "I have no regrets. I enjoy traveling and meeting new people, especially good people. People like you, Dalton."

"Thank you, ma'am," Dalton said. "I'm nothing special."

"Oh, but you are," Susan said. "You're a contest winner!"

Dalton smiled at her remark. Susan seemed very genuine to him and he was happy to have met her. He enjoyed their conversation. Susan was easy to talk to and was the type of person that when you meet them, you feel like you have known them all your life.

"So, Susan," Dalton said. "Do you have any children? A special man in your life?"

"Are you hitting on me, Dalton?" Susan asked with a grin. "I've never found a man that could occupy my time, let alone tolerate for years on end. Since there's no man, there's no kids. I've found with what I do, it's best that I navigate this crazy life alone. But how about you, Dalton? Do you have any children?"

"No, ma'am, I don't," Dalton said. "Thankfully after my divorce, the only thing that needed to be split up was our movie collection and who got to keep the dog."

"I'm sorry," Susan said. "So, you were married, huh?"

"Yes, ma'am, I was," Dalton said. "For about three years. Just couldn't make it work. I'm sure I was to blame for a lot of it, but sometimes things aren't meant to be."

"Was this recent?" Susan asked.

"Oh, no," Dalton said. "It was about six years ago. I can't honestly tell you what she's doing now or anything. We had our final words with each other and that was that."

"I see," Susan said. "I've heard marriage is hard work. It certainly isn't always sunshine and rainbows."

"No, ma'am, it sure isn't," Dalton said.

"You ever think you'll get married again?" Susan asked.

Dalton took a deep breath and responded as honest as he could. "I really don't know. I've dated a bit here and there, and I may have even been close to considering it, but to be honest, I'm not sure."

"Fair enough," Susan replied as she finished up her meal. "This meal was absolutely horrible. I wouldn't feed it to my dog."

Dalton laughed hearing Susan talk about her food. He tried to finish up what he could eat as he noticed the attendant coming by to collect the trays from everyone. While he was trying to finish, Susan touched him on the arm.

"I think it's time to visit the ladies' room," Susan said.

Susan got up from her seat, avoided the flight attendant and disappeared behind the curtain where the bathroom was located.

"Are we all done here?" the flight attendant asked Dalton as she was forcing the last bite down.

"Yes, ma'am, I believe I am," Dalton said.

"Great!" the flight attendant said. "We hope the meal was to your satisfaction."

"It was fine," Dalton said, lying through his teeth. *Little white lies that make people feel better never hurt anything*, he thought. "I think the woman beside me is finished too if you would like to take her tray as well."

"I hope she enjoyed her meal also," the flight attendant responded. "Thank you!"

"I'm sure she did," Dalton said with a smirk.

As the flight attendant took everything and made her way to help the other passengers, Dalton took another sip of his water. He thought to himself, *I wonder how much longer this flight is?* Dalton looked at his watch and saw they had been in the air for a few hours now. *Of course, we have. The movie was about two hours.* Dalton looked out the window into the clouds and wondered again about the letter. *What could this Escape-*

ment be? How in the world, out of all the people on this earth, did I get picked? I wonder what Las Vegas is like? I bet she would've enjoyed being here...

"Ladies and Gentleman, this is your captain speaking. We will be experiencing a bit of turbulence in the next few minutes. Seems to be a little storm we have to fly through. Nothing to be concerned over. Please fasten your seatbelts and try to sit back and relax. We will be through this little band soon enough."

Dalton, who was lost in his thoughts, was immediately brought back to reality once the captain began to speak. He had heard of turbulence, but only knew what he had read. He compared it to being on a bumpy dirt road back home in North Carolina while your car's suspension was about ten years old. He wasn't far off.

The first little bump came and Dalton was quick to grab the armrests again. He made sure his seatbelt was buckled and pushed himself deeper into the seat. *Humans aren't meant to fly,* Dalton thought as the second bit of turbulence hit. As the plane shook, he noticed that Susan had not come back from the bathroom yet. *I really hope she's not sitting on the toilet while all this is happening.* He turned his head to look at the clouds, but the once clear blue sky had turned to a darker shade of gray. *If there is anyone up there listening to me, please let this plane make it through the storm,* Dalton thought to himself.

Dalton was still in his thoughts when the next wave of turbulence hit. This time was much rougher than before. He was thankful that the seat was bolted down. The shaking and movement scared him. The first wave wasn't that bad. This time, reality set in. He was in a pressurized vessel going 575 mph and the only exit was a 35,000 ft. drop. He didn't like his odds. The plane shook again, harder this time. *If I didn't have to go to the bathroom before, I do now, and where is Susan?* Dalton thought.

"Ladies and Gentleman, this is your captain again. We are almost through the roughest part of this little storm. Sit back and remain calm. We are going to get through this."

Easy for you to say, you've been through this before, Dalton thought. He wanted to unbuckle his seatbelt and check on Susan. He also wanted to sit right where he was and hold on tight. While he was debating what to do, one of the attendants walked right by him.

"Excuse me, ma'am?" Dalton said.

The flight attendant stopped and grabbed onto his seat to keep her balance as the plane shook again. "Yes, sir, how can I help you?"

"My friend went to the bathroom and she isn't back yet," Dalton said. "I was wondering if I could go up there and see if she's okay?"

"I'm sure she's fine, sir," the attendant said. "I'm actually headed that way and can check on her for you if you would like."

"That would be great," Dalton said. "Thank you."

"No problem at all," the flight attendant said. "Make sure you stay seated and that seatbelt stays fastened."

"Yes, ma'am," Dalton said. "Be careful walking that way, all this shaking is pretty scary."

"This must be your first flight," the attendant said. "This is nothing. Been through much worse. Sit tight. It will be smooth skies soon enough."

There was only one more rough bit of turbulence before things got back to being calm. What seemed like a lifetime to Dalton had really only been five minutes, he realized as he looked at his watch. Over the intercom, the captain spoke again.

"Ladies and Gentleman, we've made it through the storm. You may now unbuckle your seatbelts and relax. Seems to be smooth skies ahead for the remainder of our trip together. We will be landing before you know it."

Dalton released his grip on his armrest and unbuckled his seatbelt. He began to get up and go check on Susan when he saw her stumble back through the curtain. It seemed that she had probably had one too many to drink.

"Thank you, thank you. No autographs, please," Susan said. "Should've known better than to drink so much, I suppose."

"Are you okay?" Dalton asked.

"Oh, I'm fine," Susan said. "I thought I'd slept off what I drank. Apparently, I didn't. As soon as I sat down on the commode, I knew I was going to have a rough time getting up. Then the plane started shaking and shit. I didn't stand a chance. At that point, a nice lady knocked on the door and asked me to return to my seat and I told her I would if I could!"

Dalton laughed. Susan continued.

"She asked if I needed help and I told her I was fine. Once the damn plane stopped shaking so much, I was able to compose myself and make it back here to you, safe and sound."

"Well, I'm glad you did," Dalton said.

"It sure would've been a mess if my fat ass would've fell in the aisle," Susan said.

Dalton and Susan both laughed as the plane continued to Las Vegas.

"Susan, are you sure you're okay?" Dalton asked.

"Yes, dear, I'm fine," Susan said. "Don't you go on worrying about me. You have plenty of other things to think about. For instance, what do you think that big event is that you're going to find out about soon? And don't tell me you haven't thought about it!"

"Oh, I've thought about it, but I don't know," Dalton said. "Maybe it's a lot of money. Maybe it's a job opportunity. I try to think about what really changes people's lives. Things like winning the lottery could do it. Moving somewhere would too. I really don't know."

"Well, I don't either," Susan said. "But it's fun to sit and think about. What if they give you a million dollars?"

"That sure would be nice," Dalton said. "But if it were a money prize, I'm sure they would've announced that. People do that all the time."

"Well, maybe this Riker fella' don't like all the attention that comes with that," Susan said.

"If he didn't like all the attention, why the commercials and the year-long plugs about this Escapement?" Dalton asked.

"Beats the hell out of me," Susan said. "You'll surely find out soon, though."

"Not soon enough!" Dalton said.

They both smiled at this statement.

"Dalton," Susan said. "I hate to cut our conversation short again, but I believe I'm going to lean my seat back and try to sleep off some of this alcohol. I'm still a bit woozy from the bathroom incident and probably need to rest."

"You know, a nap isn't a bad idea," Dalton said. "All that turbulence took something out of me, too."

"That sounds like a plan," Susan said. "There's nothing like a good nap. And who knows, maybe when you wake up, I'll have a surprise for you."

"A surprise?" Dalton asked. "What kind of surprise?"

"Don't you worry about that," Susan said. "Get some rest. I'm going to do the same."

Susan patted Dalton on the hand and turned away from him. Dalton smiled and leaned his seat back as far as it would go. He closed his eyes and hoped that sleep would come soon, and it did. If he would've known what was going to happen when he woke up, he probably would've never fallen asleep.

CHAPTER
THREE

T HE SUN HAD already been out for a couple of hours in beautiful Las
Vegas when Carl Gilbert jumped up quickly from his slumber.

"Shit! I'm late!" he said while glancing at his clock.

Carl jumped up from his bed, forgetting about drinking himself to
sleep the previous night, and knocked over the half-full bottle of vodka
that sat on his nightstand.

"Shit!"

As the bottle fell to the hardwood floor, it shattered into a thousand
tiny little pieces.

"Great! Guess I can cut my damn foot off before I get in the shower!
Damn! I'm so late!"

Carl tip-toed as fast as he could to his bathroom. He turned on the
shower and stared at himself in the mirror. *What am I doing with my life?*
Carl thought as he rubbed his eyes and his hands through his hair. He
reached above the sink and grabbed a washcloth and towel. He threw the
towel down on the floor and stepped into the shower.

"Hot! Hot!" Carl cried as the water hit his skin. He quickly reached
for the shower handle and turned it more toward the cold setting.

"Ah, that's better," Carl said as he pulled the shower curtain closed.

Carl knew he didn't have a lot of time to enjoy his shower, plus he
needed coffee and aspirin as soon as humanly possible. He was supposed
to be at work at 9:30 a.m. He knew from looking at his clock before
jumping in the shower it was already five after nine. He was never late.
This type of thing didn't happen to him. *Why of all days is it happening
now?*

Carl didn't stay in the shower long, maybe three- or four minutes tops. Long enough to wash the smell of the vodka and last night's smoky atmosphere from his nostrils, all while taking a quick piss to save time. He stopped the water and pulled the shower curtain back, again, seeing himself in the mirror. He had gained a good thirty pounds in the past several months. He had been drinking more, and to him, it was starting to show. He noticed he needed to shave, but that would have to wait until tomorrow. Carl tried to keep his beard trimmed, but the past few days he had overlooked it. He bent over and took the towel off the floor and began to dry off.

Once dry, he threw the towel back into the shower and ran into his bedroom. *At least I put out my clothes before I went to bed.* He grabbed his boxer briefs and put them on quickly, then threw on his button-up, plain white dress shirt. Once he buttoned it, he put on his black dress pants, socks, and shoes. He grabbed his tie and threw it around his neck, not tying it, before going back into the bathroom to run a comb through his hair.

"9:14, damn, damn, damn…Good enough!" Carl said to his reflection in the mirror.

Carl rushed out of the bathroom and grabbed his suit coat. The broken glass on the floor would have to wait until he got home. He needed to go, and he needed to go now. Carl jogged out of his bedroom, down the stairs of his townhome and into the main room where his keys hung on the hook by the door. He grabbed the keys, opened the door, and stepped out quickly, closing the door behind him. Once he locked the door, Carl made his way to the black company car he had parked crooked in the driveway the night before. He wanted to jump on the hood and slide to the driver's side, but he realized he was already late enough, no need to critically injure himself and lose the day altogether. Once Carl got to the driver's side door and unlocked it, he remembered something that he had forgotten in his rush to get to this point.

"My damn badge!" Carl said out loud.

Carl ran back into the house. Lying on the coffee table, right where he had taken it off the night before, was his badge. Carl Gilbert, Riker Industries. Carl grabbed the badge while glancing at the clock above his television. 9:19 a.m. After a deep breath, Carl was off again.

When Carl turned on the engine, the radio knocked him backward.

"Do you think you could hear it last night, Carl?" he said to himself while turning the volume all the way down. He put the sedan in reverse, whipped it into the road, and thought, *I really hope the coffee is hot and someone has some aspirin when I get there.* Once the car was in drive, Carl prayed that the local law enforcement wasn't going to be setting up any speed traps today. If they were, he would be a lot later than he was already.

There wasn't much to look at on the way to Riker Industries. Mostly desert. Mountains were in the background and he could see the beauty in it on most days. Today, however, they were a blur in the window. Mr. Riker had told him specifically to be there this morning at 9:30 a.m. sharp. The clock on the radio read 9:23, and he was still fifteen minutes away.

"I guess I better call them and let them know I'm en route," Carl said aloud. "Where is my...damn!"

Carl shook his head and wondered whether or not he should turn around. Even if he did, would he know where to look? Of all days, why did he have to leave his phone at home today?

"Screw it," Carl said aloud as he pressed down on the gas pedal a bit harder than usual and sped his way toward Riker Industries.

Luckily for Carl, traffic wasn't bad for a Monday. There also weren't any cops on the stretch of pavement from his driveway to the gates at Riker Industries (or at least none he saw). As Carl's sedan pulled into the security check at Entrance A, the clock read 9:33 a.m.

"Nice to see you made it to work today, Carl," said the scrawny security officer manning the front gate.

"Suck it, Larry," Carl said. "I'm late and don't need your shit this morning. Let me through the damn gate."

"Now, Carl," Larry said. "I wouldn't be doing my due diligence if I didn't ask for your credentials, now would I? You see, you have to show your ID badge for me to grant you access in here. We can't just let anyone in this place, you know?"

And you can't just have any foot up your ass either, can you, you prick? Carl thought to himself as he pulled out his ID badge and handed it to Larry. "Is this satisfactory, captain? Let me through, Larry. I'm late!"

"Well, now, with all the technology these days, who's to say this wasn't made at home?" Larry asked with a smile. "You see, the Carl Gilbert we all know around here is always on time. Are you an imposter, sir? Do we need to call in for a strip search?"

"Larry, I don't have time for your shit," Carl said. "Mr. Riker told me to be in his office at 9:30 sharp. It's 9:35 right now. Do I need to inform Mr. Riker that the reason I'm late is because his top-notch security staff at Entrance A, mainly Larry the Sentinel, was dead set on cracking jokes and trying to be a damn comedian? I'm sure that'll sit well, Larry. I've been here twenty-four damn years and have seen pieces of shit better than you fired for a whole lot less. See that badge in your hand, Larry. It's yellow. How many other people you see come through here have yellow-level clearance? How many, Larry?!"

"Carl, I was only..." Larry began.

"You were only what, Larry?" Carl asked. "I don't have time for this shit! If I wasn't late, sure, the funny banter and back and forth would be fun, hell, we do it most of the time. You're a good guy, Larry, but today is not the day. I haven't had coffee, I have a headache, I'm late, and you are playing 'God of the Gate'! Now give me my badge, press your little button, and let me through this damn checkpoint!"

Larry handed Carl his badge and could not press the button to raise the boom gate fast enough.

"Asshole," Larry said as Carl quickly drove through the boom gate and made his way to his space outside of Riker Industries.

It was 9:40 a.m. when Carl pulled his sedan into his regular parking space. The good news was he knew when he swiped in, there was no secretary or front desk personnel to speak to. One single elevator would take him to the top floor where Mr. Riker's office was located. The bad news, however, is that he was ten minutes late, so far. He knew Mr. Riker trusted him, that's why he was asked to this meeting today. He didn't know what it was all about, but he was pretty sure it had something to do with their contest winner coming into town.

Carl got out his sedan in a hurry, shut the door, and made his way to the office. He pushed the double doors open with both hands and hit the 'up' button on the elevator. It opened immediately. He stepped in and pressed the button that would take him to the top floor where he would have to explain his tardiness and hopefully, still be a part of the meeting that started twelve minutes ago.

As the doors to the elevator closed, Carl closed his eyes and took several deep breaths. He made sure his shirt was tucked in and tied his tie into a tight knot. He brushed off his shoulders and looked at his reflection in the elevator doors. He looked down and sighed.

"Great. This shit keeps getting better and better," Carl said, as he noticed he was wearing two different shoes.

As the elevator came to a stop and both doors slid open, Carl stepped out and walked directly to Cindy Porter's giant desk. Cindy was Mr. Riker's personal secretary, and all business, big or small, went through her first.

"Good morning, Cindy," Carl said.

"Carl!" Cindy cried. "Carl, are you okay? I've been trying to call you for the past twenty minutes! You're always here and never late! I was so worried!"

"I'm okay, Cindy. I was halfway here when I realized I didn't have my phone, and I didn't want to keep Mr. Riker waiting. I'm sure he's upset enough at the fact that I'm late as it is," Carl said.

"Nonsense!" Cindy said. "You know that Mr. Riker is a reasonable man. If he has a problem with you being late one time during your tenure here, he can take it up with me! Besides, he told me to tell you to wait right here until he calls for you, anyway. He had a phone call to take and said it could be a while. He told me to apologize to you for making you wait."

"Well, son of a bitch. How 'bout that?" Carl said.

"Now, you can go to your office or have a seat over there, I don't care which one. You know I'll call you when he's available," Cindy said.

"Thank you, Cindy," Carl said. "I do believe I need to get some coffee in me and a few aspirin. Maybe I can do that before he gets off the phone."

Cindy smiled and pointed to the table beside the wall. "There's a fresh pot right over there and I think I have some Aleve in my purse. Are they okay?"

"More than okay," Carl said. "Thank you again, Cindy."

Cindy reached in her purse, found her bottle of Aleve and shook two out to give to Carl. He thanked her again and threw them in his mouth. He had them swallowed before he ever made it over to the coffee pot. He grabbed the coffee pot and a Styrofoam cup that sat in the corner and poured. Once he sat the pot back down, he walked with his cup to the nearest chair, sat down and began to sip his coffee.

After five minutes and a half cup of coffee, he heard the phone ring at Cindy's desk. He turned his attention to her as she threw up her hand and motioned for him to come over. Carl drank one more sip of coffee before throwing it in the wastebasket. He walked to the desk and waited patiently for Cindy to hang up.

"Mr. Riker is ready to see you, Carl," Cindy said, placing the phone back onto the receiver.

"Thank you again, Cindy," Carl said. "Can I ask you something before I go in there?"

"I'm already married, Carl," Cindy said smiling.

"I know you are, Cindy. Jack is a lucky man," Carl said. "But do you know what this meeting's all about?"

"Darn right! Jack is lucky. Best decision he ever made in his life!"

Cindy said with a laugh. "Sorry, Carl, I don't. All he told me is who he was meeting with today and not to let anyone interrupt. I'm pretty sure it has to do with that guy coming in from North Carolina, though. You know, the one that won his little contest, whatever that is."

"You mean you don't even know what this contest is about? He tells you everything," Carl said.

"Apparently not," Cindy said. "If he did, I would know. Maybe if you get your ass in there, he'll tell you. Now get to your meeting, Carl."

Carl smiled at Cindy and started walking toward Mr. Riker's office. It was at the end of a short hallway and took up a big portion of the space on that floor. He had met with Mr. Riker many times, but never in his office, one on one. It was either in the boardroom, in passing, or in the elevator leaving or arriving at work. When Carl got to Mr. Riker's door, he raised his hand to knock. As he did, the door opened.

"Come in, come in," Jeffrey Riker said, surprising Carl. "We have quite a bit to discuss, my friend."

CHAPTER
FOUR

JEFFREY RIKER WAS an intimidating presence. He graduated high school when he was 14 and graduated from MIT at 17. Mr. Riker has countless charitable organizations and was on Forbes top ten list of the richest people in America for the past eight years. He started Riker Industries from the ground up and it is now the leading source in America for robotics, technological research, electronics, and internet technology. He did not want to overtake Google, instead, he worked alongside their company and changed the game for how the internet performs and how search engines operate. Jeffrey Riker was also voted 'Time's Man of the Year' three years ago for his work with climate change and his online presence alone. Everyone knew that this man was a genius, and he didn't seem to have any enemies or negative attributes against him. Mr. Riker was well loved by everyone inside and outside of his company. He believed in hard work and treating people the way you would want to be treated. This golden rule had served him well for the 57 years he had been on this Earth and if he was lucky enough to live another 57, he would follow the same rule. He loved doing things for people and people respected him for doing so. Carl especially.

"Nice to see you, Mr. Riker," Carl said as he walked through the door.
"Carl, my good man," Jeffrey Riker said, using his hand to hit Carl's shoulder a few times. "How long has it been since you and I sat in a room and talked, just the two of us?"

"I honestly don't know if we ever have," Carl said.

"Please, have a seat, Carl. Can I get you anything to drink? Coffee? Juice?" Mr. Riker asked.

"I actually had a cup of coffee outside while I spoke with Cindy," Carl said.

"Well, I'm going to get you another if that's okay? When you're drinking coffee, it's always nice to have someone to drink it with. Besides, the world's most important conversations are made around either a cup of coffee or rounds of beer and shots. Too early for the latter though, right?" Mr. Riker asked.

"I guess it is, Mr. Riker. Coffee will be fine. Black, please," Carl said.

"Done!" Mr. Riker said.

Carl watched Mr. Riker go to his desk and press a button on his phone.

"Cindy, please bring two cups of coffee. Thank you," Mr. Riker said.

Carl admired the size and scope of the office while he was standing. He walked over to the giant glass window that looked out over the mountains surrounding Las Vegas and the city itself. The view was breathtaking.

"Great view, isn't it?" Mr. Riker asked.

"It sure is," Carl said.

"Why don't you come sit down, Carl. Cindy will be in here soon with the coffee and we can get down to business," Mr. Riker said.

Carl turned from the window and directed his attention to Mr. Riker, who motioned for Carl to sit down on the black, leather couch against the wall by the entry door to his office. Carl sat down and continued to take in how nice this office was. Not only was there a view, but the furniture was fantastic as well. From where he was sitting, he could look to his left and see the big-screen television mounted on the wall, with a door to the right of it. Carl didn't know what was behind the door, but on the television, the news was playing and stocks were streaming across the bottom of the screen. Directly ahead of him, besides the view, was a very nice glass table and another black, leather sofa, which Mr. Riker had made himself comfortable on. To his right was Mr. Riker's desk, which had two very nice leather chairs facing the front of the desk, and his personal computer sitting on top of it. The computer consisted of three monitors. Carl knew Mr. Riker practically lived in his office and was always on the cutting edge of technology, so he had probably built the computer himself. Carl's attention was taken from him by two knocks on the door to his right.

"Come in, Cindy," Mr. Riker said.

Cindy opened the door and placed two cups of coffee on the table. Mr. Riker thanked her and she disappeared as quickly as she arrived. Carl watched Mr. Riker pick up his cup and take a sip, followed by some lip-smacking that Carl could only attest to meaning the coffee was up to his standards. He sat the cup back down and leaned back into the sofa, crossing one leg over the other, before he began to speak.

"Let's get down to business, Carl," Mr. Riker said. "You've been with me for a long time. Twenty-four years if I'm not mistaken. You are a very loyal and respected employee. Before we start, I want you to know that I appreciate all you do here for me and my company."

"Thank you, sir," Carl said. "I do what I can. I enjoy being a part of your company, and hope to be here for as long as you'll let me."

"Well, before we go any farther, please know that your job is not in jeopardy. I know the past few months have been rougher than usual, but I wanted to make sure you know that I appreciate all you do for me and I truly hope things are getting better," Mr. Riker said.

"Thank you," Carl said. "I appreciate you and the company working with me, and each day gets a little better. Not easier, but better."

"Understandable," Mr. Riker said. "Just know that we are always here if you need anything, Carl. Now, all that aside, we have a few matters to discuss."

"Yes, sir," Carl said as he reached for and sipped on his cup of coffee.

"Carl, I need you to focus all of your attention on a new assignment I have for you. I know that you work hard at your job for me, but this is like a promotion of sorts," Mr. Riker said. "I've not made anyone else aware of this, not even Cindy, because I wanted to talk to you first. Are you familiar with our Escapement promotions?"

"I am," Carl said. "I have seen the commercials and such, but I really don't know all the details."

"No one does, Carl," Mr. Riker said. "No one but me, and maybe five other people. When I tell you and the people around the world that it's truly life-changing, I'm not exaggerating."

Mr. Riker grabbed his cup of coffee and continued to sip on it.

"Well, that's great, sir. What is it?" Carl asked.

Mr. Riker smiled as he sipped on his coffee and heard the question come from Carl's lips. Mr. Riker placed his coffee back on the table and leaned forward to answer Carl.

"I can't tell you. Not yet," Mr. Riker said. "But if you accept the position I'm about to offer, you will find out before anyone else will."

"I see," Carl said. "What's the position?"

"Carl," Mr. Riker began. "We have a winner for this event. The world knows the event is closed, but they have no idea who has won. Only a few people that work here are actually privy to the fact that our winner is coming into town. I will not share it with the world either unless our winner wants me to. Through our databases of customers who have bought our products and registered them, and a random generator of those people around the world, the name that was chosen was Dalton Mallet. All I can tell you about him, for now, is that he bought a television and a computer that we manufacture. He registered both of them and his name was selected. He is actually from America. North Carolina, to be exact. If he accepted our offer, his flight will be landing at McCarran today around noon. What I'd like you to do, Carl, is pick him up, take him to the Bellagio or anywhere else he would like to go, and bring him here to meet me tomorrow by 10 a.m."

"So, you want me to pick up a guy, babysit him for the night, and bring him back here tomorrow?" Carl asked. "That's the promotion?"

"This is not a babysitting job," Mr. Riker said. "Carl, I trust you. I know you'll see to it that Mr. Mallet is taken care of and treated properly. I know you will do the job right. I also know you are thinking anyone can do this job, why me? Well, Carl, you have been a model employee for a long time. I have known you and Cindy the longest, and she needs to be here to run the day-to-day operations with me. Other analysts will be taking over your current job while you are taking care of this. Think of it as time out of the office. The promotion is not this, per se, Carl. It's after this. If you can take care of this for me, I want you working directly under me. Your record speaks for itself. You're a smart man. You will have your own team and answer to no one but me on special projects your group is assigned. The team's first order of business will be helping me deal with the aftermath of our Escapement if Mr. Mallet chooses what I think he will."

With this, Carl's mouth opened and hung agape. He sat back in his chair and stared back at Mr. Riker in disbelief.

"You're going to give me my own team?" Carl asked. "And we'll only be doing projects that you directly ask us to do? How can I say no to that?"

"Hopefully, you won't," Mr. Riker said. "The media frenzy and storm we could have after the Escapement is going to be crazy. If all things go as planned, the world as you know it will change overnight. Mr. Mallet's world will be forever changed if he chooses for it to be."

"Mr. Riker," Carl said. "I don't mind picking this guy up and dropping him off. I don't mind hanging out with the guy. I don't even mind bringing him back here. What does concern me, however, is all the secrecy. If I'm going to get this promotion and help with this so-called media frenzy and world-changing stuff, shouldn't I know what it is?"

"Yes, you should, and you will," Mr. Riker said. "But not right now. You will find out at the same time Mr. Mallet does. I trust you, but I wouldn't want you ruining the surprise for him before Tuesday by accident."

"Is anything about the Escapement illegal?" Carl asked.

Mr. Riker began to laugh. He stood up and walked over to his desk and rested against it.

"I don't know, Carl," Mr. Riker said.

"You don't know?" Carl asked. "Mr. Riker, you know everything. You analyze every situation before you do anything and that's what makes you a great boss and leader. How do you not know if something's illegal or not? How am I supposed to accept a job that I may be questioned about without knowing the legalities of it?"

"I understand your concern," Mr. Riker said. "I will happily answer that question, but I'm going to need to know if you'll accept this position first. I'm going to need you to trust me."

"Can I have time to think about this?" Carl asked. "I really don't know how to answer without knowing what's going on."

"If we would've spoken yesterday, that would've been possible," Mr. Riker said. "But with Mr. Mallet landing shortly, I'm afraid time is of the essence. Can you trust me, Carl?"

Carl got up from his seat and walked to the window of the office. He placed his hand on the wall and leaned toward the glass, looking out over the city of Las Vegas. He knew in his heart that he trusted Mr. Riker. Mr. Riker had provided him a stable job and income for twenty-four years. Mr. Riker was a great boss and leader. Carl also knew that the vagueness of his answers and the question of legality made him question the whole thing. If Mr. Riker would just tell him what was going on, he could use all the information and make a sound decision, but he knew that wasn't going to happen.

"Mr. Riker," Carl said. "This promotion, how much does it pay?"

"Well, how about we double what you're making now," Mr. Riker said without hesitation.

Carl turned from the window and faced Mr. Riker.

"Double?" Carl asked.

"Double," Mr. Riker said.

Carl walked over to the plush, leather chair sitting in front of

Mr. Riker's desk and sat down. He looked up at Mr. Riker who was still resting on the edge of his desk.

"Mr. Riker, I trust you. You're a good man, and I'm sure you have your reasons for keeping this event quiet. I do have my reservations, but you haven't led me astray yet. And where I come from, money talks. I do believe I'll have to accept your offer." Carl said.

Carl stood up and extended his hand to shake Mr. Rikers. Mr. Riker smiled and stood upright, extending his hand into Carl's. They shook hands. As Carl began to pull away, Mr. Riker squeezed his hand a bit tighter and pulled him closer.

"Thank you for accepting, Carl, and a promise is a promise. You asked if the Escapement was illegal and I said I didn't know. That was an honest answer. How can I know if something is legal or illegal if it has never been seen or done in the history of mankind before?"

CHAPTER
FIVE

Mr. RIKER RELEASED CARL'S hand and Carl sat back on the couch.

"What do you mean it's never been seen or done before?" Carl asked.

"I meant what I said, Carl, and that's truly all I can and will say on the matter at this time," Mr. Riker said. "I'm truly glad you will be taking this on with me. Truth be told, you deserved this promotion much sooner."

"Well, thank you, sir. I'll do my best," Carl said, still struggling with the comments he had heard.

"Now then, let's talk some business. Do you have anything in your company car that needs to be taken out?" Mr. Riker asked.

"I don't think so," Carl said. "It could probably stand to be cleaned a little before I go pick him up."

"No need, Carl," Mr. Riker said. "Hand me your keys."

Carl reached in his pocket and took out his key chain. He pulled the sedan keys off of it and handed them over to Mr. Riker. While doing this, Mr. Riker reached into his own pocket and pulled out another pair of keys to give Carl.

"With a new promotion comes a new ride, Carl," Mr. Riker said. "When we leave the office, I'll walk you to it. It's already cleaned, gassed up, and ready to go."

"Wow, thank you," Carl said.

"No need to thank me, Carl. It comes with the job. It was time for a new company car for you, anyway," Mr. Riker said. "Now, as I stated before, our Escapement winner is Dalton Mallet and his plane will be arriving around noon. It's 10:30 now, so we don't have that much time. I would like for you to get to McCarran and see to it that Mr. Mallet is picked up and taken to wherever he would like to go. His ultimate desti-nation is the Bellagio. This is where he'll be staying and all the reservation and room information is here in this folder on my desk, along with a few other things."

Mr. Riker grabbed the folder and handed it to Carl. Carl quickly flipped through the pages in the folder. He saw the reservation materials, but also some legal papers and questionnaire sheets.

"What are these?" Carl asked, shuffling through all the forms.

"Well, since he was the winner of our little event, the legalities must be handled first and foremost," Mr. Riker said. "Our lawyers have gone over everything, and all he needs to do is read and sign them. Everything is very self-explanatory. Should he have any questions about anything, except the actual Escapement itself, I'm sure you'll be able to answer him. Again, another reason why I trust you with this. Also, in that little stack is a questionnaire I'd like him to fill out. A way for me to get to know him a little better before we actually meet tomorrow."

Carl found himself looking over the legal papers as Mr. Riker was explaining what they were. Mr. Riker was right; this was very self-explana-tory. Liability information and confidentiality agreements, the usual per winners of things here in Vegas. When he got to the questionnaire, he took it out to glance at it and look over the questions. Nothing too per-sonal, seemed to be general questions, like a form you would fill out if you were applying for a job. When Carl finished looking over the majority of the forms, he came to the final item. A clasped folder that was sealed with some type of digital lock.

"Mr. Riker?" Carl said. "What about this?"

"Ah, yes," Mr. Riker said. "That folder is for Mr. Mallet's eyes only. Once he opens it, he is free to share the contents of that information with you, but you only. Part of the confidentiality agreement."

Another damn secret, Carl thought to himself. "Want to give me a hint at what's in here?" Carl asked.

Mr. Riker, smiling at the comment, said, "Carl, all of this information is assuming Mr. Mallet is on that plane. I sent him one First Class ticket and hoped he would choose to come here. I do not know and will not know he accepted until you make contact with him at the airport. If he chose not to come, all legalities are out the window. If he declines the Escapement, what's inside that folder will not matter. Could I choose another person? Sure, I could, but I don't want to, for reasons you'll understand later. If you go to meet him at the airport and he's not there, you come right back here to me. Bring everything in the folder and we can open it up together. But because Mr. Mallet is the recipient, this folder must be seen by him first. I hope you understand and I can trust you to make it happen."

"You can trust me," Carl said. "I wouldn't even know how to open this thing. Is that some kind of locking mechanism?"

"It sure is, Carl," Mr. Riker said. "Made in our own lab. Only a four-digit pin number will open it. Two people have the code. Myself, and Mr. Mallet. If he inquires about it, tell him the code is in his letter. Hopefully, he brought it with him. If not, we can open it together tomorrow."

"Okay," Carl said. "I have the forms, and apparently, I have a new car. I need to be at McCarran at noon. Sounds simple enough."

"It shouldn't be that bad," Mr. Riker said. "We have made a sign that reads 'Dalton Mallet' and it's in the car already. Stand by the terminal and wait for him to make contact with you. If no one comes to you, inquire with the staff to make sure everyone got off properly and then come back here. If he does show up, take him to the Bellagio, or anywhere else he would like to go and get to know him. Go somewhere and get the forms filled out and you can bring them to me once Mr. Mallet is settled in. I'll be at the office all night, so you can bring them by when he's done. Now, shall we go take a look at your new company vehicle?"

"Sounds good to me!" Carl replied.

Mr. Riker and Carl both exited the office and headed to the lobby.

"Cindy," Mr. Riker said. "Congratulate Carl here on his new promotion. He will now be working directly under me. Can you please get me a list of some of the finest engineers and software people we have? Carl will be putting a team together soon and I would like all of our best resources to be at his disposal."

"Absolutely, sir," Cindy said. "Congratulations, Carl! Well deserved!"

"Thanks, Cindy," Carl said.

Mr. Riker and Carl continued to the elevator and proceeded to the lower level where Carl had entered the building. Once on the ground floor, they exited the elevator and then the building to the parking deck where his old car was located.

"I thought we would come out here first to make sure you didn't leave anything of value in your old car," Mr. Riker said. He unlocked the door and opened the sedan, allowing Carl to look inside.

"I'll check," Carl said. "But I'm pretty sure there's nothing in here I need."

Carl looked inside the car and found nothing. He reached under the steering column and pressed the button unlocking the trunk. He walked to the back to check and saw he was right. Nothing was in there either.

"Very well," Mr. Riker said. "I will have someone come out and take this car to be cleaned and moved on to the next person, or to be sold. How do you feel about that SUV right over there?"

Mr. Riker pointed a few spaces down, which was a little closer to the entrance, at a black BMW X5 SUV. It looked as if it had just come off the showroom floor.

"Now that is a nice car!" Carl said.

"Yes, it is," Mr. Riker said. "Yours is the one next to it."

Next to the SUV was a minivan that looked like it had seen plenty of miles. It had a spare tire on the rear wheel and some of the wood grain paneling was peeling off.

"The van?" Carl asked.

"Yes, the van! Perfect vehicle. Inconspicuous. Durable. Reliable. I bet it has 200,000 miles on it, and it's still going!" Mr. Riker said.

What the actual hell, Carl thought.

"Mr. Riker, I appreciate all you've done and continue to do for me, but if it is all the same to you, I'd rather keep the sedan," Carl said.

Mr. Riker, who could not maintain a straight face any longer, burst into a fit of laughter.

"That van was broken down on the side of the road this morning and towed here," Mr. Riker said. "As Cindy was coming to work this morning, she saw a family broken down and in need of assistance. She called Triple-A and got them where they needed to be, but since we were close, she asked if she could get the van towed here until they could come get it. You're a good man, Carl. The SUV is yours, not the van."

"Well, I didn't want to seem unappreciative, but you really got me there," Carl said.

"All in good fun, Carl. Now, I hope the new car lives up to your standards," Mr. Riker said, continuing to laugh. "Call me on this number once you've picked up Mr. Mallet. If you run into any trouble, please let me know."

He gave Carl a card with only a phone number on it. Carl placed it in his wallet.

"I will, and thank you again," Carl said.

"Thank you, Carl," Mr. Riker said. "Are you sure you would rather take the BMW instead of the van? And are you wearing two different shoes?"

Carl smiled and shook his head as he walked toward the car. Mr. Riker laughed walking back to the building.

This is one badass ride! Carl thought as he got into the car. He knew it was a top-of-the-line vehicle and it definitely had all the extras. He pushed the 'Engine Start' button, backed the vehicle up, and proceeded back to the gate where he entered. He made it a point to pull over at the security gate to speak to Larry before he left.

"Larry," Carl said. "I apologize for this morning. I was in a hurry and was running late. It's my fault I was late, not yours, and I shouldn't have handled it the way I did."

"Yeah," Larry said. "I called you an asshole but I'm pretty sure you didn't hear me. New ride, huh?"

"Yes, it is. And I was an asshole," Carl said. "Again, I'm sorry."

"Hell, Carl, don't worry about it. We get shit every day. At least you had your badge and I didn't have to turn you around. Those situations are awkward," Larry said.

"I guess they are. Maybe tomorrow I won't be in such a hurry," Carl said.

"I'm off tomorrow. You can be an asshole to someone else," Larry said with a smile.

"You got it, buddy. See you when I see you," Carl said.

Carl got back in his car, waved at Larry, and drove back past security. He made his way back to the highway and proceeded to the airport. Carl couldn't help but notice how much smoother the ride was in this vehicle compared to his other car. He thought about the events of the day so far and reality started to set in.

"Holy shit!" Carl said aloud, realizing how much exactly he would be making now, and how far he had come. It had been a rough couple of months, but maybe things were turning around. He turned on the radio and sang the wrong words to the songs that were playing as he made his way to the airport.

By the time Carl had gotten through traffic, parked the car, gotten the sign from the back and walked into McCarran International Airport, it was a little after noon. He saw that the flight from RDU had gotten in about five minutes ago and was about ready to begin the deboarding process. He stood near the exit, way before the luggage carousels so the people getting off the plane could see him as he held up the sign that had Dalton Mallet's name written on it. Carl saw lots of people walk past him to get their luggage as they exited the plane. Many of them were excited, *their first time in Vegas,* Carl thought. Some looked to be people going from one place to another, or busybodies, as he liked to call them. As the people started to thin out, no one had come to him yet. He turned and saw there was still luggage and other items going around the belt, and no pilot or flight attendant had walked by, so he continued to wait.

Five minutes turned into ten, and ten into twenty, when finally, a man with his head hung down came walking slowly out of the terminal to the area where Carl was standing. The man looked surprised, like he had seen a ghost. He continued to walk slowly toward Carl, like a zombie in one of those old movies, focused on the sign as he walked.

"Mr. Mallet?" Carl asked. "Mr. Dalton Mallet?"

The man spoke almost too quietly to hear.

"I'm...Dalton...Mallet," said the man.

"Mr. Mallet, are you okay?" Carl asked.

"No, sir, I'm not sure that I am," Dalton said as he stumbled, grabbing onto Carl's shirt as he fell forward.

Carl grabbed Dalton as he fell and went to the ground with him.

"I need some help over here!" Carl yelled, helping Dalton to the ground. "I need some help now!"

CHAPTER
SIX

As Jeffrey Riker walked away from Carl Gilbert, who was about to get into his new SUV, he continued to laugh.

"He really thought it was the van!" Mr. Riker said aloud to himself.

Jeffrey Riker walked back into his building and waited for the elevator doors to open. Once they did, he entered the elevator. Instead of pushing a button, he took out a key from his pocket and placed it into a small keyhole by the button keypad. Once he turned the key, the doors shut immediately and the lights went out in the elevator, replaced instead by a red glow. All cameras inside the elevator stopped recording and began to play on a loop, a loop of an empty elevator. A panel also opened below the buttons of the elevator floors. There was only one button inside this panel, and it was labeled 'T'. He pressed the button and the elevator began to move downward. After a minute had passed, the elevator came to a full stop and the doors opened only to show another, larger set of doors.

Mr. Riker walked out of the elevator and faced the closed doors. He stood in front of an electronic keypad, the kind you would find on a desktop computer. Above the keypad was a screen. The screen read, 'ENTER PASSCODE.' Mr. Riker typed in the passcode and the screen changed from 'ENTER PASSCODE' to "PASSCODE SUCCESSFUL! YOU MAY ENTER.'

Both doors opened to a new room. Inside this room were multiple monitors, electronics, and various other lab equipment. Cables were running across the floor and the ceiling. Electronics were mounted up high and the room looked as if it were running by machines, just like the

Matrix. The most interesting thing in this room, however, was what looked like what is best described as an old phone booth, the kind one would previously find on many street corners in the city. It had no glass, but a smooth metal casing around it. It seemed to be covered with buttons, wires, and switches. Mr. Riker pulled one of the switches and it opened just as you would expect an old phone booth to open, but inside there was no phone. Mr. Riker stared into the contraption. *Everything looks good to go on the inside,* he thought.

"Mr. Riker," a voice said. "Good to see you down here. What do you think?"

Mr. Riker turned to see a figure coming from a doorway near the back of the lab. He was wearing horn-rimmed glasses and a white lab coat. Mr. Riker could tell right away from the spiky hair, tie-dye t-shirt he could see through the open lab coat, and the black Crocs that it was Scott Brown, one of his longtime engineers and physicists. Scott was a little unusual, but extremely intelligent and a tremendous asset for Riker Industries.

"Is it ready, Scott?" Mr. Riker asked.

"Absolutely," Scott replied, as he grabbed a clipboard off of t he wall and began to run down what looked like a checklist. "We have double and triple-checked every aspect of it. It seems to be in fine working order."

"That's good, Scott," Mr. Riker said. "That's really good. We can't, and I strongly emphasize the word can't, have what happened before happen again."

"We are well aware of that and have taken every precaution and data point we had to ensure that this time is successful," Scott said. "I've run all the numbers myself personally. Three times even."

"Excellent, because the world may be watching, Scott," Mr. Riker said. "The world may be watching. And whether they tune in or tune out, this will change everything. We only have one more shot at this. This time, it has to work. We can't allow what happened before to..."

"It'll work, sir," Scott said, placing the clipboard back on the wall, cutting Mr. Riker off mid-sentence. "We have crossed every t and dotted every i. We have learned from everything and have no doubts about our success this time. What happened before will not happen again. When can we proceed?"

"Soon," Mr. Riker said. "Very soon. I have sent Carl Gilbert with the paperwork to meet our Escapement winner. If our winner shows up, and I'm quite certain he will, he'll be escorted here tomorrow, and we should be ready to go Wednesday or Thursday. Three days tops, Scott. Three long days."

"Are you going to bring him to the lab?" Scott asked. "How will you present everything to him?"

"Not sure yet," Mr. Riker said. "I would first like to talk everything over with him. Get to know him a little. Explain what I can to him so that he can make the decision himself. If he requests to see it, I will call down to you so that everything is well taken care of."

"That sounds like a plan, sir," Scott said. "Do we know the direction we're headed? It's very important to know what direction we're headed."

"Not yet," Mr. Riker replied. "We'll know Thursday at the latest. It would be nice if we knew tomorrow, but a decision like this will take some time to process. Are you certain we are multi-directional, just in case?"

"To the best of our findings, research, and trials, we are working at full potential in both directions, sir," Scott said. "It's really magnificent to think of what we've done here."

"Yes, it is, Scott. And to think they said it would never be done," Mr. Riker said.

"It hasn't," Scott said. "Not yet, anyway. Well, not successfully. With humans."

"Things are about to change, Scott. Things are about to change," Mr. Riker said as he patted Scott on the back.

Mr. Riker pushed the switch that he pulled earlier and the door to the contraption closed shut. As Scott walked back into the lab in which he had appeared from, Mr. Riker walked back to the door from where he entered. Before he walked out and back to the elevator, he turned one last time to look at the contraption in the center of the room.

Mr. Riker smiled and nodded his head.

"The world changes very soon," Mr. Riker said before stepping back into the elevator.

Mr. Riker closed the panel with the 'T' button and removed his key. He pressed the button that would ultimately lead him back to his office. As he did so, the red glowing lights dimmed and the overhead lights came back on. He was full of excitement about what was to come later in the week. He could not wait.

When the elevator doors opened on his office floor, Mr. Riker stepped out and made his way over to Cindy.

"Mr. Riker," Cindy said. "Carl is a good man. You made a fine choice promoting him. He's had a rough go of it lately and I know this will boost him up quite a bit. I can't even imagine how he can still come to work and function like he does."

"Carl has earned it, Cindy," Mr. Riker said. "He's been with us a long time and comes through on everything he's tasked with, without hesitation or complaint. It's people like that who continue to make our business a success. Life can always throw us curveballs, Cindy. I believe Carl is handling the situation as best as one can."

"He's a good guy," Cindy said. "I truly hate what happened."

"I do too, but he seems to be as okay as he can, given the circumstances," Mr. Riker replied.

Mr. Riker's conversation with Cindy was cut short by a ringing in his jacket pocket. Mr. Riker did not recognize the number.

"This has to be a misdial. The only people that have this number are the ones I program into it," Mr. Riker said before he answered the phone. "Jeffrey Riker, Riker Industries. May I ask who this is?"

"Mr. Riker, this is Carl. We may have a problem..."

CHAPTER
SEVEN

D ALTON OPENED HIS eyes and his first thought was, *where am I?* After a quick observation of his surroundings, he realized he was still on the plane, but was unsure of how long he had been asleep. He glanced over to where Susan was sitting and noticed she was still asleep. Dalton moved his seatback to its upright position and figured he needed to use the restroom. He got up from his seat and quietly walked toward the curtain in front of him. He noticed that the restroom was unoccupied, so he opened the door and entered.

The bathroom was very small. Dalton was amazed that all of the things one would find in a regular-sized bathroom would fit in such a small area. He maneuvered himself inside the tiny space and used the restroom, flushed, washed his hands, and proceeded back to his seat.

Dalton tiptoed past Susan, not wanting to wake her, and noticed a small box sitting on his seatback tray. He sat back down quietly and began to investigate the box. It was black and the size of a small jewelry box. There were three squares on top of it that looked like glass, two in the top corners and one in the middle near the front of the box. A small, LED light was by each square. A series of LED lights seemed to be embedded in the side next to an array of tiny holes that formed a circle. Dalton sat up in the seat and looked around at the passengers only to notice that most everyone was asleep, including Susan. He decided to inspect the box a little further.

Dalton picked the box up carefully with both hands and tried to open it, but the top wouldn't budge. There was one drawer in the front and it wouldn't open either. On each side of the drawer was a button, and beside each button, a tiny light. One button would press in but the other one would not. It reminded Dalton of a modern-day Japanese puzzle box. Etched into the front of the box were the letters 'E-M-G-E-E'.

"Fancy little box, isn't it," a familiar voice chimed in while Dalton was trying to figure out what exactly was in front of him.

"It sure is," Dalton said, putting the box back down. "You wouldn't happen to know where this box came from, would you, Susan?"

"It's your surprise, Dalton," Susan said.

"What is it, exactly?" Dalton asked.

"Before I explain what it is, let's have a drink. We should be landing soon and I want to finish these little bottles. I have two left. One for me and one for you. Whaddya' say?" Susan asked.

"Sure, why not," Dalton said, still intrigued by the box in front of him.

Dalton watched Susan turn around and reach in her purse for the two bottles. When she turned back around, she was nothing but smiles, bottles in hand.

"One for you and one for me," Susan said, passing Dalton one of the tiny bottles.

"Thank you, Susan," Dalton said. "This box is too much, really."

"We'll get to the box. For now, how about we toast to new friends and new adventures. Now bottoms up, young fella," Susan said, lifting up her bottle to toast Dalton before pressing it to her lips.

Dalton took the cue from Susan and put the bottle to his lips and turned it up. Whatever was in the bottle didn't go down smooth at all. Dalton felt his cheeks get flushed almost right away. Once he finished with the bottle, he brought it down and immediately felt different. He saw Susan's entire expression change. What he once saw as smiling and funny, turned dead serious after he ingested whatever was in that bottle.

"That is some tough stuff, Susan," Dalton said as he coughed. "What is it?"

Dalton tried to focus on the bottle, but the words on it were becoming too blurry to read. He felt Susan touch his arm and saw her lean in closer to him.

"Sorry about the drink, Dalton, but it had to be done," Susan said.

"Had to be done?" Dalton asked.

"Stay quiet and listen to me, Dalton," Susan said. "I don't have much time, so I'll only tell you what you need to know. The drink you just had will make you woozy and make it look like you're drunk, but you aren't, and the effects will wear off very soon. It's meant to put you to sleep, but in no way is it going to hurt you. When you open your eyes, you'll forget this plane ride. You'll forget ever talking to me, actually, and that's probably for the best. In your mind, you'll think you've slept the entire time and are waking up with a terrible headache."

"What are you saying..." Dalton said.

"The only thing you'll remember from this trip is getting on the plane and someone giving you this box," Susan said. "I call it an EmGee box. Think of it as a mystery box of sorts. It has a flip-top lid and one drawer. The drawer needs to be opened before the lid. That's the only hint I can give you and one you will be sure to remember. Put it in the seat next to you. When you wake up, put it in your carry-on bag."

"Okay," Dalton said, feeling the effects of the drink getting stronger.

"You will not be able to open this by yourself, and don't show it to anyone that you don't trust. Thank you for the conversation and for being kind to an old woman. Time for me to repay the favor. Wish we could speak more, but everyone around here will be waking up soon. Catch ya' later, Dalton." Susan said.

Dalton felt Susan's hand squeeze his arm a bit tighter. He turned to look at her and thought he saw her smiling at him. Dalton watched Susan look to the left and right and saw her take what looked like a remote out of her purse and press a button. She smiled one last time and her skin began to turn clear. It was as if parts of her disappeared into thin air while he was watching. She vanished right before his eyes. Dalton tried to speak but couldn't. His mouth would open but the words wouldn't come. He tried to reach out toward her but his arms didn't work. The feeling in his legs was gone. His eyes started to feel very heavy and Dalton passed out in his seat.

"Ladies and gentlemen, this is your captain speaking. We have safely arrived at McCarran International Airport. Let me be the first to welcome you to the city that never sleeps, Las Vegas!"

The captain's voice over the loudspeaker caused Dalton to open his eyes. His face felt hot and he didn't know why. People were getting up around him and moving to the exit. Dalton put his hands on his face and pressed his cheeks together, trying to make sense of when he fell asleep and why he felt the way he did. It was like he had a sober mind inside of a drunk body. He reached to his waist to remove his seatbelt and saw a box in the next seat.

I know the box is mine...but where did it come from? Dalton thought to himself. He tried to remember the plane ride, but his mind wouldn't let him. As his brain shuffled through the memories of the past few hours, Dalton only remembered boarding the plane, putting his carry-on bag in a compartment over his head, and the importance of the box beside him. That was it. He had no memory of the plane ride altogether. *Was I sleeping the entire time?* Dalton thought as he tried to compose himself.

Dalton waited for the aisle to clear around him before he tried to stand up. He sat quietly as the plane cleared, rubbing his eyes and trying to gather his thoughts. Once the plane was almost devoid of people, Dalton used his hand on the armrest for balance and stood up. His legs were a bit wobbly, but he managed to get upright and open the compartment above his head, removing his carry-on bag. Dalton placed it in the seat he had gotten up from and unzipped it. He carefully picked up the box and placed it inside of his bag.

"Everything okay, sir?" a voice behind Dalton asked.

Dalton turned and noticed a flight attendant staring at him.

"Yes, ma'am, just trying to get my things together," Dalton said.

"Very good, sir," the flight attendant said. "Enjoy your stay here in fabulous Las Vegas!"

The flight attendant made her way back to the coach area of the plane, leaving Dalton to himself in the First Class section. He still didn't feel like himself, but considering everyone was off the plane, he decided to leave as well. Dalton walked very slowly down the aisle to the door in a trance-like state. He stumbled through the terminal alone, walking even slower, trying to maintain his balance. Everyone else was long gone. He didn't feel right. Dalton had never experienced anything like this.

As Dalton continued to walk through the terminal, he staggered a bit, but he balanced himself on the desk in the lobby area.

"Are you okay, sir?" one of the employees asked.

Dalton smiled and continued to walk. He felt as if all his energy was gone. He started to shake a bit and his face felt hot again. He kept looking down while walking, trying to keep his balance so he wouldn't fall over. Dalton raised his head and thought he saw his name on a sign. He tried to walk toward it and felt like he would never make it there.

"Mr. Mallet?" a well-dressed gentleman asked. "Mr. Dalton Mallet?"

Dalton shuffled his way over to him, feeling like he could fall over at any moment.

"I'm...Dalton...Mallet," he said.

"Mr. Mallet, are you okay?" the man with the sign asked.

"No, sir, I'm not sure that I am," Dalton said as he stumbled, grabbing onto the man's shirt as he fell forward. The noise around him stopped. Everything went dark.

CHAPTER
EIGHT

WHEN DALTON BEGAN to come to his senses, he realized he was on the floor of the airport. Four people were squatted down beside him. One looked like an EMT.

"Are you okay, sir?" the EMT asked.

"I think so," Dalton responded. "What happened?"

"Seems you got off the plane, walked in and passed out," the EMT said. "The gentleman over there at the desk caught you and was yelling for help. I ran over here and he went to the phone."

Dalton turned his head to look at the desk and saw a man in a suit on the phone. He was moving his hands as he spoke and seemed very animated. When he made eye contact with Dalton, he rushed himself off the phone and made his way over the group that was kneeling beside him.

"Mr. Mallet, are you okay?" Carl asked.

"I think so," Dalton said. "Don't remember much of the flight, so it could just be air sickness, if that's a thing."

"It can be," the EMT said. "Could be a variety of things. We could always get you to a hospital. Get you checked out."

"I think I'll be fine," Dalton said.

"Do you think you can stand up? Walk?" the EMT asked.

"One way to find out," Dalton said.

The crowd backed away slowly. Carl extended his arm and Dalton grabbed a hold of it. He pulled Dalton up to his feet and allowed Dalton to balance himself by placing his other arm on his shoulder.

"You good?" Carl asked.

"I'm good. Maybe walk beside me, just in case," Dalton said.

"Sure, man," Carl said. "The car is right outside. There's a bench out there you can sit on while I go pull it closer. Do you have any luggage or anything?"

"Yes, sir," Dalton said. "Black bag. Tag should have my name on it. Also had a carry-on."

"I've got it right here. You kinda threw it at me when you fell. I'll go get your other bag while this guy makes sure you're good," Carl said as he left to go find Dalton's luggage.

"You sure you're okay?" the EMT asked. "I'd feel a lot better if you would at least go get checked out."

"I'll be fine, I think," Dalton said. "Been through a lot worse. I guess flying hit me harder than I thought it would."

"If you aren't used to it, it can do that, I suppose," the EMT said. "If you continue to feel like this, go get checked out."

"I will," Dalton said. "I just need some rest and I'll be good to go, I'm sure."

"Are we all good?" Carl asked, returning with a black bag of luggage.

"I think so," Dalton said. "But who's luggage is that?"

"The damn tag says 'D-a-l-l-a-s...' shit...be right back," Carl said.

Carl ran back to the luggage carousel. Dalton laughed a little to himself.

"Who's that guy?" Dalton asked the EMT.

"He said his name was Carl, I think," the EMT said. "Told me he was here from Riker Industries to pick you up. You fell right into him when you walked in. He caught you and called for help. When I got over here, he ran to the phone. Said he had to call his boss or something."

As the EMT was finishing, Carl arrived with the correct bag in hand.

"That looks a lot better," Dalton said. "Thanks."

"No problem, Dalton," Carl said. "If you want the other bag, we can go back and get it too, no one else was over there."

"I'm fine with my bag," Dalton said.

"Mr. Mallet, get some rest and take care," the EMT said. "Carl, get him somewhere so he can rest. If he continues to feel like this, get him to a doctor or something."

"Thank you so much, mister?" Carl asked.

"Tommy," the EMT replied. "Tommy Dodds"

"Thank you, Mr. Dodds," Carl said.

"Thank you!" Dalton said.

Tommy walked away and left Dalton and Carl to their business.

"I don't think I have officially introduced myself. I'm Carl. Carl Gilbert," Carl said.

"Nice to meet you, Carl," Dalton said. "You can call me Dalton."

"Sounds like a plan, Dalton," Carl said. "Shall we get you to the Bellagio?" Carl asked.

"I'm fine with anywhere that has a bed if I'm being honest," Dalton said.

Dalton walked with Carl out of the airport and Carl helped him sit down on one of the benches right outside the doorway. Carl walked back to his new car, got in, and drove it to where Dalton was sitting. Carl got out and helped Dalton into the back seat. He picked up his luggage and put it in the back. As he got back into the car, he asked how Dalton was feeling.

"You still okay back there?" Carl asked.

"I'm going to be fine," Dalton said. "Just a little shook, that's all. I can't believe I passed out in an airport."

"It's okay," Carl said. "I've passed out in worse places. Long flight, I guess. Shit happens."

"I guess so," Dalton said.

"Have you ever been to Las Vegas?" Carl asked.

"I've never been out of North Carolina," Dalton said.

"No shit?" Carl asked.

"Plenty of places to visit there without leaving the state. Mountains.

Beach. Big cities. Small towns. I actually don't even like leaving the small town I'm from, Carl. It doesn't even have a stoplight," Dalton said.

"Bullshit!" Carl said.

"Seriously, man," Dalton said. "We have a post office and a mom and pop's store. Nearest big city is twenty minutes away, but nothing compared to this. We live a lot slower back home."

"Well, damn man," Carl said. "Whole new world out here. Sin City, baby. What happens here, stays here. Except herpes. That shit stays with you, like that movie 'The Hangover' said."

As Carl looked in the rearview mirror, he saw Dalton smiling at his last comment.

"Take it all in, Dalton," Carl said. "This place never sleeps. And where you're staying, the Bellagio, by far the best place on the strip. Good food. Good location. You can spend hours staring at the fountains alone."

"I'll stick to getting some sleep first, then maybe I can take some of the city in," Dalton said.

"Sounds like a plan. I'd be happy to show you around," Carl said.

"That's okay with me. I don't know where anything is," Dalton said.

As Dalton looked out of his window, Carl watched his expression in the rear-view mirror. He knew that seeing Las Vegas for the first time was an experience. Carl sometimes wished he could see it through new eyes himself. He loved this city and was a mainstay here. What he didn't love, however, was the traffic. It was slow getting to the Bellagio, but they even-tually made it. They passed the Luxor, Tropicana, M GM Grand, New York, New York, and Paris casinos and hotels before finally arriving. He could tell by the look in Dalton's eyes he was enamored with this place.

"You got anything in North Carolina like this?" Carl asked.

"Not at all," Dalton said. "This place is crazy. You even have escalators on the outside of the buildings!"

Carl pulled his car right up to the Bellagio's front doors. He got out, took the luggage from the back, and helped Dalton out of the backseat.

"You okay, Dalton?" Carl asked.

"I'm good, probably just need a nap. Been a long flight and a rough landing," Dalton said.

Carl helped Dalton into the Bellagio and walked with him to the front desk. Dalton couldn't help to be taken aback by this place. There were all kinds of sounds coming from the casino floor, which happened to be right past the lobby. People were cheering. Slot machines were ringing. Above him was a tremendous glass sculpture that contained every color he had ever seen. Columns lined the entryway. The entire place was immaculate and lined by the red velvet ropes he had only seen in movies.

"This place is ridiculous," Dalton said, taking it all in. "There is nothing like this back where I'm from. Nothing."

"Nothing like it anywhere, I imagine," Carl said. "Let's go get you squared away."

Dalton walked with Carl to the front desk. He watched as Carl leaned onto the counter and listened as he spoke to the receptionist.

"Hello, young lady," Carl said to the woman at the front desk. "This here is Dalton Mallet. Riker Industries has reserved a room for him, actually the Penthouse Suite, according to my folder here. Confirmation number is 8-1-5-9-3."

"Yes, sir. We have him here through Friday. Everything is paid for. Looks like room service is handled as well," the woman said. "Anything you would like to eat, feel free to order, it's taken care of."

"Wow," Dalton said. "Thank you so much!"

"Dalton," Carl said. "Excuse me for a moment. I'd like to call Mr. Riker and let him know you're doing better. I'm sure this beautiful lady will give you all the information you need. Give me one second."

Dalton nodded and watched Carl walk to the end of the counter and ask for a phone. He listened to the woman behind the desk explain where his room was, how to get to it, and how his key worked. Dalton was fascinated that his keycard must be inserted into the elevator in order to access his room. Once the elevator doors opened, he would use the card again to access the door. No one could get to the Penthouse Suite unless they had the card. It was the coolest thing he had ever heard. Once he had listened to all the information and had the keycard in his hand, he saw Carl walking back towards him.

"We all set?" Carl asked.

"Good to go," Dalton said. "I'm going to go up and get some rest."

"Would you like me to help bring your bag up? You sure you're good?" Carl asked.

"I'm fine. Thanks anyway," Dalton said.

"Dalton," Carl said. "I'll be back later today to show you around and whatnot. I have some paperwork we need to fill out for this Escapement, according to Mr. Riker. What would be the best time?"

Dalton checked his watch and it read 4:15 p.m.

"It's already after four?" Dalton asked.

"No," Carl said. "You're going to have to reset that. You are still on time back east, my friend. It's only 1:15 right now."

"That's right," Dalton said. "I'll reset this when I get to my room. I'll also turn on my phone. I wasn't taking any chances my first time flying. Maybe come back around four or five then?"

"Sounds good," Carl said. "I'll have them call your room when I come back. Get some sleep, my friend. Tonight, we can explore Vegas a bit."

"I'll do my best," Dalton said. "Thanks for the ride."

"Don't mention it," Carl said before shaking Dalton's hand and exiting the Bellagio.

Although the receptionist behind the counter offered to get someone to carry his luggage for him, Dalton decided to carry it himself. It was only one bag, besides what he carried on. He packed light. He was a simple man. Couple of changes of clothes and some toiletries. If he needed anything else, he had the five-hundred dollars that was given to him for winning the Escapement that he could use. Dalton followed the directions of the lady behind the counter to get to the elevator that would take him to his room.

Of course, I have to walk through the casino, he thought. This was unlike anything Dalton had ever seen. There were slot machines everywhere. Game tables too. Dalton was not much of a gambler. He would play cards with his friends every now and again, but he didn't see the fun in throwing your money away hoping to get more.

Dalton made his way through the Bellagio's giant casino floor. He saw the Blackjack tables, Poker tables, and Roulette tables. There were lots of people gathered by the Craps tables and everyone was on their feet. Dalton had only seen Craps on movies and had always been interested in it, but never found the time to learn to play. Dalton saw at least twenty-five television screens down a row of stairs, each showing different sports. There were leather couches and recliners as well, so people could watch the games and gamble while feeling relaxed and at home. Once Dalton made it through the casino, he finally reached the room full of elevators. There were at least six to his count and only one was labeled the Penthouse elevator. As soon as he pressed the button, the doors opened. He stepped in alone and saw a spot for his keycard to go in. He put in the keycard, the doors closed and the elevator began to move.

When the elevator finally stopped, the doors opened and he found he actually was the only room on the floor. He walked out of the elevator to the only door in front of him. He used the same keycard from the elevator and entered his suite.

This place is bigger than my house, Dalton thought. He stood at the entryway and stared. The giant room had a big couch directly in front of him facing what looked like a 70" television. The wall of windows was facing the fountains and the Las Vegas strip. Dalton knew that would be one hell of a view come nightfall. To his immediate right was a full bar, to his left, a giant bathroom. There was also a door that led to a bedroom. Inside was a king-size bed in front of another big screen television. All the furniture was, in Dalton's mind, way above his pay grade. He didn't stay in places like this. If he had to work out of town, he was a Motel Six guy. If it was good enough for Tom Bodett, the spokesman for Motel Six, it was good enough for him. He was sure Tom didn't use the Bellagio as his company model.

Dalton put his toiletry bag in the bathroom and sat his luggage on the bed. He pulled his cell phone out of the front pocket of his jeans and sat on the couch. He turned the phone on and placed it beside him, waiting for it to load. Dalton grabbed the television remote and attempted to figure out the channels, eventually landing on ESPN. He grabbed his phone and saw there were no new messages or voicemails, so he scrolled through his contacts and finally landed on her number. Dalton touched the screen and put the phone to his ear as he listened to it ring. The call went to voicemail, so he left a message.

"Hey. It's me. Landed safe. Was a rough flight and I don't really remember much of it, which is weird. Hotel is nicer than anything we have back home. This place is unreal. Wish you were here. I miss you. Hope everything is okay in your part of the world."

Dalton ended the call and put his phone back beside him. He thought about his day and couldn't understand why he couldn't remember anything from the plane, except...

Dalton walked back to the bedroom and unzipped his carry-on bag. He carefully removed the box from his bag and brought it into the main room with him, placing it on the table. *What is this thing? How does it work?* Dalton thought. He continued to stare at the box. Dalton tried as hard as he could to remember how he acquired it, but he couldn't. He also couldn't believe he was here, in this city, in this room. He couldn't believe he would be meeting Jeffrey Riker. He couldn't believe he was the winner. Dalton's mind raced with all these thoughts, all at one time, until he drifted off to sleep on the couch.

CHAPTER
NINE

ARL EXITED THE Bellagio and made his way back to his new
BMW X5.

"A nap would be really good right now," he said aloud. "I can also get my damn phone!"

Carl started the ignition and began to drive back to his house. He knew he had some glass to clean up, and a phone to find. His only concern right now for the company was Dalton Mallet. Mr. Riker had made that very clear. If Dalton was going to get some rest, so was he. He couldn't help but think of all Dalton had been through upon arriving in Las Vegas. He shook his head and hoped Dalton would feel better. Sometime during this ride, Carl also thought about his wife and wondered what she was doing right now, or where she was for that matter.

The thoughts lingered as he continued home. He was focused on getting there. Carl pulled into his driveway around 1:40 p.m. Traffic was a little worse in the afternoons with everyone coming from or going to lunch, not to mention the tourists. Carl got out of the X5 and went into his house. Same place as it was before. It needed cleaning, but that wouldn't happen today, except the glass from his vodka bottle. He took his overcoat off, placed it across the couch and walked to the kitchen. Inside of the kitchen was a broom and dustpan, so Carl grabbed them and proceeded upstairs to the bedroom. He swept up all the glass and walked back downstairs to place it in the trash. After putting the broom and dustpan back in the kitchen, Carl grabbed a bottle of water from his refrigerator, went back to his bedroom, and sat on the bed. He opened the bottle of water, took a sip, then placed it on his nightstand beside a picture of a woman. Carl took off his two different shoes and tossed them beside their correct matches on the floor. He stood up and emptied his pockets, placing his keys, wallet and loose change on top of his dresser. Carl loosened his tie and took it off, hanging it on the knob of his dresser. He turned to sit back down and saw his phone face down on the floor, almost under the bed. He picked it up.

"Five missed calls," Carl said aloud.

Carl entered his lock code on the screen and pressed the button that allowed him to see the missed calls. All from this morning. All from work. He also saw the notification icon for four text messages. Three were from Cindy at work.

"Where are you?"

"Carl, are you okay?"

"Please call or text back"

The other message was his friend Bill, who he hadn't seen since everything happened three months ago.

"Thinking of you, buddy. Stay strong. If she's smart, she'll come back"

"If she's smart, she'll stay gone," Carl said aloud.

Carl put his phone on the charger atop his dresser and set the alarm for 4:30 p.m.

If I can sleep until 4:30, that'll give me time to get up, shower, change clothes, and get back to the Bellagio by 5:30 or a little after. Dalton probably needs the rest. He should be good to go by then.

Carl sat back on the bed and laid back, resting his head on the pillow while staring up at the ceiling. He turned over and grabbed the picture off the nightstand and held it in front of his face.

The woman in the picture had short, brown hair and it was curly. Her eyes were brown. She had freckles and a beautiful smile. She was standing and pointing in the picture, her smile seemed to come from a laugh. She was wearing a blue top with a backpack, a pair of shorts, and running shoes.

"I miss you every day, kiddo," Carl said. "I wish I could change things. I wish I could've been a better husband to you. I don't know how many times I've tried to call because I quit counting. I've left you so many voice-mails that I probably filled the damn thing. I just wish you would let me know you were okay. A call. A text. A damn letter. Something. Was I really that bad?"

Carl's eyes began to tear up and he wiped them away as quickly as they came. He placed the photo back on the nightstand and opened the top drawer. Inside was a flask. He unscrewed the top and took a sip while looking at her picture.

"Here's to us, kiddo, and what might have been," Carl said.

Carl screwed the top back on the flask and set it in front of the water bottle.

"I need to fill you up again," Carl said, before laying back down.

He closed his eyes and waited for sleep to come.

The alarm rang on his phone at 4:30 p.m. It went off for ten minutes before Carl realized what the noise was.

"Shit," Carl said. "Here we go again."

Carl sat up and rubbed his eyes. He stood up long enough to turn off the alarm on his phone and sat right back down. Grabbing the flask off the nightstand, Carl unscrewed the top and drank what little was left inside. He placed it back on the nightstand and decided to shower in the morning. Carl figured he would just change clothes before he left to pick up Dalton. He threw the white shirt he was wearing on the floor, walked to his closet, and picked out a light blue, button-down shirt to wear. No tie this time. The pants he was wearing were good enough. Carl slipped the shirt on and buttoned it except for the top two buttons. He unfastened his pants to tuck his shirt in, then refastened them. Carl walked back over to the dresser and looked down at two pairs of shoes.

"I'll be wearing the same shoes this time, dammit," Carl said with a smile.

Carl slipped on his shoes and walked to the bathroom to wash his face and comb his hair. Once finished, he grabbed his keys and loose change and put them in his front pocket while putting his wallet in his back pocket. He took his phone off of the charger.

"Not going to forget you this time," Carl said.

Carl also grabbed his flask from the nightstand.

"You either. Bartender, Jobu needs a refill," Carl said, smiling.

Carl walked down to the kitchen, flask and phone in hand. He laid the phone down on the table and then opened one of the cabinets.

"Choose your poison, Carl," he said. "Except for vodka. You busted that shit this morning."

Inside the cabinet was a wide variety of liquor. Carl sorted through them before deciding on a bottle of Jameson.

"Maybe a bit of Irish luck tonight," Carl said.

Carl poured the Jameson into his flask and placed the bottle back into the cabinet. He screwed the top back on the flask and walked into the living room to grab his sport coat. After putting it on, he placed the flask in his left jacket pocket and his phone in the right one. Before leaving, he turned on a lamp in the living room so he could see when he returned later. Carl walked out the door, shut and locked it, got into his car, and drove back to the Bellagio.

He parked his car right outside the door and informed one of the valet's that he was picking up a client. They allowed him to park in the area and he walked to the front desk.

"Hello, young lady," Carl said. "I'm Carl Gilbert. I work for Riker Industries and one of our clients is staying here. I'm supposed to meet him in the lobby and told him I'd call when I arrived. His name is Dalton Mallet and he's in your Penthouse suite. Could you call his room and let him know I'm here?"

"Absolutely," the lady behind the desk said. "Just one moment."

The lady, whose name tag read Cheryl, called Dalton's room.

"He'll be right down," Cheryl said while she hung up the phone.

"Thank you, Cheryl," Carl said. "Please let him know I'm waiting out by the fountains."

"Our biggest attraction," Cheryl said, smiling.

Carl walked back outside and informed the valet he spoke with earlier that his client was on the way down. He also informed him that he would be standing by the fountains if he needed to move his car. Carl walked over to the rail by the fountains and leaned over to watch. It wasn't long before Dalton joined him.

"Hey, Carl," Dalton said.

"Hey, man, you feeling any better?" Carl asked.

"I am, actually," Dalton said. "Just needed some rest is all. Was quite a scene earlier."

"I hear that," Carl said, pulling a flask from his jacket pocket. "Drink?"

"No, thank you. I'm good for now," Dalton said.

"Yeah, I probably shouldn't either," Carl said before taking a swallow.

"I come here sometimes just to watch the water show. Helps me think through things. Gives me something to do, I guess."

"I can understand that," Dalton said. "Know of anywhere good to eat around here?"

"I was hoping you were hungry. I'm starving," Carl said. "What are you in the mood for?"

"Kind of day I had; I don't care. Anything would be good right now," Dalton said.

"Okay then. Let's go to the car. I know a nice little place not far from here. We can get a bite to eat, get the paperwork figured out, and go from there," Carl said.

"Let's do it," Dalton said.

Dalton walked with Carl to his car parked in front of the Bellagio. They got in and made their way to one of the premier steakhouses on the

Las Vegas strip, courtesy of Riker Industries. It was only a few miles away from the Bellagio.

As they made their way down the strip, neither Dalton nor Carl had any idea they were being followed, but they would find out soon enough.

CHAPTER
TEN

DALTON COULD DO nothing but stare out the window and admire the sights and lights that Las Vegas had to offer. It wasn't fully dark yet, but the city was lit up in all kinds of neon and flashing lights. The buildings were massive. People were walking along the sidewalk with excitement and energy, not seeming to have a care in the world besides hitting it big.

"Is it always like this?" Dalton asked.

"Every damn night," Carl said. "This place is one of the biggest attractions in the world, and for good reason too. People come here hoping to hit it big, but most go home with less than they came with."

"But they keep coming back?" Dalton asked.

"It's Vegas, baby," Carl said with a smile.

After a short ride down the strip, Dalton noticed Carl turning into another hotel and casino, named the Venetian.

"Is the restaurant in the hotel?" Dalton asked.

"Most of em' are, pal," Carl said. "One of the best is in here though. Delmonico Steakhouse. One of Emeril's places. Best damn steak you'll ever eat."

"This place looks fancy," Dalton said. "I'm way underdressed."

"You're with me," Carl said to Dalton. "And because you're with me, you're associated with Mr. Riker. Don't worry about the clothes. Let's go eat."

Dalton watched Carl as he got out of the car and tipped the valet. He exited right behind him and followed Carl into the Venetian. It was every bit as nice as the Bellagio. The lobby looked like a cathedral, and off in the distance, he actually saw a small boat on a canal inside the place.

"Do you see that?" Dalton asked.

"Don't be a tourist," Carl said with a laugh. "This place is modeled after Italy. They have canals running through here and you can take gondola rides. It's really popular with the 'Just Married' crowd."

"That's insane," Dalton said.

"You aren't in Kansas anymore, Dorothy," Carl said.

Dalton walked behind Carl in awe of the scenery. Giant statues. Huge columns. The man on the back of the gondola was rowing and singing in Italian while a couple held each other. There were even lampposts inside this place. It wasn't long before they were standing outside Delmonico Steakhouse. Dalton knew this from the giant lettering across the top of the establishment that read simply Delmonico. The host greeted them at the entrance with a smile.

"Good evening, gentleman," the host said. "Just two of you tonight?"

"Absolutely," Carl said.

"Right this way," the host replied and escorted them to their table.

Dalton was fascinated by the giant chandeliers, the walls full of wine bottles, and all the fancy décor.

"I'm way out of my league, Carl," Dalton said.

"Me too, buddy," Carl said. "This is on the company's dime. If it was just you and me, we'd be getting a burger from McDonald's."

"I'd be totally okay with that," Dalton said.

"I'm sure you would," Carl said. "You won the event, Dalton. Let's enjoy it a little."

Dalton and Carl were shown to their table close to a window and were quickly greeted by their waitress for the night.

"Welcome to Delmonico!" the waitress said. "I'm Nancy and I'll be serving you tonight. Can I start either of you off with a glass of our finest wine?"

"I'll have a Scotch," Carl said.

"Do you have sweet tea?" Dalton asked. Carl laughed.

"We have unsweet," Nancy said. "You can add sweetener to it if you would like."

"I'll just have a beer," Dalton said. "Whatever you have on tap. Don't need to let this guy drink alone anyway."

"That sounds great," Nancy said.

"I'm actually ready to order if you are," Carl said to Dalton. Dalton nodded.

"Nancy, I'll have the Prime Ribeye, medium rare, with a baked potato," Carl said.

"I'll have a New York Strip if you have it, medium, with a baked potato as well," Dalton said.

"Simple enough," Nancy said. "I'll bring your drinks and we will have that food right out for you."

"Prepare yourself, Dalton," Carl said. "This will be the best steak you've ever had in your life."

"Right now, anything would be good. Every time I swallow, my stomach is saying thank you," Dalton said.

They both laughed. As they waited for their food to arrive, Dalton and Carl started to get to know one another.

"So, Dalton, what do you do for a living?" Carl asked.

"I'm what you would call a handyman, I suppose. Little electrical, plumbing, construction. I can do a little bit of it all. Money isn't bad, keeps the bills paid," Dalton said.

"I hear that," Carl said. "I've never been handy with anything, except computers. I've done this kind of work most of my life."

"How long have you been with Riker Industries? What exactly do you do?" Dalton asked as the drinks showed up.

"Well, without getting technical, I take people's ideas and turn them into a technology they can use. I've got a pretty decent head on my shoulders. Actually, I received a promotion today and get to head up my own team," Carl said.

"That's awesome, Carl!" Dalton said. "Congratulations!"

Dalton raised his beer as a toast to Carl's promotion.

"Hell yeah, we can drink to that," Carl said, raising his glass of Scotch.

"Mr. Riker gave me a chance in his company when I was 22 and fresh out of college. I had a degree, but no damn clue what I was doing or where I was headed. I applied and he must've liked what I wrote. Called me within a week for an entry-level position and I've made my way through the company ever since. That was a long time ago. I'm getting old."

"You can't be that old," Dalton said.

"46 and counting," Carl said.

"46 isn't that old," Dalton said.

"Says the youngest one at the table. How old are you, 25?" Carl asked.

"I'll be 30 in a few days," Dalton said.

"Well, another reason to toast. Here's to your birthday," Carl said, raising his glass and drinking another sip.

"Where did you go to college?" Dalton asked.

"California Institute of Technology, computer engineering and programming. Grew up here in Vegas, but went to school out in Pasadena. Wasn't bad. Got my degree and moved back to my normal, which is right here in Vegas. Got my chance at Riker's and been here ever since," Carl said.

"You seem to be a pretty smart guy," Dalton said.

"When you're working for Mr. Riker, you have to be," Carl said as the food arrived.

"This looks delicious," Dalton said.

"Bet it tastes that way too, let's eat," Carl said.

Dalton and Carl ate and continued to make small talk. Every bite of steak Dalton ate was better than the last. The steak was cooked to perfection. It was juicy, tender, and loaded with flavor. It didn't take them long at all to devour the meal that was placed in front of them.

"I don't have the words to describe that steak!" Dalton said.

"Best steak in Vegas, hands down," Carl replied.

They both pushed their plates forward and sat back in their seats, full from the meal they had eaten. Dalton pushed his chair back a bit to exhale and Carl picked up his drink to take another sip. Dalton glanced down at the table and noticed a ring on Carl's left hand.

"So, how long have you been married?" Dalton asked, pointing at the ring.

Carl stopped drinking and put his glass down on the table. He glanced down at his wedding ring.

"I was married. Not anymore. She left. Can't say I blame her. I'm probably not the easiest person to live with," Carl responded, pausing between each sentence.

"Sorry, Carl. I saw the ring and..." Dalton said before Carl cut him off.

"No worries, man," Carl said. "I guess I'm still hoping there's a chance, you know? I don't know if I'll ever take the ring off. She was the one. Don't know if you've found the one or not, but if you do, do everything you can to keep her," Carl said, finishing his drink.

Nancy, the waitress, seemed to arrive as Carl was finishing.

"Looks like you two have finished these plates up. Can I take them out of your way?"

They both nodded.

Nancy grabbed the plates and asked if they would like a refill on their drinks.

"Absolutely," Dalton said.

Nancy smiled and told them she would be right back.

"Things will work out, Carl," Dalton said.

"If you knew the whole story, you wouldn't be saying that. But I appreciate the effort. How about you? No ring I see. Anyone special in your life?" Carl asked.

"That's a long story too, my friend. Probably should've known you earlier and I would've taken you up on your advice," Dalton said.

Nancy returned with the drinks just as Dalton finished his sentence.

"Any dessert tonight?" she asked. Dalton and Carl both shook their heads no.

"Well, no rush gentleman. Stay as long as you would like. I'll leave the bill right here and take it when you're ready," Nancy said.

"Thank you, Nancy," Carl said as Nancy continued to help other customers.

Carl raised his glass to Dalton.

"Here's to the one that got away," Carl said.

Dalton raised his glass to meet Carl's, then they both drank.

"Dalton," Carl said. "Let's liven this conversation up a bit."

Carl took out the folder that Mr. Riker had given him and opened it up.

"First and foremost, congratulations to you on being selected as the winner of this Escapement, whatever the hell it is."

"You don't know?" Dalton asked.

"According to Mr. Riker, only he and five other people know. I'm not one of them. I wish I was, man. Sorry," Carl said. "Anyway, we need to get this paperwork filled out. I have to get it back to Mr. Riker tonight before we meet with him tomorrow. Now, I've looked over most of it, glancing really, and it looks like general liability information. Insurance forms, waivers, etcetera. If you would read it and sign them, I'd appreciate it."

Carl slid the forms to Dalton and he began to read them. As Dalton was reading and signing, Carl remembered something he had read earlier in the forms.

"Dalton, one of those forms is a confidentiality agreement. Once that's signed, you can't talk about anything that happens during the meeting tomorrow or after the meeting. Apparently, this is some top-secret shit," Carl said.

Dalton laughed.

"Whatever this so-called Escapement is, Mr. Riker doesn't want anyone to know. At least, not until he discusses it with you," Carl said.

"Got it," Dalton said. "This is a lot to fill out."

"Mr. Riker is a smart man and leaves nothing to chance. If it's been thought of, it's in those forms. If you have any questions about anything, let me know. If I can't answer it, we will call the man himself," Carl said.

Dalton took about ten minutes to read and sign the forms. While he was doing this, Carl placed his company card on the table beside the bill. Nancy soon arrived and picked it up.

"Is that it?" Dalton asked.

"Not yet," Carl said. "This next form is a little better though. It's like a questionnaire. Kind of like if you were applying for a job, but some of the questions on here seem like he's trying to find out more about you."

"Okay," Dalton said. "Slide it on over."

Carl slid the questionnaire to Dalton while collecting the other forms. As Dalton completed the questionnaire, Carl looked over the legal forms and ensured everything was in order before placing them back into his folder.

When Dalton finished, he handed Carl the paper.

"Mind if I look over it?" Carl asked.

"Be my guest," Dalton said.

Carl read over the form.

"Braves baseball? Seriously?" Carl asked.

"What do you mean, seriously? Who else should I pull for?" Dalton asked.

"I'm a Dodger man," Carl said. "Living out here, it's Dodger baseball or nothing. Growing up watching Kirk Gibson hit that grand slam, seeing El Toro and Hershiser pitch, can't get much better than that," Carl said.

"Well, back where I'm from, it's Braves baseball. Atlanta is the closest team to home, so that's who I grew up watching. Dad liked 'em, too. And my granddad. I guess it's a tradition," Dalton said.

"At least it isn't the damn Yankees," Carl said.

"Damn straight!" Dalton said.

Carl finished reading over the form and placed it into the folder.

"Are we all finished?" Dalton asked.

"We have just one more thing," Carl said. He took out the clasp folder with the digital lock and slid it across the table to Dalton.

"What in the world is this?" Dalton asked.

"Your guess is as good as mine," Carl said. "Mr. Riker wouldn't tell me anything about it. Said it was for your eyes only. If you wanted to share the contents, you could, but the only ones who would know what's inside would be you and him."

"Is this a lock code?" Dalton asked.

"Apparently, so," Carl said. "Mr. Riker said he designed it himself. Said only you and him knew the code to get in."

"I don't know any code," Dalton said as Nancy brought back Carl's card and set it on the table.

"Mr. Riker said the code was a four-digit pin number, and it was in your letter or something like that," Carl said. He grabbed his card and placed it back in his wallet.

"The letter!" Dalton said. "It's back in the hotel. I saw the pin number on the top but I wasn't sure what it meant. Now I know."

"Well, do you remember it?" Carl asked.

"Sure don't," Dalton said. "I guess we'll have to go back and get it."

"I'm ready when you are," Carl said.

"Then let's go," Dalton replied.

Dalton offered to leave the tip and Carl declined. He watched Carl take out enough cash to leave the waitress a very generous tip. Dalton was anxious to see what was inside the folder and figured Carl was as well. Carl grabbed the paperwork Dalton had filled out and they made their way back to the car and headed toward the Bellagio.

"I wonder what's in here?" Dalton asked aloud, holding the folder up to the window, trying to peek inside.

"Must be important if it has a damn lock on it," Carl said.

"Are you sure you don't know anything about this Escapement thing?" Dalton asked.

"I tried to get it out of Mr. Riker and he wouldn't tell me. He's keeping this very close to his vest. I hate saying this, but curiosity is starting to get the best of me about this whole damn situation. Right now, I really want to know what's in that folder," Carl said.

"Well," Dalton said. "I'll know soon enough. Maybe we both will."

"Mr. Riker said it's for your eyes only, but if you want to share, I won't stop you," Carl said, jokingly.

As they pulled into the Bellagio, Carl stopped the car and told Dalton he was going to call Mr. Riker and let him know that the paperwork was in order.

"That's fine," Dalton said. "I'll go ahead to the room and take out the letter so we can have the pin number."

"Wait," Carl replied. "The room you're in, I can't get up there without the keycard. I'll make the call quick if you'll hang out for a minute."

"No problem," Dalton said. "Do you need to speak privately?"

"Not at all," Carl said. "Give me one second."

Carl grabbed his wallet and pulled Mr. Riker's card from it. He programmed the number into his phone before calling.

"Carl!" Mr. Riker said. "Good to hear from you. How are things?"

"Things seem to be going well," Carl replied. "We went out to dinner and Mr. Mallet completed the paperwork, so I should be bringing it by soon."

"Excellent. Did he happen to open the folder yet?" Mr. Riker asked,

"Not yet. He left the letter in his hotel room and we're going up to get it," Carl said.

"Are you going up with him?" Mr. Riker asked.

"Well, he seemed like he wanted me to be there. I told him it was for his eyes only, just as you instructed," Carl said.

"Do me a favor, Carl. When Mr. Mallet opens the folder, see if he'll give you an answer," Mr. Riker said.

"An answer? An answer to what?" Carl asked.

"I'll see you soon, Carl," Mr. Riker said, ending the call.

That was weird as hell, Carl thought to himself.

"An answer?" Dalton asked.

"We'll see soon enough," Carl said. "The man speaks in riddles sometimes."

Dalton grabbed the folder. He exited the car with Carl and they walked into the Bellagio. After the walk through the casino and the elevator ride, Dalton used the keycard again to open the door.

"Let me go get the letter, make yourself at home," Dalton said.

Carl walked over to the bar and propped himself against it while Dalton disappeared to the bedroom. It wasn't long before Dalton reemerged with the letter in one hand and the folder in the other.

"Here's the letter. How do I put the numbers into this thing though?" Dalton asked.

Dalton gave Carl the folder and he looked over the locking mechanism.

"This is interesting," Carl said. "These LED outputs are touchscreen."

Carl tapped the first box and a '1' came up. When he tapped it again, a '2' registered on the little screen.

"Oh, okay," Dalton said. "Easy enough."

Dalton placed the letter on the bar and got the folder from Carl. He began to tap the mechanism. While he was doing this, Carl looked over the letter. He was not blind to the fact that the blue ink on the bottom was a woman's handwriting. He decided that now was not the best time to bring it up.

"4-8-1-2," Dalton said aloud as he tapped the numbers into place.

Once the final number was entered, the mechanism made a noise and fell off of the folder.

"I guess it can be opened now," Carl said.

Dalton took the folder over to the couch and sat down. He pulled open the clasp and then opened the folder. He stuck his hand inside and pulled out a single piece of paper. Carl could tell it had words on it, but he couldn't make out what they were. Dalton read the paper and then set it down on the table, beside the folder.

"Dalton, you good?" Carl asked.

"Yeah," Dalton responded. "I'm good, just thinking of an answer."

"An answer?" Carl asked. "An answer to what?"

"Apparently, it was a question he left off the questionnaire. He wants to discuss it tomorrow and try to get to know me better. Said it would help him see what kind of person I was, in a sense. This is a tough question," Dalton said.

Carl knew from speaking with Mr. Riker earlier that he wanted to see if Dalton would give him an answer, he just wished he knew the question.

"What's the question, Dalton?" Carl asked. "If you don't mind me asking."

"Come see for yourself," Dalton said as he sat back on the couch and continued to think.

ELEVEN

Mr. Mallet,

Welcome to Las Vegas!

I was betting that you would come. I hope the flight wasn't too bad and everything is up to your standards thus far. I look forward to meeting you tomorrow and discussing the Escapement with you in person.

By now, you have signed all the legal documents and answered your questionnaire, and for that, I thank you. I would like to propose one more question to you. Take your time to think it out, because there is no single correct answer. I like asking questions that require thought. The kind that makes your brain hurt a little. I like to think of them as conversation starters.

Here is the question:

If you had the choice to either change something in your past or see your future, which one would you choose and why?

Take some time to ponder this. These types of questions are fun!

See you tomorrow!

Jeffrey Riker

CEO Riker Industries

CARL PLACED THE letter back on the table after he finished reading it and looked at Dalton. He shook his head, stood up, and walked to the bar.

"What?" Dalton asked.

"Mr. Riker loves those kinds of questions," Carl said, looking through the bottles of alcohol. "I remember back when I first started, can't remember when exactly, but he had us all in a room and asked if we were all going to be stranded together on an island, what item would we bring and why? And we couldn't all bring the same thing. There were fourteen of us. You should've seen us trying to explain all that stuff."

Carl found a bottle of vodka and poured himself a glass.

"This question could go so many different ways," Dalton said.

"Yes, it could. But a word of advice," Carl said, sipping some of the vodka from the glass. "When you answer, come up with an answer for both scenarios. Mr. Riker loves the thought process. He enjoys back and forth between people and finding solutions to tough questions. The man has built a career on it."

"Thanks, Carl," Dalton said. "I could seriously go either way on that answer, anyway."

"I think we all could," Carl said.

Carl finished his glass and set the empty container on the bar.

"Dalton," Carl said. "I need to get these forms back to Mr. Riker. It won't take long at all I'm sure. Would you like to ride along?"

"Well, I need to make a phone call first. And I probably need to shower," Dalton said as he stood up.

"No problem," Carl said. "I can wait, or, if you would like, I can swing back by and give you the grand tour like we talked about."

"Can we take the grand tour tomorrow? After the plane ordeal, and that meal we just had, I think I'm going to call it a night," Dalton said.

"Of course, we can, Dalton. Consider it done. But it's only a little after nine, and this is Vegas. You're calling it a night already? Even after your nap?" Carl asked.

"Afraid so. We live a lot slower back east than y'all do out here. It's also midnight back home. I'm not much of a gambler either, so the casino isn't for me. I'm fine with getting a shower, having a drink, watching some sports and calling it a night," Dalton said.

"No harm in that, but no fun either," Carl said. "I respect it, though. Have a good night, Dalton. Unless I hear otherwise, I will be in the lobby at 9:30 in the morning. Here's my personal cell number if you need anything. Nice meeting you, my man. Think about that question, but not too hard. You don't need a headache tomorrow. Big day for you. Hell, big day for me. I get to find out what this damn Escapement actually is, too! Try and get some rest."

Carl took out a business card from his wallet and gave it to Dalton.

"Thanks for the dinner, Carl," Dalton said, taking the card from Carl. "And for the company. See you tomorrow."

Carl began to walk out the door and stopped as he got to it.

"Before I go, can I ask you something?" Carl asked.

"Sure," Dalton said. "What's that?"

"That thing on the table. The box-looking thing. What is it?" Carl asked.

Dalton turned his head to look at the table and realized through all the excitement he had left the box from the plane sitting out in plain sight.

"To be honest with you, I have no idea what it is," Dalton said.

"No idea," Carl said. "Was it here when you came in?"

"Not exactly," Dalton said. "When I woke up in the plane it was beside me. I somehow knew it was mine, but I still don't know where it came from. I know that makes no sense."

"Not a damn bit," Carl said. "You think someone gave it to you?"

"Yeah, I do," Dalton said. "I know I didn't bring it from home. It was just there."

"Can't open it, can you?" Carl asked.

"How did you know?" Dalton asked.

"Because if you could, it would be on the table open and not closed," Carl said. "Mind if I have a look?"

"Be my guest," Dalton said. "I've tried everything."

Carl walked back over to the couch and sat himself down in front of the box. He picked it up and turned it many different ways, looking at it from all angles. Dalton sat down beside Carl and watched him.

"I've never seen anything like it," Carl said.

"Me, either," Dalton said. "I've tried to remember that plane ride since I woke up on the floor. For the life of me, I just can't. I know the box is important. I also know for some strange reason, the drawer in the front has to be opened first, but I can only get one button to press in."

"I saw that," Carl said. "The button on the left is the only one that will press in. Damn thing is like an electronic puzzle box."

"The left button?" Dalton asked, confused.

"Yeah, this button right here," Carl said, lifting the box again to show Dalton.

"The right button was the one that pressed in for me," Dalton said.

"No way," Carl said. "Show me."

Dalton took the box from Carl and used his thumbs to press both buttons on the front of the box. Only the right button went in.

"Dalton, set the box down on the table," Carl said.

Dalton sat the box down. Carl put his right hand on the top of the box to stabilize it and pressed the button on the left. It went in easily.

"Dalton, press the other button," Carl said, keeping his thumb on the box.

Dalton pressed the button on the right and the box emitted a chime. It sounded like the noise from Super Mario Brothers when Mario grabs a coin. Once the sound effect had finished, they heard the drawer in the front unlock and it opened automatically.

"Holy shit," Dalton said.

"Guess we needed two different people pressing two different buttons," Carl said.

Inside of the drawer was a label that simply read 'For Dalton' taped to the top of a small box. Dalton took out the box and opened it. Inside was a wristwatch. The watch had a brown, leather strap and it looked to have an etching on the side, but most of it had been worn off. The watch had a digital face and reminded Dalton of an old Casio watch from the eighties, but it seemed much bulkier. The time and date were set correctly and it had no buttons.

"Well, this is a weird-looking watch," Dalton said.

"Most digital watches don't have leather bands, buddy," Carl said. "They also have buttons on the side so you can set them. Where are the buttons?"

"Damned if I know," Dalton said. "Why a watch?"

"No idea, man," Carl said. "But it's yours apparently. Might as well wear the damn thing. You sure you don't know where this box came from?"

"I really don't, Carl," Dalton said. "I wish I did."

"Well, shit, that's enough excitement for one night," Carl said. "Let me get this paperwork back to Mr. Riker. I'll be back in the morning. We can look over that box some more before we leave."

"Okay, Carl," Dalton said. "Thanks again for everything. If you don't mind, please don't mention the box to anyone, not right now at least."

"It's your box, kid, I just helped open it," Carl said with a grin.

Carl stood up and walked to the door. Dalton walked behind him and closed the door after he left. He made his way back to the couch and programmed Carl's number into his phone. He thought about making another phone call like he did earlier, but he decided against it. Dalton took off his old watch and replaced it with the one he had just discovered. Dalton couldn't help but think of how weird everything was getting. He pushed the box to the middle of the table and picked up the letter he had received from Mr. Riker to give it some more thought.

Seeing my future would be interesting. Maybe in the future, things are different and we are together. If I could go back, I could change some things and we wouldn't be where we are now. Dalton put the paper down, grabbed his phone, picked up the box, and walked to the bedroom. He sat the box on the dresser then unzipped his bag and took out the charger for his phone. He plugged it into an outlet and hooked his phone up to it. After Dalton saw his phone was charging, he went back in the bag for his gym shorts and a t-shirt.

Dalton walked to the giant bathroom and turned on the shower. While the water was getting hot, he took off his clothes and threw them on the floor. Dalton took off the watch and placed it on the sink. He grabbed a towel and placed it beside the sink before getting into the shower.

After bathing, Dalton turned off the water and reached out of the shower for the towel. He dried himself off and pulled on his gym shorts. He used the towel to clean the steam off the mirror. After doing this, Dalton took out what he needed from his toiletry bag. He brushed his teeth, combed his hair, applied deodorant and then put the watch back on as well as his t-shirt.

Dalton grabbed his clothes from the floor and walked them back to the bedroom. He placed them in a garbage bag he had brought with him, then walked back to the main room to turn off the television and turn out the lights.

Dalton walked back into the bedroom and closed the door. He took his luggage off the bed and placed it on the floor. He turned the sheets back on the bed, grabbed the remote, and laid down. *Damn this bed is comfy.* Dalton turned on the television and flipped through the channels. He stopped on ESPN Classic. They were showing all of Mike Tyson's fights from earlier in his career. *That man was a beast!*

Dalton glanced at the alarm clock beside the bed and saw it was a quarter past ten. He set the alarm for seven, just in case he didn't wake up, although he was usually up at six each day. He rolled back over and watched the fights, hoping it would bring sleep. Dalton thought about his day and what was to come tomorrow. He would find out what the Escapement was, and maybe his life would change forever. He thought his excitement would keep him up longer, but sleep found him instead.

Thirty minutes after he had drifted off to dream, Dalton's phone lit up. The phone had been placed on silent, so there was no ringtone to wake him. The phone vibrated on the dresser in the room several times. Dalton never heard it.

When the phone finally stopped vibrating, all that was on the screen was a notification that read 'Missed Call', but that notification quickly turned into 'New Voicemail'. Underneath the words of the notification, was a single letter.

'B'

CHAPTER
TWELVE

CARL WAS ON his way to deliver the folder to Mr. Riker when he started thinking about the question posed to Dalton in the letter.

"If I had the choice to either change something in my past or see my future, which one would I choose and why?" Carl asked himself aloud. "It's a damn no-brainer, I'd choose you every time, kiddo. I'd go back in a heartbeat and fix whatever I did wrong."

Carl's mind was flooded with images of her, the good times and the bad. He remembered when they met, how he proposed, the wedding, followed by the fights, the tears, and her leaving. He remembered her laugh, and how she would snort when she couldn't stop. He remembered how she cried when he hurt her feelings for the last time. The vacations, nights out, nights in, long days and even longer nights. Carl remembered it all, constantly. That's why he drank. It helped him deal with it. It helped him remember and forget all at the same time. Most of the time he acted okay, but deep down he hurt. Carl longed for something that he was afraid he would never get back. He missed her, and he missed her badly. If she would just call him, text him, anything, maybe he could at least apologize and set things right, but it had been months now. It was apparent she didn't want to hear from him. Carl had to learn to live without her, which is something he never imagined himself doing. But here he was.

The night security was at the gate and after showing his badge, Carl proceeded to the building. He swiped his card and made his way to the elevator. Once at the top floor, he walked past the desk where Cindy would usually be and went directly to Mr. Riker's office. He knocked twice.

"Come in," he heard from behind the door.

Carl opened the door and saw Mr. Riker sitting behind his desk at his computer. He seemed to be very focused on what he was doing.

"Mr. Riker, here are the forms you requested. Sorry it took so long," Carl said.

"Nothing to be sorry about," Mr. Riker said, looking up from his computer. "Lay them on the desk. I'll look over them before I leave for the night. Big day tomorrow. Trying to make sure everything is in place. Have a seat, Carl."

"I understand, sir," Carl said, as he sat down in the chair in front of Mr. Riker's desk. He placed the folder on the desk.

Mr. Riker pulled the folder closer to him and moved it to the corner of the desk. He sat at attention, looked at Carl, and smiled.

"Did he answer?" Mr. Riker asked.

"Well, if you're referring to everything in the folder, yes. If you're referring to the question inside of the locked folder, he said he still needed some time to think about that," Carl said.

"That's what I wanted to hear," Mr. Riker said. "Nothing I enjoy more than actual thought put toward an interesting question. I'm sure he showed you the question."

"He did," Carl said.

"What would you decide, if you were presented with that choice, Carl?" Mr. Riker asked.

"I don't need to think about it at all. I'd change the past. No questions asked," Carl said.

"And your reasoning?" Mr. Riker asked.

"Vanessa," Carl said.

Mr. Riker sat back in his chair and shook his head.

"Carl, I'm so sorry. I didn't mean to bring it up. How are you doing with everything, given the circumstances?" Mr. Riker asked.

"I'm okay. I just miss her. If I could go back, I would," Carl said.

"And still no word?" Mr. Riker asked.

"Not a one," Carl said.

"Maybe she just needs time, Carl," Mr. Riker said.

"It's been months," Carl said. "If I could go back and change things, I would, but I can't. I don't know what I did that was so bad...that she can't even speak to me."

"Carl, we're all here for you," Mr. Riker said.

"I know," Carl said. "Cindy's been great about it, so have you and my coworkers. I appreciate all of you working with me through it all 'til I could get my life somewhat together. Each day brings its own new challenges, but overall, I think I'm better than what I was."

"We can all tell you're doing better. Doesn't mean it makes it easier," Mr. Riker said. "We all loved Vanessa. We all know you did too."

"Still do," Carl said.

Mr. Riker nodded.

"Thank you for bringing the forms in, Carl," Mr. Riker said. "If you would like to stay and talk some more, we can."

"I'm okay. It's getting close to ten now. Probably need to get some sleep. Big day tomorrow for our winner. He seems like a nice guy," Carl said.

"Okay, well I'm only a phone call away," Mr. Riker said. "I'll be leaving shortly myself. I'm going to look over these answers in the folder, reply to a few emails and call it a night."

Carl got up from his chair, thanked Mr. Riker for the talk, and made his way back to the car. On the way home, he stopped at one of the local liquor stores to make sure he got another bottle of vodka. He didn't turn on the radio for the trip home. He decided to ride in silence. Carl was still fighting a battle within himself to move on or stay put. The world kept turning, but he remained at a standstill. He didn't want to give up hope that she would come back. He couldn't. Twenty years of his life had been with her; good, bad or indifferent. Vanessa was the love of his life.

Carl pulled into his driveway and turned off the engine. He got out, vodka in hand, and clicked the button that locked the car. He stared up at the sky and didn't see any stars. He noticed some lightning in the distance and heard thunder. *Going to storm soon. Maybe it'll pass over tonight.* Carl pulled up the weather app on his phone and saw that rain was in the forecast for the remainder of the night and all day Tuesday. He put the phone in his pocket and shuffled through his keys to find the key that unlocked his front door. As he approached the door, he stopped to look at the envelope taped to it.

The envelope had his name, Carl Gilbert, written on the outside of it in black ink, probably from a Sharpie. It was sealed. He pulled it off and turned around. Carl looked left and right but saw nothing out of the ordinary. He unlocked the door and walked in.

Carl closed the door behind him and locked it. He was glad he had left the lamp on in the living room. He sat down on the couch. On the coffee table in front of him was a glass he used from the previous night. He unscrewed the cap from the vodka and poured some into the glass. Carl took two sips before opening the envelope. Inside was a single piece of paper that read:

Carl Gilbert,

We need to meet.

Tomorrow night.

Bellagio. 7 p.m.

I may have some information about your wife.

But I also need your help.

I'll find you in the casino.

A friend

CHAPTER
THIRTEEN

S HE HAD BEEN following him most of the day. She had tailed him going to the airport, the Bellagio, and then back to his home. She needed to talk to Carl but didn't know how to approach the subject matter. She decided to wait.

Day became afternoon and afternoon turned into night. She saw Carl come out of his house and followed him again. Back to the Bellagio where he picked up the same man he dropped off hours ago. She followed them to the Venetian. While they ate steak, talked and did whatever, she ate her sandwich she had packed. Ham and cheese, nothing out of the ordinary.

A few hours later, they left the Venetian. She followed. Not too close. She didn't want to be spotted. Not yet at least.

They actually parked at the Bellagio this time. They both went inside. She waited.

Around 9:06 p.m., Carl came back out. He had paperwork with him. She followed him to Riker Industries. When he went through the security check, she turned her car around and drove to Carl's house.

She didn't know how long she had, but she didn't want to waste time. She left the car running on the side of the road. She grabbed her notepad from the passenger seat and wrote Carl a note. She needed to speak with him, and the sooner the better. She was fairly certain that the man Carl was escorting around town was the winner of the thing she had been seeing all over television. She, like every other person in the world, knew the event was over. No one knew the winner, though. Putting two and two together, she would bet that this guy had won, so whatever it was had to be happening soon.

She put the note she had written in an envelope and wrote Carl's name on the outside of it. She sealed the envelope. She took some tape she had in the glove compartment and pulled a piece off. She got out of her car and ran to Carl's front door, used the tape to stick the envelope to it, and ran back. She drove down a couple of houses and pulled into the driveway of a home that had a 'For Sale' sign. From the driveway, she could see Carl's house.

She saw Carl when he arrived. She saw Carl stumble out of his car. Most importantly, she saw him grab the note and take it inside.

"Tomorrow night," she said aloud. "Tomorrow night, maybe we can both get some answers."

She turned the key in the ignition and drove away, disappearing into the night. She would meet Carl at the Bellagio very soon, but Carl wouldn't be ready for everything he was about to find out. Carl's life, too, was about to be forever changed.

CHAPTER
FOURTEEN

THE ALARM GOING off beside the bed woke Dalton up. His left hand came out from underneath the bedsheets quickly, hitting the top of the alarm clock and stopping the noise. He opened his eyes to a replay of SportsCenter. The clock read ten minutes past seven. He hadn't slept past six in a long time, but he was on vacation, so why not? He pushed himself up so that he was sitting upright with his back and head against the headboard. Dalton rubbed his eyes and tried to get the sleep out. There were only two and a half hours until Carl would arrive. *Today is the day,* he thought. He picked up the hotel booklet beside the bed and found the options for room service. One was the Bellagio Express and the other was the Bellagio Classic. The express menu contained yogurt, oatmeal, continental breakfast or a breakfast sandwich and would arrive faster than the classic. But the classic...the classic was worth the wait, plus, everything was already paid for. He picked up the phone and dialed the extension.

"Bellagio Classic! How can we serve you today?" said the voice on the other end of the phone.

"Hello, yes, I would like to order the American Breakfast, please," Dalton said.

"How would you like your eggs?"

"Scrambled"

"Bacon, Ham or Sausage?"

"Could I get bacon and sausage?

"Of course, you can. And to drink?"

"An orange juice and a hot cup of coffee."

"And can we get you anything else, sir?"

"I think that's good, thank you so much!"

"It will be up shortly, sir. Thank you!"

Dalton hung up the phone and placed the hotel booklet back on the nightstand. He decided to get out of bed and get himself ready for the day. He got up from the bed, walked to the bathroom and turned on the shower. While the water was warming up, he went ahead and used the bathroom. When he was finished, Dalton took off his shirt and shorts, grabbed another washcloth and got into the shower.

Once bathed, he turned off the water and grabbed another towel to dry himself off. He stepped to the sink and opened his toiletry bag. He grabbed his toothbrush and toothpaste and proceeded to brush his teeth. Once he finished, Dalton walked back into the bedroom and opened his luggage. He took out a pair of jeans, a polo shirt, a pair of boxers and his socks. Once he put his clothes on, he grabbed his belt off the floor and put it on as well. He took out his Braves hat and put it on, followed by his new watch. As he sat on the bed to put on his shoes, there was a knock at the door. Dalton quickly laced up his shoes and walked to the door.

When he looked through the peephole, he saw it was room service. He opened the door.

"Here is the breakfast you requested, sir," the man with the bow tie said. "We hope it's to your satisfaction."

"I'm sure it's fine," Dalton said. "It smells good! Not sure if you can accept tips, but please take this."

"Thank you, sir," the man said. "Do enjoy."

"I will," Dalton said.

The room service attendant left the room and Dalton closed the door behind him. He went to the bar and took the cover off the food. *Damn, this looks good,* he thought to himself. He moved the plate of food to the coffee table and turned on the big television to the local weather channel. He walked back to the bar for his juice and coffee, before returning to the couch to eat.

While Dalton enjoyed his meal, he saw from the weather report that rain was expected all day. While he was eating, he flipped through the channels and landed on an old Three Stooges episode. This passed the time as he ate.

When Dalton finished his breakfast, juice and coffee, he saw that he still had over an hour before Carl would arrive. He knew time would go by slow. Especially today. He was nervous and excited all at the same time. To relieve his nervous energy, Dalton decided to walk around the casino and do some exploring on his own around the hotel. The book he looked through this morning to order breakfast also had many of the amenities and different shops the hotel had to offer. Before going down, he needed to grab his phone, just in case.

Dalton walked to the bedroom. He felt like he was frozen in time when he looked at the phone's lock screen. He unplugged the charger and carried the phone with him to the couch. He sat down and stared at it.

'New Voicemail'

'B'

He remembered the time difference. *Shit, when I called her it was actually three in the morning.* He tapped the notification icon and put the phone next to his ear.

"Please enter password," the digital voice that guarded his voicemail replied.

He typed in his code.

"You have one new message," the digital voice stated. "First new message."

"Hey Dalt, it's me. On break at work. It's so much different here, but I don't regret it. Glad you landed safe. Hope you're doing better. I've seen pictures of the Bellagio. I know it's fancy. I wish I was there, too, but you know it's for the best. Like I told you before you left, decisions are the hardest thing to make, especially when it's a choice between where you should be and where you want to be. I know where you want to be, but is it really where you should be? Sometimes things just don't work out like we want them to. No one's to blame. Life happens. Maybe we need this time away to work on ourselves. I miss you, too, Dalton, and no matter what, I'll always love you."

"End of message. To delete this message, please press..."

Dalton ended the call. He could hear her voice crack near the end of her message. He thought back to the morning he proposed to her.

He had planned it for a month. Dalton never thought he would get married again, but she was special. She knew they were going on vacation because they always tried to do something, but she was unaware of what was to come.

Dalton had taken her to the beach. She loved the beach. She could sit and watch the waves crash into the shore for hours and not say a word. Especially at Emerald Isle. He took her out as the sun was getting ready to rise. They liked to walk on the beach early before it got crowded. When the sun started to make its way over the horizon, Dalton got down on one knee before he took out the ring. She cried. She also said no.

She turned to walk away and Dalton grabbed her hand. She turned around, still crying.

"I got accepted," she said. "I have to leave."

"Accepted?" Dalton asked. "Already? I thought it took months, years even to be accepted."

"I was going to tell you tonight. I found out before we left. We both knew this could happen. You know in my heart I've always wanted to do this," she said.

"I know, it's just..." Dalton said before she cut him off.

"You know you can't leave because you have other responsibilities. I understand that and I love you for it," she said. "Decisions are the hardest thing to make, especially when it's a choice between where you should be and where you want to be. I have to do this. It's where I should be. I want to be with you, but you know where you need to be. It's not fair to you for me to ask you to come with me."

"It's not fair to you for me to ask you to stay," Dalton said as he pulled her to him, hugging her tightly. "How long will you be gone?"

"At least a year, maybe longer," she said.

"Where'd you get accepted?" Dalton asked.

"The European Union, so I'll be stationed in either Germany or France," she said.

They left the beach that day and not much was said on the trip home. They were both hurting, but neither knew the right way to communicate how they felt without upsetting the other.

She had always wanted to travel overseas. The opportunity became available to work abroad, while making a difference. Only a handful of nurses are chosen. He had no doubts she would be a finalist. He never imagined she would be accepted into the program. Nursing abroad is a great opportunity to make a difference internationally. It was something she was born to do. He just didn't think it would happen so fast.

She and Dalton remained civil and friendly to each other. They would talk at least once a week and continue to text back and forth. Every conversation was tough. Life isn't fair.

Although they had been living together, she thought it best to move her things into her parents' home. Dalton helped her.

The last time he saw her was in a little restaurant outside of their hometown. She had agreed to meet him there so he could tell her about the trip. She couldn't believe he had actually won until he let her read the letter. He told her that the television and computer were hers, so when she left, he had to buy new ones. He figured that was how he became an entrant into the Escapement. She smiled. Dalton always made her smile.

"I miss you," Dalton said.

"I miss you, too. Every day," she said.

"I'm lost without you, if I'm being honest. Just feels like a big part of my life is missing. Without you, I don't know if I'll ever find it," Dalton said.

"Dalton," she said. "You're a great guy, and I'll always love you."

"When's your flight?" Dalton asked.

"Tomorrow night," she said.

Dalton excused himself and walked to the bar. She grabbed a pen and left a note on his letter. She folded it up and placed it back into the envelope.

Dalton returned from the bar and she handed him his letter back. He placed it in his pocket without looking at it.

"When do you leave?" she asked.

"Two weeks," Dalton said.

"Is your sister going to..." she began.

"Yeah," Dalton said, cutting her off. "I've spoken with the doctors. Told them I wouldn't be there for at least a week. Nothing I can do anyway, except be there."

"That's good, I always thought a lot of your sister," she said.

"She misses you being around, I'm sure," Dalton said.

"Try to have fun out there. Las Vegas is a big place. And congratulations, Dalton. Do you even know what the Escapement is?" she asked.

"I don't think anyone does, but I will soon," Dalton said. "Please be safe out there. You know I'll worry about you."

"You always do, but I'll be fine," she said. "It's such a great opportunity. I can help so many more people and learn so much."

They made a bit more small talk before they had to part ways. He hugged her tight. She hugged him back.

He felt the tears coming down his cheek as he remembered. He wanted to call her back, but he didn't. He put the phone in his pocket and wiped his eyes. He took the original letter from Mr. Riker out of his coat pocket and read what she had written again.

'I hope you are able to find what it is you've been missing...Love, B'

Dalton put the letter down on the table and walked to the window. He pulled back the curtain and stared out at the rain falling down from the sky. He put his hand on the glass and leaned into the window.

"What I've been missing is you, Britney," Dalton said aloud. "It's always been you."

CHAPTER
FIFTEEN

C ARL DIDN'T THINK he slept. If he did, it was in spurts, and not good sleep. He never made it to his bed. It wasn't even because of the alcohol this time.

'I may have some information about your wife'

Carl kept reading that line, over and over, in his head.

What kind of information?

He debated calling Vanessa's sister and decided against it. She never really liked him, anyway. He didn't have any of her best friends' numbers, and if he did, how could he call them after so much time had passed? He hoped Vanessa was okay.

Who would leave a note like this?

Carl remembered running outside after reading the note and looking around. He was trying to see if anyone was watching him. Who could've left this on his door? He saw nothing. Nothing but street lights, dark skies, and rain. It had rained all night. It was still raining.

Carl looked at the clock on his satellite receiver and saw it was a little past eight.

Have I really been sitting here all night?

He was tired. He was cranky. He needed caffeine and more aspirin.

Carl got up from the sofa and walked to the kitchen. He scooped out some coffee and put it in the filter of his coffee pot, filled the pot with water and turned it on. As the coffee was brewing, he walked to the medicine cabinet in the bathroom that was down the hall from the kitchen. Carl opened it and took out the bottle of Tylenol. He shook four out, closed it, and placed it back in the medicine cabinet. When he walked back to the kitchen, he took out a small glass and filled it with tap water. He quickly washed down the pills. The coffee continued to brew. The smell alone was enough to make any dark day a bit better. Carl looked at the fridge and stared at her picture that was hanging from a 'potato chip' clip. She was giving him the finger and making a face with her tongue out. She hated pictures. She was always quick to tell him so. He took them anyway.

"Please be okay, kiddo," Carl said aloud.

The coffee continued to brew.

Carl thought back to when they met.

He had been with Riker Industries for four years and was moving up within the company. Mr. Riker was making all the right moves and the company was doing well. Mr. Riker had arranged for a company weekend retreat at the Grand Canyon. Carl was driving to the retreat and saw her sitting against a car on the side of the road, crying. He pulled over to help. He parked his car behind hers and approached her.

"Everything okay?" Carl asked, knowing it wasn't.

"No, two flats and my phone doesn't get a signal out here," she said, wiping her tears away.

"My phone works. You can use it if you'd like," Carl said.

"I don't even know who to call," she said, tearing up again.

"How about we call a tow truck to begin with and go from there," he said. "I'm Carl."

"Vanessa," she said. "Call the cheapest one you know."

Carl stepped away and made the call. When he ended the call, he walked back and extended his hand to help her up.

"They'll be here shortly. I got it as cheap as I could," Carl said.

"What's the damage?" Vanessa asked.

"Free," Carl said.

"I'm not a charity case," Vanessa said.

"I'm sure you aren't," Carl said. "I have Triple-A through my work. I never use it, or haven't yet. Tow is free to wherever you need it to go. My company takes care of us. I made sure it could be used for any car and they said it was fine. You're good to go."

"Thank you so much!" Vanessa said as she hugged him.

"Easy there, kiddo!" Carl said, lifting his hands in the air. "Next thing you know you'll be grabbing my ass and telling me you love me."

She laughed. He remembered how much he loved her laugh.

"Don't count on it," Vanessa said, smiling.

Carl waited by the car with Vanessa until the tow truck arrived. They got to know one another through small talk and found they were into a lot of the same things. Carl also recommended a place to tow the car. Vanessa thanked him. Once the car was hooked to the truck, he helped her into the cab.

"If you need anything else, please let me know," Carl said, handing her his business card.

"I do, actually," Vanessa said. "I need to repay you for helping a girl out."

"You don't need to repay anything," Carl said. "Hope everything works out for you, kiddo."

"Do you mind if I use your phone really quick?" Vanessa asked.

"Sure," Carl replied, handing her his phone.

After a few seconds, Vanessa handed him the phone back.

"What did you do?" Carl asked.

"Smart guy like you, you'll figure it out," Vanessa said with a smile. "Thank you again, Carl."

"You are truly welcome, Vanessa," Carl said as he walked back to his car.

When Carl sat back down behind his steering wheel, the tow truck was headed west while he was about to head east. Vanessa seemed sweet

and was absolutely stunning. The little bit of time spent with her capti-
vated him. Before starting his car, he took out his phone.

"Now what did you do to this phone," he said aloud.

Carl looked through his contacts and saw there was nothing new. He
checked the text messages. Nothing. He didn't have a lot on his phone.
He wasn't on social media. He didn't have any apps or games. Carl started
clicking everything he could. He finally got to what looked like a notepad.
He clicked it and saw a new note.

'Thanks again for the help. Thanks even more for the company. Would
love to continue our conversation if you would. I owe you dinner.
Vanessa.'

Her phone number was underneath the note with a heart emoji.

Carl smiled and saved the number in his phone.

The coffee pot beeped letting Carl know it was ready. He took the
mug and poured himself a cup. He usually liked it black, but today,
some Bailey's would go well with this breakfast of champions. Carl took a
bottle of Bailey's out of his liquor cabinet and poured some into his mug
with the coffee. After he put the liquor back, he took his mug into the
living room and sat back on the couch to drink his coffee. The clock read
8:20 a.m.

Carl turned on the television as more of a distraction than as
entertainment. He watched the news until he had finished his coffee.
He was still tired, but Carl knew he had a big day ahead of him. Not as
big as Dalton, but a big day nonetheless. He needed sleep, but knew he
wouldn't get it. He also needed a shower, and that he could do.

Carl walked upstairs and put his phone on the charger while he got
himself a shower. He got himself dressed. Carl actually had time to shave,
but he chose not to. His beard was getting longer but he didn't care.
Maybe tomorrow, he thought. Once he had got himself together, he saw
it was 9 a.m. Carl took his phone off the charger and walked back down-

stairs, gathered all he needed for the day and walked out of his house, locking the door behind him. He jogged to the X5 to avoid the rain as much as he could. Once he sat down and closed the door, he started the engine and turned on the heat.

"Get to the Bellagio as soon as I can. Dalton to Mr. Riker by ten. Be at the Bellagio again tonight at seven. That's the most important thing," Carl said aloud.

He drove to the Bellagio and arrived by twenty after nine. He made his way to the front desk and asked one of the employees to call Dalton's room.

"He's not answering, sir," the employee said.

"He's probably on his way down, thank you," Carl said.

Carl sat in the lobby and realized he hadn't eaten. He knew he needed to, but the coffee would have to do until the meeting was over.

"Ugly outside, isn't it?" a familiar voice asked.

Carl turned toward the voice and saw Dalton standing behind him.

"Hey, Dalt," Carl said. "You snuck up behind me there. I was expecting you to come through the casino."

"Yeah, I came down early and walked around a bit. There's a lot going on in this place," Dalton said.

"City never sleeps, my man," Carl said. "Big day today, huh?"

"Yes, it is," Dalton said.

"Were you able to get any sleep?" Carl asked.

"I did," Dalton replied.

"Well, how about we go and find out what all this Escapement shit is about?" Carl asked.

"I'm ready when you are," Dalton replied.

Dalton followed Carl outside to his car. They made their way to Riker Industries. Dalton asked questions about Mr. Riker and Carl answered what he could. They made some small talk, mostly about baseball. Dalton was excited, but he was also nervous. Carl was anxious, but mostly about meeting this mystery person at the Bellagio later in the evening. Neither man knew what to expect from this meeting. Neither Dalton nor Carl could have prepared themselves for what was yet to come.

CHAPTER
SIXTEEN

CARL AND DALTON arrived at Riker Industries right before 10:00 a.m. They made their way through the security check and parked in Carl's spot outside of the office.

"So, this is it, huh?" Dalton asked Carl.

"Yep," Carl said. "My home away from home. This is the main building, where most of the offices are located, including Mr. Rikers."

Carl pointed to the other surrounding buildings explaining what went on in them while Dalton listened.

"If you want a tour, I'm sure we could arrange that," Carl said.

"I'm good," Dalton said. "This Mr. Riker, he's a bit of a genius, right?

"Oh yeah," Carl said. "Genius is probably an understatement. All this you see in front of you, he built from the ground up."

"Bit intimidating," Dalton said.

"He's a nice guy. Been with him a long time. He's run all kinds of promotions before and it's always a media frenzy. He didn't want that this time unless you did. I'm sure he'll discuss that with you," Carl said.

"I'm fine with us, no media," Dalton said.

They got out of the car and Carl swiped his security badge, allowing them to enter the building. They walked up to the elevator and entered it.

"Next stop, maybe some answers, hopefully," Carl said.

Dalton nodded his head.

The doors to the elevator closed and they rode in silence. When the doors opened, they walked toward Cindy's desk.

"Cindy, this is Mr. Dalton Mallet. We're here to see Mr. Riker," Carl said.

"Of course, you are," Cindy said. "He is expecting you. Congratulations Mr. Mallet!"

"Thank you," Dalton said.

"Okay, Dalt," Carl said. "Let's go."

They both walked to Mr. Riker's door at the end of the hall. Carl knocked twice.

"Come in," Mr. Riker said from the other side of the door.

Carl opened the door and allowed Dalton to walk in ahead of him. Mr. Riker was walking out from behind his desk, clapping. Carl closed the door as he entered behind Dalton. Mr. Riker extended his hand to shake Dalton's.

"Mr. Mallet! Welcome! Congratulations on being selected as the winner of our Escapement!" Mr. Riker said, shaking Dalton's hand. "Make yourself at home. Please, let's have a seat."

"Thank you," Dalton said, as he shook Mr. Riker's hand.

Dalton sat on the couch beside the door he entered from. Mr. Riker sat down beside him.

"Carl," Mr. Riker said. "Why don't you have a seat with us."

Carl sat on the couch opposite of them, forming a bit of a triangle. Mr. Riker started.

"Mr. Mallet," Mr. Riker said.

"Dalton, please," Dalton responded.

"Dalton, I heard about your flight in. I do hope you're feeling better," Mr. Riker said.

"Much better," Dalton said. "Like Carl and I talked about earlier, could've been a variety of things. I'm all good now, though, thank you."

"I have no doubts you are. And this was your first flight?" Mr. Riker asked.

"Yes, sir, it was," Dalton said.

"To be from North Carolina and not fly often? They were the first in flight, correct?" Mr. Riker asked.

"Yes, my state was, but not me," Dalton said. "I usually drive wherever I need to go."

"And what do you think of our fair city?" Mr. Riker asked.

"A lot bigger than home," Dalton said. "Again, thank you so much for the flight and the nice hotel room. I'm pretty sure my house can fit inside of the suite I'm in."

"A winner of any contest my company holds should receive nothing but the best," Mr. Riker said. "I'm glad the accommodations are to your liking. Now then, I've looked over the paperwork from last night and everything looks good, but I'd like to review one of those forms. Is that alright?"

"Totally fine, sir," Dalton said.

"Splendid," Mr. Riker said, pulling two folded pieces of paper from his jacket pocket. "This is the confidentiality agreement you signed last night. It states that anything we discuss here cannot be discussed outside of this office. You signed that you agreed."

He handed the form to Dalton to look over again.

"I did," Dalton said. "I don't have anyone here to discuss them with, except Carl over here, and we mostly talk about baseball."

"Excellent, which brings me to this next piece of paper. Carl, I will need you to sign this same form if you're going to sit here with us," Mr. Riker said.

"Sure thing," Carl said, taking a pen out of his pocket.

Mr. Riker slid the paper across the table to Carl for him to fill out and waited for him to do so. Once he was finished, Mr. Riker took the paper and placed it back in his jacket pocket.

"Now that all of this is complete, I'm curious to hear your answer, Dalton," Mr. Riker said.

"My answer?" Dalton asked.

"To the question I left you in the folder. I'm sure Carl has explained that I love asking questions like this. I consider them my icebreakers," Mr. Riker said.

"Oh, the question asking about the past or the future?" Dalton asked.

"Yes," Mr. Riker replied. "If you had the choice to either change something in your past or see your future, which one would you choose and why?"

Dalton sat back in his chair. He collected his thoughts before he answered.

"Mr. Riker, I sat and thought of this question last night before Carl left. I even showed it to him and we talked about it. My answer could honestly go both ways, however, I'm only supposed to pick one. If I had the choice, I'd have to see my future," Dalton said,

"Is that so?" Mr. Riker asked, smiling.

"You know," Dalton began. "The past made me who I am. There's a lot of pain in the past, too. Maybe if I could see the future, and know all the pain was worth it, I'd be okay. Nothing I can do to go back and change someone's mind. I can't go back and save my parents. Maybe in the future, my sister will be awake and I can be with the person I'm supposed to be with."

"Your sister?" Carl asked.

"My sister's in a coma, Carl," Dalton said. "My parents lived a good life. A long life, and they died. It happens. My sister took it hard and turned to drugs. She overdosed one night and has been in a coma ever since."

"Dalton, I'm sorry," Carl said.

"It's okay, Carl," Dalton said. He turned to Mr. Riker. "Could I go back and stop her from overdosing, maybe, but she'd do it again. Maybe in the future she'll wake up and get the help she needs, then I don't have to constantly be there. Maybe my future is where I'll be happy."

"Completely understandable," Mr. Riker said. "I spoke with Carl last night, and he chose the past, for reasons that are only known to him and myself. Should he want to share them with you, that's totally up to him."

"I'd go back and save my marriage, simple enough," Carl said.

"Both great answers. Both worth their weight in gold," Mr. Riker said.

"How about you?" Dalton asked.

"Me?" Mr. Riker said. "I'd have to go to the future. See if all my hard work continues to pay off. See what's ahead. Keep looking forward."

Dalton finally asked the question that had been weighing on his mind since the day he read the letter.

"Mr. Riker, what is the Escapement?" Dalton was finally able to ask.

"I'm so glad you asked," Mr. Riker said. "An Escapement, by definition, is a mechanical linkage in mechanical watches and clocks that gives impulses to the timekeeping element and periodically releases the gear train to move forward, advancing the clock's hands. An Escapement, by my definition, is an escape through time. A reset button. A do-over. Dalton, are you ready for your life to change forever?"

"Depends on what all of this actually is," Dalton said. "I read in the letter you sent me that I have the right to refuse the option as well. I'm just eager to see what all the fuss is about."

"I am too," Carl said.

"Well, I shall not keep you waiting any longer," Mr. Riker said. "First off, Dalton, you do have the right to refuse the Escapement. Like I said in the letter, no harm, no foul. But, if you refuse, that's it, no one else will have this opportunity. That I can elaborate on later."

"Okay," Dalton said, patiently waiting.

"Dalton, what if I told you time travel was possible?" Mr. Riker asked.

"What?" Dalton asked.

"If I were to give you an actual choice, to either go back to the past or go forward into the future, would you still choose the future?" Mr. Riker asked.

"Hypothetically?" Dalton asked.

"No," Mr. Riker said. "Actually."

"Hold up," Carl said. "Mr. Riker, are you saying that Dalton can choose whether or not he wants to travel through time?"

"That's exactly what I'm saying, Carl," Mr. Riker said.

"Time travel?" Dalton said. "That's science-fiction movie stuff. There's no way that's possible."

"Oh, but it is," Mr. Riker said. "And you get to decide whether or not you'd like to be the first man to successfully travel through time."

"Mr. Riker, are you serious?" Carl asked. "How?"

"Carl, when I first started this company, that was the ultimate goal," Mr. Riker said. "I kept it close to the vest because it's always been close to my heart. Time has always fascinated me. What if we could go back and change things? What if we could see the future? Can you imagine the possibilities? The money to be made? The fame to be had? I hired the best scientists, engineers and tech-savvy people I could find. To make money to fund the research, I went into the production business. We worked with Google. We made electronics. We're always on the cutting edge of technology and it's brought us here. Time travel IS possible. For the past ten years, we've made ultimate strides toward making it happen. We've finally figured it out."

"I need a drink," Carl said, standing up from the couch.

"Make that two," Dalton said.

"Three would be better," Mr. Riker said. "A celebratory drink."

Carl walked to a small cabinet beside the window where the liquor was kept and poured three glasses of straight Jack Daniels. He walked them back over, handing one to Mr. Riker and one to Dalton.

"To time!" Mr. Riker said, raising his glass in the air. Dalton and Carl looked at each other and both started drinking.

"I said your life would change," Mr. Riker said to Dalton. "How it changes depends on you. You have three options. Option 1, refuse, enjoy the rest of your stay and fly back home like nothing ever happened. Option 2, accept and go to the past. Option 3, accept and go to the future. The choice is yours, Mr. Mallet. Choose wisely."

"How much time do I have to think about this?" Dalton asked.

"The sooner the better, Dalton," Mr. Riker said. "Tomorrow would be ideal, Thursday at the latest."

"This is crazy!" Dalton said.

"I assure you, it's not," Mr. Riker said.

"How is all of this even possible?" Carl asked.

"Don't worry about the how's or why's," Mr. Riker said. "Carl, that promotion you received will place you on the cutting edge of this technology. This is what your department will be in control of. Our time branch. Could probably use a better name, but we can talk semantics later."

"A time travel branch?" Carl asked. "My team will be overseeing this part of your operations? I don't even understand how the hell it's all possible!"

"You will, Carl," Mr. Riker said. "All in due time."

"No time like the present!" Carl said.

"My concern right now is more the past, or the future, depending on which way Mr. Mallet would like to go," Mr. Riker said.

Dalton sat back on the couch just shaking his head back and forth, trying to make sense of all he was hearing.

"I'm just...I'm finding all this hard to believe," Dalton said.

"Believe it, Mr. Mallet," Mr. Riker said. "The possibility of time travel can and will change your life!"

"I have so many questions, but I don't even know how to ask," Dalton said.

"You have questions? Hell, I work here and I don't know what's going on," Carl said.

"Only five people other than myself know about any of this," Mr. Riker said. "They're all housed in the lab and have been working non-stop to make this a reality."

"The lab on the east side of our headquarters?" Carl asked.

"Not exactly," Mr. Riker said.

"Could I see the lab?" Dalton asked. "I'm assuming that's where it's going to happen."

"You assume correctly!" Mr. Riker said. "Let me see if the lab is available for you to visit."

Mr. Riker walked behind his desk and pulled open a drawer. He took what looked like a cell phone out of it and pressed a button on its side.

"Scott, this is Mr. Riker, can you hear me?"

"Go for Scott."

"Scott, is the lab available? Mr. Mallet would like to see our operation."

"Lab is available, sir. Come on down."

"Ten-four. We will be there momentarily."

Mr. Riker placed the phone back into his drawer and closed it.

"Would you two accompany me to the lab?" Mr. Riker asked.

"Absolutely," Dalton said. "Was that a phone, or a walkie-talkie?"

"A bit of both actually," Mr. Riker said. "Like the old Nextel's, only better."

Dalton nodded his head and looked at Carl. Carl shrugged.

"Ready to see the lab?" Dalton asked.

"Hell yeah, why not?" Carl said.

"If you happen to have any questions while we're down there, don't hesitate to ask, Dalton. I want you to know every bit of information you need to know before making this decision," Mr. Riker said.

All three men walked out of the office and through the hallway.

"Cindy, we're moving our meeting elsewhere. Hold all my calls. I'll be back soon," Mr. Riker said, walking past the reception desk.

"Yes, sir," Cindy said.

Once they got into the elevator, Mr. Riker pressed the 'L' button to go back down to the lobby.

"This is crazy," Dalton said.

"Who you tellin'?" Carl asked.

Once the elevator doors opened on the lobby floor, Mr. Riker took out his key and inserted it back into the small keyhole beside the panel. The doors immediately closed and the lights faded out, replaced by red, glowing lights. A small panel opened below the elevator buttons to reveal a button labeled 'T'.

Dalton and Carl both looked at each other in disbelief.

"I've been working here for years, and I never once questioned that keyhole or knew there was another button," Carl said.

"You wouldn't begin to believe everything you don't know, Carl," Mr. Riker said, pressing the button that made the elevator proceeded downward.

CHAPTER
SEVENTEEN

THE ELEVATOR DOORS opened to two bigger closed doors.

"Excuse me, gentlemen," Mr. Riker said. "I need to use the keypad over there to open these doors."

Mr. Riker stepped toward the keypad. Dalton turned to Carl.

"Can you believe this shit?" Dalton asked.

"I don't have the words, Dalt," Carl said.

The doors opened into another room.

"Gentlemen, follow me," Mr. Riker said.

"After you," Carl said, extending his arm and stepping aside.

Dalton and Carl followed Mr. Riker into what looked to be a perfect, circular room. There was a tall, slender, metal contraption in the middle of the room connected to all types of wires. Different types of machines were scattered all over the place. Wires ran from side to side across the floor and ceiling. There were three people walking around the contraption, using various electronic equipment on it. Mr. Riker walked past all of this to a man standing with a clipboard by several computer monitors. To Dalton, the man looked out of place.

"Scott," Mr. Riker said. "This is Dalton Mallet. He's our contest winner and wanted to see our little operation first-hand. Behind him is Carl, who you already know. He'll soon be helping all of you with our new time division we've established down here."

Scott turned away from his monitor, took off his glasses and starting cleaning them furiously.

"Hello, I'm Scott," he said. "We don't get many visitors down here."

"How long you been down here, Scott?" Carl asked. "I thought you'd quit?"

"About a year," Scott answered. "We keep a nice little place down here, but we aren't mole people or anything like that. Far from it. We each get two days off a week. Both in a row. We can go home and rest and relax like you do, but we pretty much choose to stay right here, because this, this is more important than being home. This is going to change everything. Has Mr. Riker told you what all of this is?"

"He said it was some kind of updated Port-o-Potty, right Dalton?" Carl said. Dalton laughed.

"Port-o-Potty?" Scott asked, confused. "This isn't a Port-o-Potty at all!"

"He's pulling your leg, Scott," Mr. Riker said. "I have told them mostly everything they need to know."

"Oh, okay," Scott said, putting his glasses back on. "It's a modern-day miracle, that's what it is. We can't wait to see this baby in action! Do you know which way you're going, Mr. Mallet?"

"Which way?" Dalton asked, still taking everything in.

"Mr. Mallet," Mr. Riker said. "He means in what direction will you be traveling. To the past or the future."

"Oh," Dalton said. "When the question was hypothetical, I said the future. Now that it's real...is this real?"

"Absolutely!" Scott said. "We have run the diagnostics, tested everything, and our trials..."

Scott was cut off by Mr. Riker before he could finish.

"Let's just say I've been very hands-on with this entire operation," Mr. Riker said. "We are ready and more than excited to jump to the past or the future. Now, Mr. Mallet, you have a big choice here. One that would normally take longer than we can allow you to take. If you'd like to do all this privately, without media, that's totally okay, however, we will be filming it. This needs to be documented for the world to see. This is the next big thing!"

Dalton looked at the contraption in the middle of the room.

"Is that," Dalton began to ask, pointing to the contraption in the center of the room. "Is that it?"

"Yes, it is," Mr. Riker said. "Sally, open up the door to the machine, please."

The lady with the lab coat standing beside an array of switches, buttons and levers pulled one of the switches down and the contraption opened. Dalton and Carl both walked to the front of it and looked inside.

"Well, it sure ain't no hot tub," Dalton said.

"Or a DeLorean," Carl added.

Mr. Riker walked up behind them and looked into the machine as well.

"We don't really have a name for it yet, gentlemen," Mr. Riker said, putting his arms around them. "That will be something you can think of, Carl. The way it works is quite simple. You tell us where you want to go. It takes some time to program, that's why we need to know early. It's not like the movies where you can just say it or type it in and go. Once you program it all in, in layman's terms, you hit a few switches, push a few buttons, pull a few lever's and it's ready. After you enter the machine, the door will close. A countdown will begin on the screen inside, while also relaying messages to you of what to do. The machine will tell you to close your eyes. When you open them again, you will not be in the present."

"How does it work?" Dalton asked.

"Have you ever watched Star Trek?" Mr. Riker asked.

"I've seen a few episodes here and there," Dalton said. "I'm not an expert or anything."

"Remember when they get beamed down or beamed up? It works very similar to that," Mr. Riker said.

"How do you know it works?" Dalton asked.

"How do you know if anything works?" Mr. Riker asked.

"You've tried it?!" Carl asked.

"In science, experiments must be done. Trials, as well as errors, have to be made," Mr. Riker said. "We learn from our mistakes. Once we had a working version, we tested. Material things, lab animals, things we could track."

"Ever tried it on a human?" Dalton asked.

Dalton heard Mr. Riker get quiet. Scott grabbed his clipboard and walked back to the room behind the lab. Everyone around them stopped working.

"Was it something he said?" Carl asked.

"I believe in being completely transparent with you, Dalton," Mr. Riker said. "You need this information to make an informed decision. We have tested four human subjects."

"Mr. Riker!" Carl said.

"All signed our waiver forms. All received payment. They answered an ad we had placed in various pop-ups and websites and we contacted them. We had them sign our legal forms and confidentiality agreements and went from there," Mr. Riker said.

"What happened?" Carl asked.

"Scott," Mr. Riker said aloud. "Please bring the test results from our four human subjects."

Scott brought four folders into the room and handed them to Mr. Riker.

"This is hard to talk about, but some of these people sacrificed themselves for Science. They were well aware of the ramifications," Mr. Riker said.

Carl couldn't believe what he was hearing. Dalton stood there, still amazed at everything, not sure how to act or how to feel. Inside his head, the thought of this being a reality shook him to the core. He didn't know what to ask or say, so he continued to listen.

"People died! People died because of this?" Carl asked.

"Carl, you know as well as I do, things are done in the name of Science at times to better our world. These people were willing participants and will get the credit they so rightfully deserve when all of this comes to light," Mr. Riker said.

"I can't believe what I'm hearing," Carl said.

Mr. Riker opened the first folder and began to explain the results of the tests.

"Each subject was tracked with a beacon. This is something we made in our lab in order to track the success of our test runs. Our first human subject was tested after successful tests with objects and various animals. The subject did not fare well. The machine overloaded and sadly the subject passed due to head trauma. We learned from this that human DNA, when beamed, I say beamed to keep the scientific jargon to a minimum, is very finicky. We have to be exact in our weight measurements, height measurements, blood samples, and everything else. If we are off just slightly, things could go awry, which we found out here," Mr. Riker said.

Carl put his hand on the back of his neck and winced. Dalton continued to stand there, listening. Mr. Riker continued.

"The second human subject was tested three months later," Mr. Riker said. "The subject unfortunately passed during the beam. We couldn't stop mid-beam. The subject had an aneurysm. The process was too much for the subject to take. We knew it worked then, because when we opened the door, the body was missing. We monitor all the vitals once our subjects are inside. The subject could have had the aneurysm anywhere, it just so happened to be during our experiment. We ran through all of our notes and data meticulously to see if it was anything from the inside or on our end. We concluded that the commotion and the toll this takes on the body during the process is rough, but the blinking lights during the beaming process can be too much on the brain, hence the closing of the eyes stipulation we added to the inside of the machine."

"The eyes must remain closed for the duration," Scott chimed in. "It is very important that they stay closed."

"Thank you, Scott," Mr. Riker said. " Our third human subject was tested two months after our second subject. Everything on our end was ready. All tests passed from the equipment to the test subject. Process went smooth as could be and we tracked the subject into the future, using our beacon. Once the subject arrived, our monitors went crazy. The beacon began to indicate the subjects' heart had stopped. Our subject landed on a street and was hit by a car. Killed on impact."

"Wait," Carl said. "Killed on impact? How do you know this if the subject was sent to the future?"

"Our subject wasn't sent years away, Carl," Mr. Riker said. "Our subject was sent forward a week. A week into the future. Upon entering, our subject was hit by a car on the Las Vegas Strip. It was all over the news. Remember the individual that appeared out of nowhere, according to witnesses. That was our third test subject."

"Holy shit! Are you serious?" Carl asked.

"This is real?" Dalton asked, looking at Carl. "This is really happening?"

"It's real alright," Scott said. "I was here. I saw it. It happened."

"Our fourth and final human subject was tested two months after our third subject. Everything on our end was ready. All tests passed from the equipment to the test subject. Process went smooth as could be and we tracked the subject into the past, using our beacon. Once the subject arrived, the beacon was active for three hours before it failed. We checked the beacon schematics and found a flaw in the design concerning the tracking of time. The flaw was corrected, but we lost contact with the subject. Subject presumed alive," Mr. Riker said.

"Someone actually did it?" Dalton asked.

"They sure did, we just had a hiccup on our beacon. That's why we know it'll work now. You also have all the information at your disposal," Mr. Riker said.

"This is crazy!" Carl said. "Have you really made a time machine?"

"We," Mr. Riker said. "This is your division now, Carl. We have made a time machine. All of our successes and failures, we shall have together."

Carl placed both of his hands on a desk that had two monitors on it and leaned forward, not believing what he was hearing. Dalton stared into the machine, in disbelief.

"Everything he's saying is true," Scott said. "I witnessed everything."

"Time travel is now a reality gentleman. It is no longer a mere fantasy," Mr. Riker said.

"I have another question," Dalton said.

"Okay," Mr. Riker replied. "I will try to answer the best way I can."

"You've only got one question?" Carl asked.

"Since the beacon messed up, on your last subject, is that why you couldn't bring them back?" Dalton asked.

"You didn't tell him?" Scott asked, looking at Mr. Riker.

"Dalton," Mr. Riker began. "The beacon has nothing to do with bringing someone back. It's just a way to track our subjects to let us know our success rate or failure."

"Oh," Dalton said. "Then why didn't you bring them back?"

Everyone in the room stopped what they were doing again. The room became eerily quiet. You could hear a pin drop. Mr. Riker looked at Dalton and simply smiled.

"My dear boy," Mr. Riker said. "This is a one-way ride. Once you make the trip, you can't come back."

EIGHTEEN

"WHAT DO YOU mean, you can't come back?" Dalton asked.

"Mr. Mallet," Scott said. "In order to make a return trip, one would need this same machine and the same amount of prep time. The machine is here."

"Think of it like this, Dalton," Mr. Riker said. "If you go to the past, you would need this machine to get you back. That means we would have to send a group to every year in the history of mankind to build one of these in order to make that happen. On the other hand, one could be built in the future, but we have no way of knowing. However, if it were already built, wouldn't someone be here by now with it? So, this is a one-way ticket. You can travel there, but there is no traveling back."

"This is a lot to think about," Dalton said. "This whole thing is just..."

"A big ol' mindfuck?" Carl added.

"That!" Dalton said, pointing at Carl.

"But what an opportunity!" Mr. Riker said.

"Why not you?" Dalton asked, looking at Mr. Riker.

"Me?" Mr. Riker replied. "My God, I'd love to! And I most certainly will! But I need to stay on this end with Carl and everyone else for the time being. We must document and educate our world on what it means and the possibilities that time travel presents."

"But you said that no one else would get the chance if I refused. You said you would explain that later," Dalton said.

"I did say that, and I meant it," Mr. Riker said. "No one will get the chance, at least, not in the immediate future. When you go, wherever you decide to go, we would like you to document everything. We want to get as much information here that you can share with us. We have designed a camera that should work as a two-way between time. It's inside of a special watch that you will wear, that also contains the beacon. With this, you can make direct contact with our lab, no matter which way you decide to go. In time, I shall follow, as well as many others. Imagine all the government funding."

"This is so heavy," Dalton said. "Wait, another thing. If I choose to go forward or back, will anything I do change time? Could I be responsible for altering the past or future as we know it?"

Dalton felt the air get heavy in the room, realizing the implications this could have. He had seen many movies about time travel, but they were just that, movies. This was real life. He didn't know what would happen and hoped Mr. Riker would have an answer.

"Can the future or the past truly be changed?" Carl asked.

"Carl, Dalton," Mr. Riker said. "I've been a student of time travel for a very long time. I've enjoyed the movies that involved it in any way, shape or form. Loved the books and stories from the fiction I've read. Now, it's a reality. We won't really know the full extent of time travel until we do it. I do have my theories and if you both will allow me; I'll share them with you."

"Be my guest," Carl said.

"I'd love to hear them," Dalton said. "Especially since it's my ass making the decision."

"There are universally three distinct theories about time travel," Mr. Riker said. "There is the fixed timeline, the dynamic timeline, and the multiverse theory. I will try to explain them to you the best way I can, without getting too scientific, of course."

"I'd appreciate that," Dalton said.

"Me too," Carl chimed in.

"I'll start with the fixed timeline. The fixed timeline theory says if someone were to go back in time, the future they left cannot be changed.

All events remain as fixed points in time. Basically, it's course correction. The future doesn't allow itself to be changed. It's like your classic Terminator movie, so to speak," Mr. Riker said.

"Is that what you believe?" Carl asked.

"Let me finish, then I'll tell you what I believe," Mr. Riker said. "The second theory is the dynamic timeline. This is like Back to the Future, which I love. If you go back in time and alter events in the past, it will directly impact the present. For instance, let's say you go back and accidentally kill your father. This would never allow you to be born, therefore, you would cease to exist and ultimately disappear from reality. Remember in the movie when Marty was disappearing from the picture? Unless he was able to get his parents to kiss, he would be gone forever. Same concept. In order to exist, he couldn't change the events that led to his birth."

"That's heavy, doc," Dalton said with a smile.

Carl shook his head.

"Precisely!" Mr. Riker said. "The third and final theory is the multiverse theory. This supports the theory of alternate timelines and an infinite number of parallel universes. This was explained very well in the last Avengers movie, Endgame, I believe. When someone travels to the past, anything they change will actually create an alternate timeline. For instance, if you go back, anything you change will not affect the present we live in now. Only the new timeline will be affected, the alternate time-line. Does any of this make sense?"

"It's all over my head, but the movie references helped," Dalton said. "Which one do you lean towards?"

"Personally, I believe in the multiverse theory. I believe there are parallel universes. Have you ever had deja vu?" Mr. Riker asked.

Dalton and Carl both nodded their heads, paying attention to every word Mr. Riker was saying.

"I personally believe deja vu is a way of letting you know you've been down that particular path before. If you don't experience it, you're going down a path you've never traveled. If you do experience it, you have made these same decisions and choices before. I could go on for days about this, but in my personal opinion, I believe in the multiverse theory. I think that you can change things and nothing in our present, here, would be affected. Wouldn't that be something?" Mr. Riker said.

"Something isn't the word I would use," Carl said. "And I'm going to end up running this operation."

"This is all so, out there," Dalton said.

Sally pushed the switch back to the up position and the door to the contraption closed. Dalton and Carl took a step back, trying to take in everything they had seen and heard. Mr. Riker said something to Scott and he disappeared again to a room outside of the lab.

"Seems I've given you quite a bit to think about," Mr. Riker said to Dalton.

"That's an understatement," Dalton replied. "When do you need an answer, again?"

"Tonight would be wonderful. Tomorrow at the latest," Mr. Riker said.

"I'd love to make this happen as soon as possible. I honestly can't wait!"

"I guess I've got some thinking to do," Dalton said.

"Yes, indeed," Mr. Riker said. "Wherever you would like to do your thinking, please do so. If it wasn't raining, I would have Carl take you to the Grand Canyon to mull things over."

"The hotel's fine," Dalton said. "I may try and walk the strip a bit. Clear my head, gain some perspective. Even in the rain."

"Wonderful," Mr. Riker said. "I'll have Carl take you back. Feel free to think everything over and then some."

"Carl," Mr. Riker added. "Once you have taken Mr. Mallet back to his hotel, do come back here so we can discuss your job a bit further, now that you know a little more of what it entails."

Carl nodded his head. They all began to walk back toward the elevator. Dalton turned his head and looked behind him, still not believing everything he was seeing and hearing.

"We are on the cusp of history, gentleman. Soak it all in," Mr. Riker said, extending his arms into the air.

Once they were in the elevator, Mr. Riker closed the panel and removed his key. He pressed the button that would take them to the lobby.

"Carl, I'll see you soon," Mr. Riker said. "Dalton, if you have any more questions, please call my direct line. Carl will give you the number. I'll answer everything I can to the best of my ability. Also, keep in mind everything we've said today is completely confidential. You may discuss it with Carl or me, but no one else. Happy thinking."

Mr. Riker stayed inside the elevator, most likely taking it to his office. Dalton and Carl exited, and walked toward the car, both in somewhat of a state of shock.

"Carl, is this really happening?" Dalton said, getting in the car.

"Looks that way," Carl said. "I need a drink."

"Me, too," Dalton said.

"A time machine," Carl said, as he shut his door and began to drive away. "A time machine. A goddamn time machine. The son of a bitch actually did it."

"Has he tried it before?" Dalton asked.

"Not that I know of, but he's always been fascinated with that kind of shit," Carl said. "I mean, have you read any of his interviews? Now that I think about it, he always mentions something about time. Hell, he practically quotes 'Back to the Future' in all the staff meetings. I just can't believe he actually figured it out. Damn."

"Man, this is way out of my league," Dalton said.

"This is out of the fucking ballpark!" Carl said. "And me? I'm going to be in charge of it all?"

"I have to decide whether or not to go through with it, don't I?" Dalton asked.

"Yeah man, you do. Shit," Carl said. "I wish I could offer you some advice, but I don't even know where to start or what to tell you. You have to answer two questions, bud. One, are you going to do it, and two, if you do, where the hell will you go? What a hell of a prize to win. What a hell of a set of questions to answer."

"His question from last night makes sense now," Dalton said.

"But that was hypothetical. When it comes down to it, and my friend, it's come down to it, does your answer from last night, or today, still hold relevance to the question asked?" Carl asked.

"I honestly don't know," Dalton said, looking out of the side window, watching the rain continue to fall. "Would your answer still be the same?"

"I'm not you, buddy," Carl said. "It's not my decision to make."

"But what if it was?" Dalton asked. "If you were to be given the same choice as me, would your choice be any different?"

They had made it to the Bellagio. Carl pulled the car around to the front door. He put the car in park and looked directly at Dalton. He never cracked a smile.

"I would go back, no questions asked," Carl said. "I lost something months ago. I'm coming to realize I may never get it back. A life without her just isn't worth living. For all the mistakes I've made, I'm sure I've paid for them and then some. I want answers. I want her. If I had the choice, I'd go make things right. I'd make life worth living again."

NINETEEN

D ALTON EXITED THE car, still in shock. Carl told him he would be back later in the evening, probably around six. It was two now. He told Dalton if he needed anything, to give him a call. Dalton nodded and walked into the Bellagio. Carl put his car in drive and proceeded back to Riker Industries.

Carl was lost in thought the entire way back. He was going to be the team lead of this world-changing event. He didn't know if he was ready for it. He knew for sure he didn't understand it, but Mr. Riker trusted him. Mr. Riker wanted him to be a part of this, for reasons even Carl didn't understand. *I am sure there are way more people much more qualified than me for this,* he thought to himself. He couldn't get back to work fast enough. All of this information was like a whirlwind. So much input. Carl knew there was so much to catch up on, and he couldn't imagine where it would start.

Carl thought of Vanessa. If she was mad at him before with all the time he spent at work, she sure wouldn't have been happy now, if she was still around. He had meant every word he had said to Dalton. In fact, he was a little jealous. *If it were me, I'd leave today. We'd be back together, kiddo.*

Carl thought about the letter he received on his door the previous night. He was supposed to meet someone at seven tonight. What did they know? Who were they? *What a freaking day!*

As Carl pulled into Riker Industries, he saw a familiar face at the security station.

"Long time, no see," Larry said.

"Larry! I thought you were off today," Carl said.

"This place can't function properly without me. Evening shift called out and guess who they call? The Gatekeeper himself, Mr. Larry!" Larry said.

Carl flashed his badge to Larry and was given a thumbs up. Carl drove right back to the spot he had left from a few minutes ago. He made his way to the elevator and straight to Cindy's desk once he arrived at Mr. Riker's floor.

"Is he in?" Carl asked Cindy.

"You know he is," Cindy said. "I'm not sure he ever leaves sometimes. Let me tell him you're back."

Cindy called Mr. Riker's office.

"Carl has arrived, sir. Yes, sir. Yes, sir. Will do."

Cindy hung up the phone.

"He said go ahead back, Carl," Cindy said.

"Thanks, Cindy," Carl said.

Carl walked down the hall and knocked on Mr. Riker's door. Once Mr. Riker instructed him to come in, Carl did just that. Mr. Riker was behind his desk at his computer. Once Carl entered, Mr. Riker stopped what he was doing and smiled at Carl.

"Please have a seat, Carl," Mr. Riker said.

"Thank you, sir," Carl said.

"Today has been eye-opening for you and our guest, I'm sure," Mr. Riker said.

"To say the least," Carl replied. Carl's stomach growled.

"Oh, my word!" Mr. Riker said. "We totally skipped our lunch, didn't we? With all the excitement, food was the last thing I was thinking about. I will call Cindy and ask her to bring us some sandwiches that were ordered earlier today. Would you like a sandwich?"

"That would be fine," Carl said. "I guess I need to eat."

Mr. Riker called Cindy and asked her to bring two ham and cheese sandwiches, if there were any left. Carl nodded in approval while Mr. Riker was talking.

"She should be in with those soon," Mr. Riker said. "Fortunately for us, there were a few sandwiches left. Until then, this is for you."

Mr. Riker slid a brown briefcase across his desk toward Carl. Carl grabbed the handle and pulled it toward him. He pressed the buttons by the handle to open it, but it was locked.

"The code is 0-8-8," Mr. Riker said. "Because when this baby hits eighty-eight miles per hour, you're going to see some serious shit."

"Appropriate reference," Carl said with a grin.

"I thought so," Mr. Riker said, all smiles.

Carl used his fingers to roll the appropriate numbers on each side of the clasps. Once he did, he pressed the buttons and the clasps unlocked. He opened the briefcase to an array of files and folders. The briefcase seemed to be full of data.

"This is the sum of the information we have on our little machine below us," Mr. Riker said.

"This is all the information on our new division?" Carl asked.

"Not all of it, but it's a start," Mr. Riker said. "You will need to familiarize yourself with all of this. Think of it as your homework. Once you have the basics, we can go through all the files, folders, videos, and everything else we have on the computers down in the main lab."

"I can do that," Carl said. "Mr. Riker, I have a question for you."

"If I could quote you from earlier, only one?" Mr. Riker asked, smiling.

"Why me?" Carl asked. "There are so many people here that work for you. Many of them are a lot smarter than me. Hell, some of them probably even designed this thing for you. So, yeah, just one question. Why me?"

"Carl," Mr. Riker said. "I told you earlier that you've been with me for a very long time. No matter what position you've held in this company, you've met deadlines and surpassed any goal we've asked. You are loyal and true to our company. Even in a time of despair, you pulled through for us on one of our greatest mergers and achievements our company has had to date. You do not allow yourself to fail. You are the perfect man for this job."

"I hope I am," Carl said. "But it seems way above my paygrade."

"You are, and it most certainly isn't," Mr. Riker said. "I wanted to bring you in last year when we started the trials, but you were busy with the other deal, and I surely couldn't afford for that deal to go south. Once it was complete, that's when you told me about the problems at home, then ultimately what happened with Vanessa. Yet, you completed all of your tasks. You proved yourself to this company and more importantly, to me. Even when life was getting the upper hand, you used work as your outlet and we thrived. I've always had you in mind for this. Now, it's official."

"Again, thank you, sir," Carl said. "But time travel? I don't even know where to begin."

"You begin with the files in the briefcase," Mr. Riker said.

There was a knock at the door. Cindy walked in with a plate of sandwiches accompanied by two cans of soda.

"Thank you, Cindy," Mr. Riker said.

"Thank you, Cindy," Carl said.

"My pleasure! I would hate to throw all these extra sandwiches away. Enjoy!" Cindy said, leaving the sandwiches and drinks before she closed the door behind her and left.

Mr. Riker called this a working lunch and allowed Carl to move himself and his items to the couch by the door to peruse the briefcase while he ate. Mr. Riker continued to sit behind his desk, work on whatever he was working on at his computer, and eat. Carl set up shop at the table. He took out the first folder from the briefcase while taking a bite from his sandwich.

"Before I forget," Mr. Riker said. "This is for you."

Mr. Riker lobbed an object across the room toward Carl. He dropped his folder on the table and caught the object in the air. It was a small key.

"This is the elevator key. Only you, me and Scott have a copy. Don't lose it," Mr. Riker said.

"Oh, I won't," Carl said. He dug his hand into his pocket and pulled out his keys. He added the key to his keyring, right beside the new car key. Once the key was added, he put the keys back in his pocket and proceeded to investigate the folder in front of him. He opened the folder on the table and read from the top:

'Main Lab Entry Protocol'

'Insert key into elevator'

'Press 'T' button (Time)'

'When elevator stops, approach main keypad'

'Password for entry is: 4-8-15-16-23-42-EXECUTE'

"Nice call on the password for the time machine room," Carl said.

"You understand the 'LOST' reference as well?" Mr. Riker asked. "I thought it was a solid touch."

"Oh, it is," Carl said, taking another bite of his sandwich. "I loved that show. To make it a password for an underground time machine. Classic."

Mr. Riker smiled and continued to work while he ate. Carl continued to look through the files in the folder. Some of the things he understood, some he knew he would have to research. He finally made it to the files on the tested subjects, but a lot of their information was blocked out like you would see in a military redacted file (according to the movies anyway).

"Mr. Riker," Carl asked. "Why is the information on the subjects blacked out?"

"In front of you, Carl, is what you need to know," Mr. Riker said. "Since you are the head of this department now, anything you can or will be asked later could be up for questioning. If you don't know about it, you can't answer it. Better to be safe than sorry. Once we have all of our ducks in a row and whatnot, we can always reveal the files later."

"You're the boss," Carl said, finishing his sandwich. He did think it was weird that Mr. Riker didn't share everything with him, but maybe he didn't need to know every little detail, not yet anyway.

"Thank you for the sandwich," Carl said. He was almost done with his soda as well. "That really hit the spot. I needed to eat something."

"Absolutely," Mr. Riker said. "Now that you have eaten, can I show you to your new office?"

"New office?" Carl asked.

"New title, new car, new office," Mr. Riker said. He stood up and walked over to the other side of the room and stood in front of a door.

"Right this way, Mr. Gilbert."

Carl closed the briefcase and stood up. He threw his empty soda in the trash can beside him and walked over to where Mr. Riker was standing. Mr. Riker opened the door to another office, right beside his own. It was almost as large as Mr. Riker's office, but still smaller by a few square feet. All of his old items from his previous office were in there, already moved.

"I had Cindy take care of this last night. You're right next to me. Only a door separates us," Mr. Riker said.

"This is really nice," Carl said. "I sat here yesterday trying to figure out where this door went. Thank you, Mr. Riker."

The office joined Mr. Rikers but had a door of its own to the outside. He had a bigger desk as well, and on top of it, a new computer.

"All of your files have already been copied and carried over," Mr. Riker said.

There was a giant window in the back, facing the strip, and the view was magnificent.

"I will leave you to it," Mr. Riker said. "Again, thank you for accepting the position. It will be a lot of work, but we will be working together. It's easier if we're right next to each other. I'll have Cindy bring you a catalog later so you can order whatever furniture you consider appropriate. Again, glad to have you aboard, Carl."

"Glad to be here, sir," Carl said.

Mr. Riker patted Carl on the back and went back into his own office.

"Holy shit!" Carl said, standing in the middle of his new office.

Carl made his way over to his desk and sat the briefcase down. He eased himself down into his new desk chair and opened the desk drawers to find all of his items and files were there. There was also a small case of cigars with a post-it note attached to the lid.

'Congrats! You deserve it. Cindy'

He smiled and took out one of the cigars, held it up to his nose, and smelled it. He spun around in his chair and looked out of his window. So much had happened in so little time. It felt like a dream. He looked out over the city that never sleeps and thought about how far he had come. He wanted to call Vanessa. He wanted to let her know, but he knew she wouldn't answer. *Is all this really worth it if I can't share it with you?*

Carl felt his phone vibrate in his pocket. He took out the phone and looked at the screen, not recognizing the number. He answered anyway.

"This is Carl Gilbert."

"Carl, this is Dalton. Do you have a minute?"

"Hey man, I didn't recognize the number. I need to program it in my damn phone. Of course, I've got a minute. Everything okay?"

"I'm not sure."

"What do you mean, you're not sure?"

"When you left, I went for a walk. The strip is a lot longer than it looks from the sky. I just needed to think."

"I can understand that. I'm still trying to process all this shit, too."

"Anyway, I had a bite to eat and came back to my room."

"Okay."

"Does anyone else know I'm here?"

"What do you mean, Dalton?"

"When I got back to my room, there was a note on my door."

"A note on your door? From room service maybe?"

"I don't think so."

"What did the note say, Dalton?"

"It said 7 p.m. Make sure you are with Carl tonight in the casino. I'm going to speak to both of you. A friend."

Carl stayed silent on the other end of the phone.

"Carl, what is all this about?"

"I don't know, Dalton. Give me about ten minutes. I'll be there soon."

TWENTY

W HEN DALTON GOT out of the car, he walked into the casino. He got as far as the front desk when he decided he needed to get out and explore. The rain had let up to nothing more than a mist for the time being, so he decided to walk the strip and think a bit. The information he had been given was indeed life-changing, and he wasn't sure how to process it. He still couldn't believe it was possible. He hoped that walking down the strip would give him some kind of clarity.

Carl left to head back to Riker Industries. Dalton knew Carl was in shock, too. Carl had to go back and learn even more of what was going on under his nose without his knowledge. Maybe Carl would learn some things that would help make this decision easier.

When Dalton walked outside, he turned and looked at the fountains. Across from the fountains was a replica, albeit smaller, of the Eiffel Tower, outside of a casino called Paris. He knew this because of the hot air balloon on the building that had the name written across it. He decided to walk north on the strip. He had already seen what was to the south. He had passed the big pyramid called the Luxor and the MGM Grand that looked straight out of Oz, with its emerald green coloring. He hadn't yet seen all the buildings to the north, so that was the direction he headed.

The buildings were massive, and because of the weather, there weren't that many people out looking. The first building he saw on his left was Caesar's Palace. It was huge. There were so many buildings surrounding it. He even thought he saw a coliseum on the property, but he wasn't quite sure. Across the street was a picture of Donny and Marie

Osmond covering the windows of a place called the Flamingo. In front of that, a little place called Margaritaville. He decided to cross the street and have himself one.

Margaritaville was very inviting, just as the Jimmy Buffett song suggests. Dalton got a table and ordered some fish tacos and, according to the menu, a perfect margarita. He tried to relax, listening to what was obviously Jimmy's greatest hits piping through the intercom system of the establishment. The tacos were right on time. He didn't even realize how hungry he was until they were placed in front of him. The margarita was as close to perfect as he had ever had. He still had a giant decision to make, but this place seemed to relax him a bit before he continued to explore the city. He tipped the waitress generously and continued on his way.

Ahead, to the left, was the Mirage. The Mirage was a big white building with plenty of palm trees in front of it, as well as a functioning, small volcano. It seemed that each building had its own theme. No building was like any of the others. Across from the Mirage was the Venetian, where he and Carl had eaten the night before. Further up the road and to the left was a hotel and casino called Treasure Island. That would be his final stop before turning back around. He wanted to see the big pirate ship in front of that place, and he did. He saw where they actually perform shows on the pirate ship. Dalton wanted to continue to explore, but he knew he had to get back. Dalton had walked well over a mile, which wasn't much, but he had taken his time. From the exploring, eating, and thinking, he had already been out an hour and a half, according to his new watch. It was already half-past three. Carl would be coming back at six, so he wanted to get back in enough time to sit and relax a bit on the couch while examining his watch and the mysterious box a bit more.

Dalton turned and headed back. The rain was starting to pick up a bit, but he didn't care. He was lost in his thoughts and the scenery. This was not an easy decision. He was hoping that maybe he could get a good night's sleep and wake up with a decision ready to go, but he doubted it. He wanted to tell Britney. Dalton knew he couldn't. He tried to think about what she would tell him to do, but she wouldn't have believed it was possible. She was more of a realist than he was. She kept him down to Earth. She was more practical. He loved her for it.

Before long, Dalton was standing at the fountains again. The rain was coming down harder. He was already wet. His watch read 4:15 across the screen, so he watched the fountains a bit longer before walking back inside. Dalton wasn't dripping wet, but he was pretty saturated and definitely needed another pair of socks. He was also glad he brought more than one pair of shoes for this trip. His feet were soaked and he couldn't stand that feeling. Dalton sloshed his way through the lobby and into the elevator. When he arrived on his floor, he saw there was a note on the door. He dried his hands the best he could and pulled the note off.

7 p.m.

Tonight

Make sure you are with Carl in the casino.

I need to speak with both of you.

I'll find you

A friend

Dalton reached in his pocket, grabbed his phone and called Carl immediately. After the conversation, Dalton went into the room and placed the note on the bar. He started undressing and took a hot shower. While he was putting on his clothes, there was a knock at his door. He yelled from the bedroom.

"Who is it?"

"Dalton, it's Carl."

Dalton walked to the door. He had on some jeans, new socks, and a dry pair of Timberland work boots. He had his shirt in his hand when he opened the door.

"Hey bud, where's the note?" Carl asked.

"Right here on the bar," Dalton said, picking up the note and handing it to Carl. "How did you get up here? I thought I had the card with the elevator access."

"I showed the people at the desk that we paid for the room and I needed to see you. They gave me a card, but I had to sign it out. Only allows me to get up the elevator, not in the room. You say this note was here when you got back?" Carl asked.

"Yeah," Dalton said.

"Shit. Yep, same person," Carl said.

"Same person?" Dalton asked. "You know this guy?"

"The only thing I know for sure today, Dalton, is that I don't know jack shit," Carl said.

"Have a seat, I think I need to show you what was left on my door last night."

"Your door?" Dalton asked as Carl walked past him. "Last night?"

Dalton closed the door, locked it, and joined Carl on the couch.

CHAPTER
TWENTY-ONE

WHEN DALTON SAT on the couch, Carl gave him the note that was left on his door the night before. Dalton read it.

"Do you have any idea who would write these and leave them for us?" Dalton asked.

"No clue," Carl said.

"You got this last night?" Dalton asked.

"When I left your place last night, yeah. It was on my door waiting for me, same as you," Carl said.

"There is no one here I know," Dalton said. "How does anyone know I'm here? How did they get up here?"

"Those are good damn questions," Carl said. "And to bring my wife into this, they've got balls. Big ones."

"I know last night you mentioned she left," Dalton said. "What kind of information could they have?"

"I don't know," Carl said.

Carl got up and walked to the bar. He poured himself a drink.

"You want one?" Carl asked Dalton.

"After the day we're having, serve it up," Dalton said.

As they drank their drinks, standing against the bar, Carl began to talk.

"She left me three months ago, Dalton. I haven't heard from her since. Is that normal?" Carl asked.

"I'm really not the one to ask about normal," Dalton said. "You haven't heard anything in three months?"

"Not a peep," Carl said. "I've called, left messages, sent texts. Shit, I'd mail a letter if I knew where to send it. I've got nothing. Came home one day and there was a note. All her shit was gone. Not so much as a scent of her perfume left for me to take in."

"Damn, Carl," Dalton said. "And you were together for a while, right?"

"Known her for twenty years," Carl said. "Married eighteen of em'. Not so much as a message left at work with the secretary to let me know she was okay."

"And the note she left. Any mention of where she was headed?" Dalton asked.

"Basically, it said shit I already knew. We had our ups and downs; we both knew that. Said she needed some time away from me. Said she needed to see if I was what she really needed, in a nutshell," Carl said as he finished his drink.

"Carl, I'm sorry," Dalton said. "I can't say I know how that feels, but I can relate."

"Can you?" Carl asked.

"I was married before," Dalton said. "She wasn't the one, though. Should've never gone through with it, but that's a story for another time. Our split was amicable. Both of us were young and stupid, and luckily, we realized it sooner rather than later. I dated after and never thought I'd marry again, but we don't get paid for thinking, do we?"

"I guess we don't," Carl said, waiting for Dalton to finish.

"Like most stories go, a few years after my divorce, I met someone that I never would've thought I'd have a chance with, and she was the one. Hell, I think she'll always be the one. And I asked her to marry me. She told me no," Dalton said.

"Damn, son," Carl said, pouring them another drink.

"She got a promotion at work. Well, more like an opportunity. She's a nurse and a position came for her to work abroad, or something like that. She went to Europe. I couldn't go, because of my sister. Nothing I can do for my sister really, except visit every now and again, but she didn't want me to make that choice," Dalton said.

"She still in Europe?" Carl asked.

"Yeah," Dalton said. "Called her yesterday. She called me back and left a voicemail. God only knows when she's coming back."

"But at least you know where she is," Carl said, walking back to the couch.

"Doesn't make it any easier, buddy," Dalton said.

"I know, man," Carl said. "Shit, none of this is ideal at all. It's still raining outside, some damn person wants to meet with us with information about my wife and God knows what else, I'm now in charge of a damn time committee, and you have to decide if you want to Marty McFly your ass somewhere. Does that about cover it?"

"Yeah," Dalton said, finishing his second drink. "I believe that about covers it. Plus, that damn box. Where the hell did it come from? Why the hell can't I remember what happened on that plane?"

Dalton and Carl sat in silence for a few moments. Carl slapped Dalton on the shoulder.

"You figured out what you want to do yet?" he asked.

"Not even close," Dalton said.

"Well, maybe after all this and some sleep, you'll know what to do," Carl said. "What time's it getting to be?"

Dalton looked at his watch.

"It's almost six," he said. "Your time."

"Glad you have a watch on Vegas time now, no matter who the hell it's from," Carl said. "Now get a shirt on, Carolina boy. We probably need to make our way to the casino. Apparently, that's where this writer of mystery notes will find us."

Dalton put on his shirt.

"I told you I'm not much on gambling," Dalton said.

"Well, that's too damn bad," Carl said. "Our presence is requested at the casino tonight, hombre. We shall gamble a bit and when this person decides to show themselves, they're going to have a bit of explaining to do."

They both walked out of the room, got in the elevator and rode down to the lobby. They stepped onto the casino floor. There were people everywhere. The rain had kept many people inside and most were trying their luck tonight.

"Before we start, let's walk over to the front desk," Carl said. "Let's see if anyone else requested a key to your room. Only way to get up there, right?"

Dalton agreed and followed Carl to the front desk.

"Excuse me, ma'am," Dalton said. "Has anyone besides this gentleman asked for a key to the penthouse elevator?"

The lady at the front desk smiled and began typing away on the computer in front of her. Dalton didn't have to wait long for an answer.

"No, sir. Just a Mr. Carl Gilbert with Riker Industries," the lady said.

"Thank you," Dalton said.

"Well, it was worth a shot," Carl said.

After returning and signing the penthouse key card back in, Carl led Dalton toward the blackjack tables.

"Have you ever played?" Carl asked.

"A little," Dalton said. "Mostly on the computer. I know the general idea."

"We need to kill some time until whoever it is shows up," Carl said. "I'm going to play a little blackjack. There are slots all around us. Roulette is to the left. Craps tables are in the middle, there. If you sit at any one of the tables or machines, they'll bring you free drinks. At least act like you are gambling."

"I'll sit with you for a few hands. Maybe it will get my mind off of it," Dalton said.

"Hell, maybe we can win big," Carl said.

Carl and Dalton both sat down at one of the blackjack tables, side by side, unaware they were being watched from across the casino.

CHAPTER
TWENTY-TWO

S HE SAW THEM walk across the casino and go to the front desk.
"Smart move," she said aloud, knowing they were trying to figure
out how she got on the elevator to leave the note on the penthouse door.

She saw them sit at the blackjack table. The clock on her phone read
6:15 p.m. She would make contact with them closer to seven, just like
she said. She needed answers. She hoped Carl had them. She didn't know
the other guy but knew he was with Carl. Better to talk to both of them,
maybe catch someone in a lie. She turned back around in the chair she was
sitting in at a table by the lobby and opened her purse to take out some
index cards and a pen. Inside the purse were also some tiny folders. One
was labeled 'Vanessa Gilbert'; the other, 'Chris Williams'.

When I get some answers, you can get some answers, she thought to herself.

She wrote something down on several of the index cards and placed
them back into her purse with the pen, except for one. She got the attention of one of the waitresses and called her over before she closed her
purse.

"Yes ma'am, how can I help you?" the waitress asked.

"Oh, nothing for me," she said. "However, there is a nice tip involved if
you could deliver this index card to the gentleman there at the blackjack
table around seven-ish. He's the handsome gentleman with the button-
down blue shirt, sitting beside the younger man with the ball cap."

"I can make that happen," the waitress said.

"Thank you, so much," she said, taking out a one-hundred-dollar bill from her purse.

"This is for you. Make sure you bring them their drink of choice around seven. Keep the rest for yourself, as long as you take this card and give it to him."

"Consider it done, thank you!" the waitress said.

"No, thank you," she said as the waitress walked away.

She reached her hand into her purse to close her wallet. Before she clasped the purse back shut, she checked to make sure the small 9 mm and .38 Special were still in there. They were. And they were loaded.

CHAPTER
TWENTY-THREE

DALTON AND CARL weren't doing well playing blackjack.
"This is why I don't gamble," Dalton said to Carl.

"Not too much longer, Dalt," Carl said. "Just keep placing the minimum bet, or do you want to try something else?"

"This is fine. What time is it getting to be?" Dalton asked aloud, looking at his watch. "Ten till seven. I'll keep my eyes open."

"For what?" Carl asked. "We have no idea who or what to look for. Whoever it is said they would find us."

"Hello, gentleman," a waitress said from behind them. Dalton and Carl turned around.

"I asked your server what you were having. Vodka and Sprite for you, sir. Carl, right?" the waitress asked.

"Yes, I'm Carl," he said.

"And a Jack and coke for you, mister?" the waitress said.

"Mallet, Dalton Mallet," he replied.

"Okay, gentleman," the waitress said. "Good luck to you. These drinks are compliments of the young woman who was sitting at the table across the way."

They both looked over to an empty table.

"She also said to give you this," the waitress said, handing Carl an index card.

"Thank you," Carl said, taking the index card.

"What does it say?" Dalton said as the waitress walked away.

"Time to go," Carl said.

He handed Dalton the card. Dalton read it as they got up to leave.

'Go to the table where I was sitting. The next card is there.'

Dalton and Carl made their way to the empty table. Nothing. Dalton dropped down to a knee and looked under the table. Taped to the bottom of the tabletop, another card. He pulled it off.

'You may want to check your rear tires.'

"Well, looks like we need to go outside," Dalton said.

"After you," Carl said.

They walked out of the Bellagio and made their way toward Carl's car. Dalton walked to the back tire on the passenger side. Carl checked the rear tire on the driver's side.

"Over here," Carl said.

Dalton walked to his side and Carl had the note in his hand.

"Looks like we are taking a road trip," Carl said, handing the card to Dalton.

'Next stop, Stratosphere. 12th floor. Room 1204.'

"Stratosphere," Dalton said. "Is that the tall one near the end of the strip? With the big needle on top?"

"That's the one," Carl said.

They both got in the car and made their way up the strip. Carl had a valet park the car when they arrived. Both of them got into the elevator and made their way up to the 12th floor. When they got to room 1204, there was a note on the door.

'Knock three times. Do not say a word when the door opens.'

Carl shrugged his shoulders at Dalton and knocked three times. The door opened. Dalton and Carl looked inside and saw no one. They entered together. The door closed behind them and a young woman stepped from behind the door holding an index card with a finger over her lips, motioning them to remain quiet.

Carl and Dalton both read the card.

'Sit on the bed. If you speak, this meeting is over. I'm going to check each of you for a wire. Put your phones on the bed beside you.'

Carl sat on one of the beds, Dalton sat down on the other. She grabbed a device close to the television and ran it over their phones and over them. Once she finished, she spoke.

"I'm Katie. We're all good. For now, anyway," she said.

"Can you explain to me what the hell is going on here?" Carl said.

"I was hoping you could do the same for me," Katie said.

"How do you know who we are?" Dalton asked.

"I don't know who you are, but I know you're with him. I'm assuming you're here for something and Carl over there is babysitting you, but we can get to all the details later," Katie said.

"How do you know who I am?" Carl asked.

"Carl Gilbert," Katie said. "Riker Industries for over 20 years. You work really close with Jeffrey Riker, right?"

"You could say that," Carl said. "How do you know me?"

"Where is Chris?" Katie asked.

"Who is Chris?" Carl asked.

"Where is he?" Katie asked again, her friendly tone subsided.

"Listen," Carl said. "I don't know any Chris. It's not ringing any bells anyway. Do you have a last name?"

"Williams," Katie said. "Chris Williams. Where is he?"

"I don't know who you're talking about," Carl said.

"I didn't want it to be like this," Katie said. She turned around and took one of the guns out of her purse and pointed it at Carl. "Where the hell is Chris?"

"Katie," Dalton said. "I think if Carl knew, he'd tell you. Please put the gun down!"

Katie turned the gun to Dalton.

"I don't remember asking you a goddamn thing!" Katie said.

"Katie," Carl said. "You said you had information about my wife."

"You first," Katie said. "Where's Chris?"

"Katie, I want to help you, I really do, but I don't know who Chris is!" Carl said.

Katie reached back into her purse and pulled out the two little folders. One read 'Chris Williams', the other, 'Vanessa Gilbert'.

"Maybe this will jar your memory," Katie said as she threw the folder labeled 'Chris Williams' in Carl's lap.

"What about the other folder?" Carl asked. "It has my wife's name on it!"

"I know," Katie said. "And I want to help you, but you have to know I need my answers first!"

Carl opened the folder. There were pictures of a man next to Mr. Riker. They were shaking hands and smiling. Another picture showed them walking into the building where he works. Carl had never seen the guy in his life. Under the photos, a waiver form of some kind from Riker Industries.

"That is Mr. Riker, but I don't know the other guy," Carl said. "Please put the gun down."

"The other guy is Chris. I told him not to go. He went in that building with that man, and he never came out. So many months have passed. None of my questions have been answered. I have been given so many excuses and straight-up bullshit, that I figured I needed to find out for myself, so I did some digging. Found out you work in that building. You work with Riker. You have for a long time. You go in every day. It's been close to a year now. Where the hell is he, Carl?" Katie asked.

"Do you think he was one of the..." Dalton said, before being cut off.

"Shut up, Dalton," Carl said.

"One of the what?" Katie asked.

Neither of them said anything.

"One of the what?" Katie said again, this time pulling the hammer back on her gun.

"Easy, Katie," Carl said with his hands up. "Apparently, there was a program at Riker Industries. People volunteered or applied for it. He may have been one of those selected."

"How do we find out for sure?" Katie asked.

"My briefcase," Carl said. "My briefcase is at work. It has some information inside, but I haven't looked over all of it yet. If it's not there, maybe I can find the information in the lab. There is a form here with these pictures. I'll need to take the form with me."

"Sounds like a great start. You probably need to go and do that. Like right now. He stays here 'til you get back," Katie said, pointing the gun at Dalton.

"I'll get everything I can, I promise," Carl said. "What about my wife?"

"You get back here with some information, then we can talk about your wife," Katie said.

"Dalton?" Carl asked. "You good?"

"I'm pretty damn far from good," Dalton said. "But do I have a choice? Go, and hurry."

"You heard him," Katie said. "GO!"

Carl got up and made his way to the door.

"I'll be back as soon as I can," Carl said.

When Carl left, Katie closed the door behind him. She turned around and made her way back to Dalton. She lowered her gun.

"I'm sorry I had to involve you in this. I've been following both of you since the airport. He's always alone. I figured you were important because he follows you around like a hawk," Katie said.

"I'm not important at all, just won a contest, you know, from the commercials?" Dalton said.

"No shit! The Escapement thing!" Katie said. "Congrats to you."

"Thanks, I think," Dalton said. "So, this Chris guy? Who is he to you?"

"He's my brother," Katie said. "My older brother. My only brother. He looked after me. Told me he was going to make a lot of money doing something he couldn't tell me about. I told him anything you couldn't speak about and get rich from couldn't be good. Of course, he told me not to worry. I followed him the day he disappeared because I had a bad feeling. That's where the pictures came from. The form I found in his room."

157

Dalton just listened.

"I'm sorry about the gun," Katie said. "I never meant to use it. I just want to know where Chris is. I want to know what happened to him. I've researched, spied and did everything I could to find out. Still nothing. I've been following your friend for a while. He's way up in that company and has been there for years. When I found out about his wife, I knew maybe I could get some answers."

"What did you find out about his wife?" Dalton asked.

"When he gets back with the information on Chris, we can all find out together," Katie said. "Until then, do you want to talk about what the Escapement actually is?"

CHAPTER
TWENTY-FOUR

CARL DROVE AS fast as could through the rain to Riker Industries. He braked hard at the security check. Deputy Larry was waiting with a smile.

"Working hard or hardly working?" Larry asked.

"Larry," Carl said. "No time for back and forth right now. I need to get to my office."

"Got'cha badge?" Larry asked.

"Damn it, Larry!" Carl said, searching his pocket for his badge.

"Protocol doesn't change, Carl," Larry said, leaning closer to Carl's car.

"You want a damn urine sample too?" Carl asked.

"Nah, the badge'll do," Larry said.

"Even though you call me Carl, you still want my badge. Here's the damn badge, Larry," Carl said, putting the badge in Larry's face.

"Much obliged. You may en-tah," Larry said as he lifted the boom gate.

Carl quickly rushed through, parked, and took the elevator back up to his new office. It looked like everyone had left for the day. Before he could walk into his office, he heard a familiar voice behind him.

"Burning the midnight oil?" Mr. Riker asked.

Carl turned around.

"Hey, Mr. Riker," Carl said, trying not to look frantic. "It's not any-where close to midnight. Dalton called me earlier and I left before I could review all of the files like I should have. He walked down the strip and got caught in the rain. I went and picked him up and made sure he got back okay."

"Good man," Mr. Riker said. "He has a grand decision ahead of him. Any inclination as to which way he's leaning?"

"Not yet," Carl said. "But I told him I would go back over tonight. Maybe show him around the town. Go to a show. Something. He'll figure it out."

"Well, don't let me keep you from working. Hopefully, all you need is in the briefcase. If not, all the files were uploaded into your computer. The ones that aren't there are below us in the lab," Mr. Riker said.

"Thank you, sir," Carl said. "Don't work too late."

"There is always work to be done," Mr. Riker said as he stepped back into his office and closed the door.

Carl walked into his office. He sat down at his desk and picked the briefcase up off the floor. He opened it and began to search through the files again. Nothing. Nothing in there that could help him in any way. The majority of the material on the subjects was redacted. Carl took out the waiver form from the file Katie had given him. He read over it and saw it had a number on the top.

'File Code: 1564874'

He turned on his computer. On the desktop, there was only one folder. It was labeled 'It's About Time'.

"Cute," Carl said, clicking on the folder.

Once Carl clicked on the folder, an ID and Password screen popped up. Carl had remembered seeing this information in the briefcase. He shuffled through the papers until he found what he was looking for and entered the information.

USER ID: CGilbert12

PASSWORD: ELOI

The screen quickly filled up with an itemized list. There were videos, spreadsheets, files, and pictures, among all the other items needed to quickly see that this had been going on for some time now.

He found a search bar and typed the numbers from the file code on the waiver form. When he hit ENTER, multiple files came up. Carl clicked the first file and saw a digital copy of the waiver form he was holding in his hand. The second file contained Chris Williams' information, along with his picture. He was the same guy in the picture that Katie had shown him. The third file contained the legal forms Chris had signed. Mr. Riker made sure that he and his company were not responsible should any accident happen. The last file was a video file. Carl opened his desk drawer and took out a pair of headphones he kept around when he needed music to make his workdays go faster. He plugged them in, turned the sound on and clicked the video.

A video feed opened on the screen. It was filmed from where the time mechanism was located earlier. He saw Chris walk across the screen with all kinds of wires and coming from his head. It looked like he was about to have neurological tests run at the hospital. He saw Scott come over and attach something to his wrist.

That must be the beacon, Carl thought.

Mr. Riker came into the frame and shook Chris's hand. He wished him good luck and walked with him to the time mechanism. Chris gave everyone the peace sign before he stepped into the mechanism. The door closed when Scott hit a switch. Four other people appeared once the door was shut and they started flipping switches, pressing buttons, and pulling levers. Lights came on outside the machine. There was a countdown that started at sixty seconds. All the people outside of the machine, Mr. Riker included, went into the other room in the lab and shut the door. When the countdown reached thirty seconds, the lights in the room started blinking. Slow at first, then faster every five seconds. When the countdown reached ten seconds, a bloodcurdling scream came from the machine. You could hear, "STOP IT, PLEASE STOP IT," coming from inside. Screaming and pleading continued until the countdown reached five seconds. Once the countdown was over, a computer voice said, "Countdown complete. Escapement unsuccessful." Everyone ran out of the room and to the machine. When they opened the doors, Chris wasn't there. Mr. Riker walked to the camera and spoke directly to the lens.

"Subject number two's vitals' were not good. We could not stop mid-beam. It is our belief the subject suffered an aneurysm of some sort. Maybe an epileptic seizure with the lights. Subjects may need to be blind-folded. Terrible loss. We must try again."

The video ended. Carl couldn't get the scream out of his head. He couldn't comprehend the fact that Mr. Riker showed no emotion to the camera. Carl took off the headphones and stared at the screen. He knew he couldn't make a copy of the files. Carl also had no idea how he was going to break this news to Katie, especially since she had a gun.

Carl closed his briefcase and locked it, then shut down his computer. He knew he had to think of something to tell her, because the truth was going to be a hard pill to swallow. Carl knew she had information on his wife, and he desperately needed to know what it was.

Carl picked up his briefcase and exited his office, noticing the light still shining from underneath Mr.Riker's door. He checked his watch. 9:25 p.m. He made his way to the elevator and eventually, to his car.

Carl drove slower going back to the Stratosphere than he did leaving. He didn't know how he was going to tell Katie that Chris was dead. What was even worse, how was he going to tell her that his death was caused by testing a time machine?

"*I can't tell her about the time machine,*" Carl thought to himself. "*Son of a bitch, what am I going to tell her?*"

When Carl made it to the Stratosphere, he sat in the car for ten minutes, trying to think of something. Anything. He knew he couldn't go back in that room with this information. He needed her to be unarmed when he told her. Carl made it to the lobby of the Stratosphere before an idea hit him. He reached for his phone and called Dalton. It rang once before Dalton answered.

"Dalton, is everything okay?" Carl asked.

"Everything is fine, man. You're on speaker. Are you in the car?"

"No, I'm in the lobby, why?"

"Making sure. I'll explain later. Katie and I are watching television."

"Just checking in with you, Dalt. Katie, can you hear me?"

"Loud and clear, Carl," Katie said. "Tell me that you have something."

"I do, Katie. I do. But you may not like it."

"I just need to know, Carl."

"I know you do, just like I need to know about my wife."

"Her folder is right here in front of me."

"Good. I'm going to need you to bring it with you."

"Bring it with me? What are you talking about Carl?"

"Things have changed. I'm going to my house. The information will be there waiting for you. You already know where I live. It's where you left the note last night. Plus, I need a drink, and I don't feel like paying for one. Bring Dalton with you. And my wife's file. See you soon."

Carl hung up the phone before she had a chance to respond. If he was going to break this news to her, it was going to be on his turf, where he knew the layout. He made his way back toward his car and headed home. Carl was halfway there when his phone received a text message. He picked up his phone and saw it was from Dalton.

'Headed that way. Katie said to not say a word inside until she checks your place for bugs.'

Carl texted him back.

'Why does she think we're wired or bugged?'

A reply came quickly after.

'Because she showed me the bug she found on your new car.'

Carl read the message, but couldn't believe it. He didn't respond, he continued home. Once Carl arrived, he got out quickly, briefcase in hand, and went inside the house and upstairs to his bedroom. He opened his closet door and pulled down a biometric gun safe from the top shelf. Carl placed his hand into the safe and it opened after acknowledging his fingerprints. He pulled out his 9mm gun and a fully loaded clip, popping the clip into the gun. Carl put the gun behind his back and inserted it into his belt, then walked back downstairs to the kitchen and poured himself a drink. He took his drink to the living room and sat on the couch, staring in the direction of the door and placed his briefcase on the table.

Carl had drunk half of his drink before he saw a set of headlights roll into his driveway.

He took the gun from behind his back and set it beside him.

CHAPTER
TWENTY-FIVE

"I CAN'T TALK about the Escapement," Dalton said.

"Why not?" Katie asked.

"I signed a confidentiality agreement regarding the circumstances around it. If I break it, my win is considered null and void," Dalton said.

"Well, I checked for wires and bugs, no one will know but us," Katie said.

"I get that," Dalton said. "But I'll know. I gave my word. I don't like to go back on my word."

"A man with morals," Katie said. "Not many out there like you."

"I'm sure there are plenty," Dalton said. "What I will say, is the paper that Carl ran off with looked a lot like one of the forms I had to sign."

"I know it was a waiver file," Katie said. "But what was he waiving? I really hope Carl finds out. It's been a year. I know I would've heard from Chris by now. We were very close. He practically helped raise me. He wouldn't sign anything that would put me at risk. I'm sure of it."

"Maybe he signed something that made him think he was trying to help," Dalton said.

"What do you mean?" Katie asked.

"You said he was going to make a lot of money. I'm sure it was going towards helping," Dalton said.

"Well, I never saw anything," Katie said.

Dalton looked at her, a bit confused.

"You never received anything?" Dalton asked.

"Not a thing," Katie said. "Well, except a swift kick in the ass away from that place."

"What do you mean?" Dalton asked.

"Once I stopped hearing from Chris, I tried to get into Riker Industries. I was on the outside looking in. Security never let me through. I tried being nice. I tried being a bitch. I even tried the legal route and was told I didn't have the funds to go against them. They were right. Every lawyer I talked to wasn't willing to help. Waiver forms carry a lot of weight, I suppose. And if by chance Chris is dead, there's no body. No body, no death. I just want answers," Katie said.

"Maybe Carl found something," Dalton said.

"Before, when Carl was here," Katie started. "You said maybe Chris was one of the, and then Carl cut you off. What were you going to say?"

"I'd really like for Carl to get back before we open that door," Dalton said. "I can tell you it's tied to the Escapement. I honestly think Chris may have helped with the research."

"Chris wasn't that smart," Katie said. "He's my brother, and I love him, but there's no way he could've been of any value to any kind of research. He was unemployed. No college. He spent lots of time in casinos trying to make a quick buck. No real skills at all, except for being a good brother."

Dalton listened intently. Katie wanted and deserved answers. Dalton knew from the earlier conversation with Carl and Mr. Riker that all subjects had received payment. He wondered to himself where the money went. If she didn't get it, who did? Or was Mr. Riker lying?

"Even if your friend doesn't bring me the information, I still want him to know what I know about his wife," Katie said.

"But you said," Dalton started before he was cut off.

"I said what I needed to," Katie said. "I needed the leverage, just like the gun."

"I see," Dalton said. "What do you know about his wife?"

"Nothing much," Katie said. "No files or folders, just pictures."

"Just pictures?" Dalton asked. "Did you know his wife?"

"I knew his wife about as much as I knew him, which is not at all," Katie said. "Once I couldn't get any answers, I started researching the company and the people near the top. I was outside of Riker Industries almost every other day, taking pictures. Early, late, it didn't matter. Anyway, when I was researching online, there were pictures on the website. That's how I found Carl. There were also pictures of company get-togethers, that's how I found his wife. She was with him in all of the pictures. I got her name from the captions."

"So how did you know she left him?" Dalton asked.

"People love to talk," Katie said. "Do you think Carl is the first person I've talked to from Riker Industries? I hear names, I write 'em down. Carl has been there for years. If anyone knows anything besides Riker, it's Carl."

"Do you know where Carl's wife is?" Dalton asked.

"Not exactly," Katie said. "I just hope she's okay."

"You hope she's okay?" Dalton asked. "What do you mean by that?"

"Look, you have your Escapement secret, I have this," Katie said. "Maybe when Carl gets back, we can put everything on the table."

"By everything, can we start with the gun?" Dalton asked.

"I told you I didn't plan on using it anyway," Katie said. "So, yes, we can start with the gun. Let's watch some TV."

Katie scooted back on the bed and positioned the pillows so she could sit up and be comfortable. Dalton did the same. Katie used the remote and quickly went through the channel lineup. She went so fast that Dalton couldn't make out what shows she was passing. She finally settled on a rerun of a Seinfeld episode.

"I love Seinfeld," Katie said. "Kramer is hilarious."

"Katie, I have a question for you," Dalton said.

"Okay, shoot," Katie said.

"How did you leave the note on my hotel room door?" Dalton asked.

"I rode up on the elevator, got out, and put it up there. Pretty simple to do, Dalton," Katie said.

"But how?" Dalton asked. "The elevator needs a key card to get up there, or so I've been led to believe."

"It sure does," Katie said. "But unlike my brother, I'm pretty smart. Let's just say I'm good with electronics and leave it at that. I didn't go in your room, that could've set off alarms. But the elevator, not so much. Did what I needed to do and bounced out."

They continued to watch most of the episode before Dalton's phone began to ring. He saw it was Carl and showed the screen to Katie. She told him to put it on speaker. When he answered, he did.

After the call was over, Katie stood up and started getting her things together.

"I should've seen this coming," Katie said. "Carl is a smart guy, too. I truly meant him no harm."

"I know that now," Dalton said. "But he doesn't. Did you really find a bug in his car?"

"More like on his car," Katie said. She reached into her purse and pulled out a small, metallic device. "This was under the car. Right by where he sits. I looked up the model number. It's a listening device."

Dalton took the device from her and inspected it.

"When did you find it?" Dalton asked.

"When I left the casino tonight," Katie said. "While you two were gambling and reading index cards, it gave me time to scan the car."

"So, that scanner thing you have, it's made to find bugs?" Dalton asked.

"Pretty much," Katie said. "If his car is bugged, then so is his house. I would bet your hotel room is, too."

"But why?" Dalton asked.

"Don't know," Katie said. "Something else we can figure out together, I guess."

Dalton gave Katie the bug and she put it back in her purse, along with her gun and Vanessa's file. Dalton grabbed his phone and they exited the room.

After taking the elevator down to the lobby, Dalton followed Katie to her car. There were fast food bags, candy wrappers, and empty cans of Red Bull and Mt. Dew everywhere.

"Excuse the mess," Katie said. "Not a lot of time to clean when you are watching everyone from your car."

Dalton shook his head and got into the car with her.

Katie drove the short distance to Carl's house and pulled over to the side of the road before turning into the driveway.

"What are you doing?" Dalton asked.

"I need to write something on an index card. We can't speak until I scan the place," Katie said.

She grabbed her purse and removed an index card and a pen. She wrote down a message and handed it to Dalton.

"When I pull in the driveway, go up to the window outside the living room and press this against the glass. I'll flash the lights and hopefully, it will get his attention and he'll read the card," Katie said.

Dalton read the card.

'We are going to walk in. Katie needs to scan the house. Turn on some music. Katie is leaving the gun in the car.'

Dalton turned to Katie as she was taking the gun out of her purse. She opened the glove box in front of Dalton and placed the gun inside.

"Thank you," Dalton said.

Katie nodded and drove the car into the driveway. Once she was stopped, Dalton took the note, got out, and walked to the window. Katie flashed her lights several times once Dalton was there. When Dalton showed Carl the card through the window, he turned and gave Katie a thumbs up to let her know Carl had read it. Katie got out of the car and joined Dalton outside of Carl's house. He was unaware she still had a second, loaded gun in her purse.

CHAPTER
TWENTY-SIX

CARL WAS SITTING on the couch when he saw Dalton approach the window. Dalton pressed an index card to the glass and Carl got up to read it. Once he did, he nodded at Dalton and turned on the television to a music channel. Carl saw Dalton give a thumbs up, then he opened the door. He pointed at Dalton and mouthed the words, "Are you okay?" to which Dalton nodded. Katie followed in behind Dalton with her purse and the RF detector she referred to as a bug scanner. She began to sweep the house and Carl sat back down near his gun. Dalton sat down beside him. Dalton saw the gun and whispered to Carl.

"You aren't going to need that."

"You never know," Carl whispered back, returning the gun to the back of his pants, hidden from sight.

They watched Katie walk around the house. She was using the device and moving it up and down. She started in the kitchen. They saw her pull something from the bottom of the cabinet and put it on the table. She held up one finger and continued to search.

Carl got off the couch and walked to the table. He picked up what Katie had sat atop the table. It was a listening device. He walked it over to the sink and ran water over it. He watched a green light on the device slowly dim and go out. He walked back to the couch and sat beside Dalton.

"She was right," he whispered.

Dalton shook his head in disbelief, wondering exactly what the hell was going on.

"Did you find out anything?" Dalton whispered.

"Yeah, I did, and it's not good," Carl responded. "Chris is dead, he was the second subject."

"Shit, he was her brother, man," Dalton said, as he leaned back into the couch and looked at the ceiling.

"Son of a bitch," Carl said.

Katie continued sweeping, making her way upstairs. She spent several minutes up there before she came back down. She put the seven other devices she found on the coffee table in front of them.

Carl's mouth dropped open and Dalton couldn't believe what he was seeing. Katie took out an index card and wrote on it.

'What do we need to do with them?'

Carl grabbed the pen. He wrote a message and Katie read it.

'Take six of them to the sink. Run water over them 'til the green light goes out. I'll handle the last one.'

Katie took six of the devices she found to the sink and turned it on. She ran water over each one, disabling them. Carl picked up the other device and winked at Dalton. He began to speak out loud, pausing after each sentence.

"Hey, Dalt, how are things? You're where? Decided to get out and explore some more, huh? You should've called. Vegas is a different place at night. Yeah, I know you have a lot to think about, bud. You think you'll come to a decision tonight or do you need to sleep on it? I completely understand. Okay, buddy, well don't stay out too long. I believe I'm going to hit up a bar close to where you are and have a few. Feel free to join me. Okay, man. Talk to you later."

Carl got up off the couch and spoke aloud again.

"Alright, time to hit the bar. I better leave the light on so I can see when I get back."

Carl turned on the lamp, walked to the door and went outside, listening device in hand. He closed the door behind him. Dalton watched him take the device and stick it under his mailbox and then make his way back into the house.

"That should be all of them," Katie said.

"What in the hell is going on?" Carl asked, walking back inside.

"The place where Chris stayed had bugs, too," Katie said. "I think it had to do with the paper I gave you. Apparently, it's not to be talked about. Dalton confirmed it when I asked him about the damn Escapement."

"You told her?" Carl asked.

"I told her I won," Dalton said. "I didn't tell her what it was."

"That's right," Katie said. "He didn't. He has morals, Carl. But what's with all the secrecy? Why is Chris involved in all of this?"

"Katie," Carl said. "You need to sit down."

Katie walked over to the love seat and sat down in front of Carl and Dalton. She sat her purse down in front of her.

"Katie," Carl began. "First things first. From this point forward, we will be honest about everything. No secrets, no nothing," Carl said, extending his hand out to her.

"No secrets," Katie said, shaking his hand.

"Okay," Carl said. He put his hand behind his back and pulled out his gun. He took out the clip and set them on the table in front of him.

"Dalton said your gun was in your car," Carl said. "I believe him. I want you to trust me as well."

Katie was taken aback by this and thanked him. She opened her purse and took out her other gun.

"Dalton was right. I did put the gun I pulled on you in the glove compartment. This is my other one," Katie said.

She sat it on the table beside Carl's.

"I don't have any guns," Dalton said. "But I'm damn sure going to move these to the kitchen."

Dalton got up, grabbed the guns, and took them to the table in the kitchen. Once he did, he returned to the couch.

"Katie," Carl said. "I found out some things you aren't going to like. I don't want to be the one to tell you, but what choice do I have?"

"I just want answers," Katie said.

"Okay," Carl said. "Katie, your brother took part in an experiment held by my company. He signed all the forms and everything. The experiment didn't go as planned."

Carl and Dalton both saw Katie tearing up. She had her hands over her mouth and was trembling.

"Katie," Carl said. "Chris...Chris is dead."

"NO!" Katie screamed. "YOU'RE LYING!"

Katie clenched her fists and pounded them down on the table. Tears rushed from her eyes as she slid off the love seat and into the floor, completely overtaken by her grief. Carl rose up from the couch and moved to where Katie had fallen to, sat her up, and put his arm around her. She hit him in the chest several times.

"Why, Carl?" she yelled. "Why is he gone? Why is he gone?"

"I'm so sorry, Katie," Carl said, pulling her into his chest as he tried to comfort her.

"This is bullshit," Katie said, continuing to cry. " Not Chris...not Chris..."

Dalton got up from the couch and jogged to the kitchen. He grabbed a washcloth from the counter and wet it, then walked back to the living room and gave it to Carl. Carl used the hand that wasn't wrapped around Katie to brush her hair back and used the washcloth to wipe her head.

"Katie, I don't have the words. I don't have the answers. I'm so sorry," Carl said.

Katie grabbed onto Carl's shirt and pushed her head into his chest, screaming one last time before she stopped altogether and cried into his shirt. Carl let her cry and rubbed her back. He continued to do so until she finally let up a bit and pulled away from him. Her eyes were red and irritated. Her nose was running and she sniffled as she began to speak.

"Deep down, I knew it," Katie said, sobbing. "Chris would always find a way to talk to me. Always."

She continued to cry and asked for a tissue. Dalton was quick to bring her one after another trip to the kitchen. When she sat up to blow her nose, Carl adjusted himself and slid closer to the furniture, staying on the floor, but resting his back against the love seat.

"Wait," Katie said, sniffling. "Where's his body? Why didn't anyone tell me?"

"This is where it gets complicated," Carl said.

"Shit. Here we go," Dalton said, joining them on the floor, placing himself beside Katie.

"What do you mean, complicated?" Katie asked, with tears still in her eyes.

"Katie, what I'm about to tell you is going to be hard to believe. Dalton and I didn't believe it ourselves. I'm not sure if Dalton believes it now, but I do. I know it to be true," Carl said.

"Is this a fact, Carl?" Dalton asked.

"Yeah, man," Carl said. "I've read the files, and I've seen some footage."

"What am I not going to believe, Carl?" Katie asked. "Where is my brother's body?"

"Not where. When," Carl said.

"When?" Katie asked.

Carl took a deep breath.

"Riker Industries has created a time machine, Katie. Your brother was a test subject. He died during the process. I don't know where he went," Carl said.

"Time Machine?" Katie said. "What do you mean a freaking time machine?"

"I know it's hard to believe, but your brother died testing a damn time machine," Carl said.

Katie didn't know what to say. She sure didn't know how to react. She just sat there. In shock. Crying.

"Was he the only one?" Katie asked.

"No, three others were tested as well," Carl said. He then explained the various situations to her, repeating what he and Dalton had heard earlier.

"This so-called Escapement, is it time travel? Or something else completely?" Katie asked.

"I have to decide if I want to go forward or backward in time," Dalton said. "Apparently, it works now. I can turn it down, or I can take it. I'm still deciding what to do."

"This is ridiculous!" Katie said. "How do you? Where do you? What the hell, man?"

"I couldn't have said it better myself," Dalton said.

"Oh my God, your wife!" Katie said.

Carl sat back. He grabbed his drink off the table and took another sip of his drink.

"What about my wife?" Carl asked.

Katie took her purse off the table and pulled out the file. She handed it to Carl.

"I've been spying, watching, staking out, whatever you want to call it, on Riker Industries for a long time now," Katie said, still sniffling. "Seems like it's been forever. I needed answers and spoke to a lot of different people and did my research. I learned that you were pretty high up in the company. I looked over the website and saw pictures of you, so I knew what you looked like. I also saw pictures of your wife. Company outings and such. That's how I knew who she was."

Carl stood up and moved to the couch. He placed the folder on the table and opened it. Inside were pictures. He looked at each one.

"I took those pictures three months ago," Katie said.

The first picture was of Vanessa getting out of her car with some of her things. Carl knew it was the night she had left him. Those were the last clothes he saw her in. She was in the same exact parking space he had picked up his new car from yesterday. The second picture was of Mr. Riker hugging Vanessa. The third was her crying in front of him and Mr. Riker putting a hand on her back. Another picture was Vanessa going into the building, with Mr. Riker following behind her. The last picture was of Scott Brown, from the lab. He was getting into Vanessa's car.

"What is this shit?" Carl asked. "What does it mean?"

"That last picture. I took it three days after the first ones. Never saw her come back out. I took the same pictures of my brother, remember?" Katie said, using her arm to wipe the remaining tears from her eyes.

"Is there any possibility at all that your wife was a subject too?"

CHAPTER
TWENTY-SEVEN

"THIS CAN'T BE right," Carl said, confused and angry. "I need another drink."

Dalton watched Carl get up from the couch and storm into the kitchen to pour himself another.

"Make that two," Katie said.

"Are you even old enough to drink?" Dalton asked.

"I'm 22, pour me whatever you've got, especially tonight," Katie said.

"Might as well make it three, Carl," Dalton said. "I'll help you."

Dalton followed Carl to the kitchen as Carl took some whiskey from his cabinet and poured drinks for all three of them. Carl kept his drink and began to drink it right away. Dalton brought the other two back to the living room, giving Katie her drink while setting his on the table. Dalton watched as Carl picked up the pictures and continued to look at them.

"Why would she go and do it?" Carl said.

"Do we even know for sure she did?" Dalton asked.

"Pretty hard to rule against it," Carl said. "Timeline matches up, that's for sure, but why? Why would she agree to do something like this?"

"Why would Chris?" Katie asked.

"This is not making my decision any easier!" Dalton said.

"Wait," Carl said. "Wait one damn minute!"

Carl moved back to the couch and opened his briefcase. He shuffled through the papers like a wild man. Katie and Dalton watched him, sipping their drinks.

"Katie, I'm sorry about your brother. You doing okay?" Dalton asked.

"I'll be alright. Thanks," Katie said, leaning into Dalton's shoulder.

"She made it!" Carl said, loudly.

"What?" Dalton asked.

"She was the fourth subject, remember? The only thing that died was the damn beacon. Wherever she went, she's still alive," Carl said.

"Carl," Katie said. "Do you know that for sure?"

"According to everything we heard today, she should be. But where is she? And why did she go? More importantly, why the hell did Mr. Riker never tell me anything?" Carl asked, throwing his glass into the kitchen. The glass hit the floor and shattered into a thousand pieces.

Katie stood up immediately and walked over to Carl. She grabbed his wrist and brought it down.

"Carl, answers were kept from me, too. I'm thankful for your help. I'm sorry. What can I do?" Katie asked before hugging him.

"What can we do?" Dalton said, standing up.

"Sounds like there is only one person who can answer our questions," Carl said.

"We've got to be smart about this, Carl," Dalton said. "Your house was bugged. I'm sure my hotel room is, too. So was your car. Everything we've talked about so far in those places has been heard...shit! The box!"

"The box?" Katie asked.

"Yeah, a box," Carl said. "Dalton got a box on his plane ride in. Something I've never seen before. Like an electronic puzzle box."

"I can't remember anything from the plane ride in," Dalton said. "When I woke up on the plane, there was a box beside me. I knew somehow it was mine, but I didn't bring it on the flight."

"Do you think it's connected to all this?" Katie asked.

"I thought so at first, but I'm not sure," Carl said. "Like you said, I've been with Mr. Riker a long time and I've never seen any tech shit like that. It took Dalton and I both to open a drawer on it last night."

"What was in it?" Katie asked.

"This," Dalton said, pointing to his watch.

Katie grabbed Dalton's wrist and looked over the watch.

"Nothing fancy, but there's something different about it," Katie said.

"Yeah, and the tag had my name on it, so whoever gave me the box wanted me to have it," Dalton said.

"There's some weird-looking stuff on top of the box, too," Carl said. "I think there's more to it, but we'll have to look at it later and away from that room."

"Agreed," Dalton said.

"Carl," Katie said. "How long do you suppose this place has had bugs in it?"

"I'm willing to bet for the past three months," Carl said.

"This Riker guy wanted to know if you would find out your wife," Katie said.

"That's what I was thinking," Carl said.

"Do you know where he is?" Katie asked.

"I'm pretty sure he's where he always is, in the office. Probably waiting for my call on Dalton's decision," Carl said.

"Are you going to go through with it?" Katie asked.

"I don't know," Dalton said. "All of this, it's crazy, right? How do I even decide on something like this? I need to call Britney."

"Who's Britney?" Katie asked.

"I'm assuming she's the one that went to Europe? The one that said no?" Carl asked.

"That's her. I didn't say anything to anyone about me being selected for this except to her. I know it's confidential, but I need her voice in my head," Dalton said.

"Screw confidential. That shit went out the window when I found out about Vanessa," Carl said.

"And Chris," Katie added.

"Okay, can I go upstairs and make this phone call?" Dalton asked.

"Be my guest," Carl said as he got the broom and began to clean up the shards of glass. Katie grabbed a dustpan and helped him. Dalton walked upstairs.

Dalton looked at the clock on the wall and saw it was a little after ten. *That would make it close to six or seven in the morning there,* he thought to himself. He found her number in his phone and pressed the call button.

"Please answer, please answer, please answer..."

"University Hospital Aachen, Dr. Elias Richter speaking."

"Britney?"

"This must be Dalton?"

"Yeah, this is Dalton. Where's Britney?"

"Dalton, we couldn't get into Britney's phone. We didn't have the lock code. We contacted her parents but were unable to phone you. Her parents were on her emergency contact form. She spoke highly of you, but we didn't know how to reach you."

"Phone me? What's going on?"

"Dalton, Britney was in an accident."

"An accident? Is she okay?"

"Dalton, she was hit by a drunk driver leaving work last night. We did everything in our power to save her."

"Did everything in your power? What are you telling me?"

"Britney died this morning. We did everything we could. I'm so sorry, Dalton."

Dalton dropped the phone on the floor and fell to his knees. All the air escaped him. He began to tremble and couldn't control it.

"No!" Dalton said, with what seemed like his last gasp of air. "Dammit! No!" Tears filled his eyes as he continued his collapse to the floor.

Carl and Katie heard Dalton fall and ran up the stairs as fast as they could. They found Dalton on the floor, crying. His hands were over his face.

"No, no, no..." Dalton said, over and over again.

He brought his knees up closer to his body into the fetal position. Katie ran over to Dalton and sat down beside him, holding his head.

"Dalton, what's wrong?" Katie asked. "Are you okay? Dalton…"

Carl observed the scene and saw the phone on the floor. He picked it up and heard breathing on the other end.

"Who is this?" Carl asked.

"This is Dr. Richter speaking. Is Dalton okay?"

"Hell, no, he's pretty damn far from okay. What's going on?"

Dr. Richter explained the situation to Carl. Carl listened and ended the call when the doctor finished. He couldn't begin to imagine Dalton's pain. He had lost Vanessa, but he still had hope she was out there somewhere. This was different. Carl didn't have the words. He took a knee beside Dalton and told him he was there for him, whatever he needed.

Katie continued to console Dalton the best she could as Carl explained the situation to her. Upon hearing it, Katie became upset again and went to the bathroom. Dalton used Carl's shirt to pull himself up. He grabbed the top of Carl's sleeve to sit up beside him. Carl could only sit there with him, trying to find the right words to say.

"Dalton, I'm sorry," Carl said. "This. This is all kinds of not right, man. Whatever you need, I'm here."

"Britney. Britney is who I need, Carl, and she's gone. She's gone," Dalton said, trying to hold back more tears that would eventually come.

Carl grabbed Dalton's arm and pulled him closer to him, embracing him like he would a brother if he had one. Dalton cried into his shoulder.

Katie emerged from the bathroom, saw them, and ran over to put her arms around them both. She cried along with Dalton. After a moment, she pushed herself away and stood over them, hand covering her mouth, still in tears.

"She was everything, man," Dalton said to Carl. "Everything. I don't know what I'll do without her. Carl, she's dead, man. She's dead."

Carl took a deep breath and looked at Dalton directly in the eyes.

"Then let's go make this shit right," Carl said.

"What do you mean?" Dalton asked, looking defeated.

Carl placed his hand on the floor and lifted himself up. He extended his arm to Dalton. Dalton grabbed it and Carl helped him up to his feet.

"You've got a fucking time machine, Dalton," Carl said. "Let's go use the bastard!"

CHAPTER
TWENTY-EIGHT

I T WAS CLOSE to midnight. Dalton, Katie and Carl were all sitting at
Carl's kitchen table. There were papers from Carl's briefcase scattered
all over the top of it. They all had a cup of coffee in front of them.

"Let's run through how tomorrow is going to work one more time,"
Katie said.

"Okay," Carl said. "First, to finish off this shitstorm of a night,
Katie, you take Dalton back to the Bellagio. We all need to try and get
some rest. I will walk you both out, grab the bug that's outside and
bring it in here with me before I call Mr. Riker."

"You'll call Riker and tell him about my decision to go back in time.
Tell him you took me back to the Bellagio and you left after you saw I
made it in the building in one piece," Dalton said.

"I'll hang with Dalton at the Bellagio," Katie said. "We'll play it off like
he met someone at the casino, that being me, and I took him to his room
because he was drunk. That will explain my voice in his room when we
enter, and Dalton will act drunk and sad."

"Which isn't too far from the truth," Dalton added, still reeling from
the news about Britney.

"Knowing Mr. Riker, he'll want me there first thing in the morning to
get everything ready for the Escapement. You're still good with tomorrow,
right, Dalt?" Carl asked.

"The sooner, the better," Dalton said quietly.

"I don't know when he'll want you there, but when we go, Katie will be joining us," Carl said. "Before Dalton goes anywhere, we're going to get our answers."

"According to the information, here," Dalton said, referring to the paperwork on the table. "They'll need my exact height, weight, and blood, among other things, in order to make sure everything is successful with the time launch, which is what they call it."

"He'll probably ask me to bring you to the lab, maybe about an hour early, before we are a go. I'll relay that information to you tonight after I call him. I'll send you a text," Carl said.

"Which brings us to tomorrow," Katie said.

"Tomorrow, I find out why Vanessa went wherever she did," Carl said.

"Why I never found out about Chris," Katie said.

"When we arrive together, we'll all go to the lab. Hopefully, Mr. Riker is in his office and we can go down there and speak with Scott. I want to know why and where he took Vanessa's car," Carl said.

"And in doing that, he'll probably radio for Riker to come down," Katie said.

"That is when you two can get your answers," Dalton said.

"The easy way," Carl said, before grabbing his gun. "Or the hard way."

They all nodded their heads. They stood up at the table and said their goodbyes until tomorrow. Carl hugged Dalton tight. He felt horrible for him and knew that Dalton wouldn't sleep. Dalton thanked Carl for being there before tearing up again. He went to get a tissue when Katie hugged Carl and thanked him for the information. Carl walked them both out quietly. He grabbed the bug from the mailbox and walked back into the house. Once he shut the door, Katie started her car and made her way to the Bellagio with Dalton. Carl placed the bug on his kitchen table and took out his phone.

The screen of the phone showed 11:55 p.m. He didn't know if it was too late to call Mr. Riker, but he truly didn't care. He found the number within his contacts and called him.

"Carl, when I asked earlier if you were going to burn the midnight oil, I didn't know you were going to take it literally," Mr. Riker said as he answered.

"Well, sir, Dalton called me to come and be with him for a while. I think he's made his decision."

"Is that right?"

"Yes, sir. He decided to do it."

"Splendid! I will make Scott aware of this information first thing tomorrow. Does he know which direction he will be going?"

"He does. He wants to go back."

"Back? A far cry from what he explained earlier today."

"Circumstances have changed in his life, sir. Quite recently."

"Do share."

"The woman he loved. She died. She was hit by a drunk driver around 5 a.m. European time. That's why I'm calling you so late."

"Oh my god! That's horrible news. And he wants to go back to see if he can change it?"

"I guess so, but can he really do it?"

"It could be possible, but we truly won't know until he's sent back. We can then document what can or cannot be done. That poor man. Is he okay?"

"He's doing as well as he can given the circumstances."

"Terrible, just terrible."

"I dropped him off and he said he wanted to gamble a bit alone. I respected his decision and came back home to let you know what was going on."

"Thank you, Carl."

"I've been reading over the documents that are here in the briefcase. When should I be there in the morning? Should I bring Dalton to get his specifics?"

"Come in around nine. Bring Dalton. We can discuss things and get his specifics. Then he can go get some rest before it's time."

"When will the Escapement be?"

"I'm thinking tomorrow evening. Make sure we have everything ready to go on our end. This time, it will be a success, and the world as we know it will change forever."

"Can't wait to start, Mr. Riker. I'll see you in the morning."

"Try and get some sleep, Carl."

Carl ended the call and sent Dalton a text.

'Be ready to go tomorrow around 8:30. He wants to get your specifics. Escapement happens in the evening.'

He quickly received a text in return.

'I'll be ready.'

Carl locked his door, turned out his lights and walked upstairs. He put his phone on the charger and sat on his bed. He set his alarm for six. He wanted to get up, shower, and eat a little something before he picked up Dalton. He also wanted to walk through the plan in his head, one last time, before he left. Carl picked up Vanessa's picture from his nightstand and held it in his lap.

Why would you go? What did he offer you? Why did you leave me?

Carl put the picture back where he had taken it from. He laid his head on his pillow, looked up at the ceiling, then closed his eyes. It was time to think about the part of the plan he failed to mention to Dalton and Katie. They would find out soon enough.

CHAPTER
TWENTY-NINE

KATIE GOT DALTON back to the Bellagio a little after midnight. They didn't say much on the way there. Dalton mostly stared out the window while Katie drove. She truly felt sorry for him and wanted to help. Katie felt a connection with him like she did with her brother, but couldn't explain it. Looking at his reflection from the glass, she saw his eyes were glazed and he was lost in his own thoughts. Katie saw his hand move to wipe his eyes more than once, but she never mentioned it. She kept driving. It was only a few minutes before they reached the Bellagio.

"We're here," Katie said.

Dalton wiped his eyes.

"Sorry, I was in my own head," he said.

"You have nothing to be sorry about at all. I can't imagine what you're going through right now. Somewhere in my own mind, I knew Chris was gone, I just needed the closure. I hoped he was alive, but we were too close for him not to let me know where he was. The finality of it all got to me in the moment and I miss my brother. I'm so sorry about your girlfriend," Katie said.

"Thank you, I am too," Dalton said, trying to compose himself.

As they stepped out of the car, Dalton's phone received a text message. It was from Carl. He read it and responded.

"Carl?" Katie asked.

"Yeah," Dalton said. "He'll be here to pick me up at eight-thirty in the morning. It'll just be me and him. The Escapement will happen in the evening. We'll all be there."

"Damn right, we will," Katie said.

They walked into the Bellagio and through the casino.

"This place sure is nice," Katie said.

"You've never been here?" Dalton asked.

"The Bellagio, no," Katie said. "Way too pricey for me. No way I can afford it on my salary of next to nothing."

When they got in the elevator, Katie took out her RF device to prepare to scan his room.

"Remember, act drunk," Katie said.

"Again, not much of an act," Dalton said.

When they walked into the room, Dalton started the charade.

"This city is never sleeping. But I'm about to be," Dalton said aloud.

"Thank you for inviting me up. Damn, this room is nice," Katie said.

"Thank you for helping me up, after the night I've had," Dalton said.

"It's been a rough night for you, let's get you to bed," Katie said.

Dalton sat on the couch while Katie scanned the room. Once she was finished, she had found four bugs. She used some tape from her purse to mark where each of them was for Dalton. She took each of them to the bathroom and placed them in the sink. She closed the door behind her and joined Dalton on the couch.

"Thank you for letting me stay," Katie whispered. "I marked where the bugs were so we can put them back when we're ready. Turn on the T.V. for background noise so we can drown out our voices. I'm not really sure how powerful those bugs are."

Dalton grabbed the remote and turned on the television. He turned the sound up before he addressed Katie.

"Thank you for everything, Katie," Dalton said. "You take the bed. I'm crashing on the couch."

"I couldn't do that," Katie said.

"Too bad. Goodnight, Katie," Dalton said.

"Goodnight, Dalton," Katie replied.

Katie got up and walked to the bedroom. She smiled at Dalton and started to close the door until the box on the dresser caught her eye.

"Dalton," Katie said. "Is this the box?"

Dalton wiped his eyes, sat up and nodded.

"Do you mind if I mess with it?" Katie asked.

"Sure," Dalton said. "Be my guest."

Katie picked up the box and sat down on the bed, resting the box on her lap. She turned it, flipped it, and held it up to her face. *This is something,* she thought to herself. The drawer was still open on the front and she looked inside of it closely, noticing wires at the back of the drawer that looked like they connected to the buttons. Upon closer inspection of the buttons, she saw something familiar to her. *No way!* She examined the top of the box again, paying particular attention to the three glass pieces. *No freaking way!*

Katie placed the box on the nightstand and did a quick jog back to the doorway to get Dalton's attention. Katie saw Dalton lying on the couch with a pillow over his face. He turned over and the pillow slid off, revealing his irritated eyes. Katie's heart sank. She grabbed a blanket from the edge of the bed and walked to the couch where Dalton was lying. Katie placed the blanket across Dalton's body and kissed his forehead. She turned to go back to the bedroom and saw his phone on the floor. Katie picked it up and heard a voice coming from the speaker. She didn't want to be nosey, but she couldn't resist. When Katie looked at the screen, it read Voicemail across the top and a repeat button was displayed. When she put it to her ear, she heard a woman's voice. She teared up listening to the message. Katie was sure Dalton had cried himself to sleep while it played. Katie stopped the voicemail, placed the phone on the table, and went back into the bedroom.

Katie closed the door quietly and got into bed. She thought of Chris. She thought of Dalton listening to the voicemail and losing the love of his life. She thought of Carl and all he had been through. Katie's eyes welled up with tears and she turned over hoping to find sleep. What she had to tell Dalton about the box would have to wait until morning.

CHAPTER
THIRTY

J EFFREY RIKER ENDED the call after speaking with Carl and placed his cell phone down on his desk. Tomorrow was the big day. Tomorrow would be the game-changer. No mistakes this time. He took out the other phone from his desk drawer and used it to contact Scott.

"Scott, this is Mr. Riker. Do you copy?"

No answer. He tried again.

"Scott, this is Mr. Riker. Do you copy?"

No answer. He placed the phone back into the desk drawer and dialed the lab directly from his desk phone. It rang four times before it was answered.

"Yes, sir," said a voice on the other end.

"This is Mr. Riker. I'm so sorry to be calling at this hour. Is Scott available?"

"Yes, sir, one moment."

After a brief pause, Scott answered the phone.

"Hey, Mr. Riker, this is Scott. We're all running some last-minute checks."

"We are definitely a go for tomorrow, Scott. They'll be here around eight-thirty in the morning, then we can get Mr. Mallet's metrics."

"That's great news, sir. Are we going forwards or backwards?"

"We will be going backward."

"Of course. The machine will be ready."

"Excellent."

"I was just inside the machine, actually, calibrating the lights. Everything is looking great, sir. I'm very excited."

"We all are, Scott."

"Is there anything else, Mr. Riker?"

"Not at all. Please try and get some rest tonight, Scott. Big day tomorrow."

"Yes, sir."

Jeffrey Riker hung up the phone and smiled. The morning was drawing closer and he couldn't wait. He looked at his watch and picked up his cell phone from the desk. He scrolled through the contacts until he saw who he was looking for and tapped his finger to the screen, initiating the call. After two rings, there was an answer on the other end.

"Mr. Riker," the voice said.

"Doctor Richter," Mr. Riker said. "I see the job has been completed."

"Yes, it has," Dr. Richter said. "It was quite easy. Find the target. Take out the target. Get the phone and wait. I followed the script you gave me; I hope it worked to your satisfaction."

"Very much so," Mr. Riker said. "The money should be in your account."

"It is," Dr. Richer said. "I will dispose of the phone and the body. No ties to me. No ties to you. Our business is complete. Goodnight, Mr. Riker."

"Goodnight, Dr. Richter," Mr. Riker said, ending the call.

If Dr. Richter is even your name, Mr. Riker thought to himself.

He placed his cell phone back on the desk and picked up the receiver to his office phone, dialing another extension within the building.

The phone rang three times before it was answered. Mr. Riker began to speak.

"I know I didn't wake you. Big day ahead of us. Mr. Mallet will definitely be going to the past, so our plan worked. Now, tell me again how this will all play out tomorrow? We need to make sure we're going to be ready for anything time decides to throw at us."

THIRTY-ONE

C ARL HAD BEEN up thirty minutes before his alarm went off. He sat upright in the bed, staring into the darkness that was his room, knowing today was going to be one hell of a day. Would any answer Mr. Riker give him hold up? He didn't know. The only thing Carl knew for sure is that he was going to find out about Vanessa, one way or another. Carl turned off the alarm to his clock and got a shower. After he was finished, he actually shaved off his beard and looked like a completely different man.

This is the man Vanessa would remember, Carl thought, moving his head back and forth, looking at his reflection in the mirror.

He took the clothes he was going to wear out of the closet and put them on, gathered everything he needed from upstairs and turned out the light. When Carl got to the kitchen, he took some eggs out of the refrigerator and began to cook. He couldn't remember the last time he had actually cooked, but it was long overdue. Carl put two slices of bread in his toaster when the eggs were almost done and laid a piece of cheese over the eggs, sprinkling some salt and pepper on top of them. When the bread popped out of the toaster, Carl placed them on a plate and scooped the eggs out of the pan, onto the bread. He sat his plate down on the table as the coffee pot turned on. He knew it would take a few minutes to brew, so he grabbed a bottle of orange juice from the refrigerator for the time being. Carl took a seat and ate his breakfast. He used to love making egg sandwiches in the morning for Vanessa, but that was something that had faded during the course of their relationship. He realized soon after she left that he didn't do much on his end to keep her. You have to show your woman that you're in love with her every single day. She deserves that and Carl realized he had gotten complacent. He thought she would always be there until the day she actually left.

Carl finished his sandwich and juice just in time for the coffee to be ready. He cleaned his plate and poured himself a cup of coffee. As he stood at the counter, looking out the window and drinking his coffee, Carl watched the sun come up. There would be no alcohol today. He needed a clear head. A focused mind. Today, he would find out why she left him.

Carl looked at his phone and it read 6:34. He still had an hour and a half before he needed to leave to go to the Bellagio. He figured he may as well put the part of the plan he failed to mention to Dalton and Katie to work first thing. Carl would still be at the Bellagio to pick Dalton up on time, but he needed to take care of something else first.

Carl left his house and drove to work. He arrived close to seven. Larry was not at the gate and security let him right through.

When Carl entered the building, he did not go upstairs to his office. Instead, he took out his key and put it in the slot beside the buttons on the panel to reveal the 'T' button. He pressed it.

When the elevator came to a stop, he walked out and entered the code Mr. Riker had given him on the keyboard. Once entered, the doors opened, and Carl walked through. No one was in the room with the time mechanism. All the computers were still on and functioning, but not a single person was to be found. Carl saw the door that Scott would always disappear into, so he walked up to it and knocked.

Carl thought he heard some shuffling behind the door. He saw a speaker system beside the doorway. It had one button on it. He thought it looked like an intercom system, but he wasn't sure. He decided to try it, anyway. He pushed the button.

"Hello," Carl said. "This is Carl Gilbert. I decided to come in a bit early, being it's the big day. Anyone working?"

He received an answer shortly after he asked his question.

"Hello, Carl, this is Scott. Most of the crew are sleeping. I was running some last-minute figures and such. I'll be right out."

Carl stepped away from the door and rested at one of the screens in the room. He looked at the monitor, even though he had no clue what the numbers on it meant. Soon enough, the door opened and Scott walked out.

"Good morning, Carl," Scott said. "Wow! You look completely different. Would you like some coffee?"

"Already had some, thanks," Carl said. "Amazing what a fresh shave can do. How's everything looking?"

"Everything is actually looking really good. Really good. We're very excited about the possibilities today will bring us, not only now, but in the future," Scott said.

"I'm sure you are," Carl said. "I was looking over all the items Mr. Riker gave me yesterday and I'm trying to get a feel for everything. This is going to be new to me, so I hope you and the crew will be patient while I sort things out."

"Absolutely, Carl," Scott said. "We're very happy to have you as a part of our team. The things you've done for this company speak volumes. We know that you'll work hard and make all of our work meaningful."

"That's very nice of you to say, Scott," Carl said. "I'm very appreciative of the opportunity. You said everyone is asleep back there?"

"Mostly everyone, yes," Scott said. "It was a late night last night for all of us. We were all making sure we are good to go today."

"I get that," Carl said. "Scott, we're going to be working really close together, right?"

"To my understanding, yes we are," Scott said. "I'm looking forward to it."

"Can you do me a favor?" Carl asked.

"Sure," Scott replied.

Carl positioned himself out of the view of the cameras in the room. He had noticed them earlier when he and Dalton were down there. He took an index card out of his coat pocket and he gave it to Scott. Scott read the card.

'Don't say another word. Turn off the cameras and disable the listening devices now.'

Scott put the card on the table. He turned and smiled at Carl until he saw Carl was pointing at a gun holstered in the front of his pants. His expression changed just as quickly as he had smiled. Carl held up another index card.

'Don't cause any alarm at all, or else.'

Carl took out the picture of Scott getting in Vanessa's car and held it up.

Scott swallowed hard and scurried to the computer. Carl watched everything he was doing. Carl saw the green lights on the cameras go to red. He saw a screen pop up for sound in the room and watched as Scott muted it. Scott turned to Carl.

"I'm beyond sorry, Carl! I was ordered not to tell you," Scott said. "You have to believe me!"

"I figured as much," Carl said. "I'm not here to hurt you, Scott, but I will if I have to. Know that. We have to work together and we need to be able to trust one another. I'm just looking for answers."

"I was only told to move the car," Scott said. "I didn't even know who she was until after the fact, Carl. I swear."

"Where's the car?" Carl asked.

"I moved it to a place in the desert. Middle of nowhere. I was told to take it there and leave. That's what I did," Scott said. "I didn't know until later it was her car. I promise."

"Scott, I'm not here to ask you about this picture. I'm not here to blame you. Your job consists of doing things for Mr. Riker, no questions asked. I get that; however, we need to have a conversation that stays strictly between us. That's what I'm here for. Are you okay with that?" Carl asked.

"Absolutely, Carl," Scott said. "Anything. I am so sorry; I couldn't tell you."

"Is there any way we can lock that door you just came out of?" Carl asked. "I'd hate for us to be bothered."

"They're all still sleeping, but I can make that happen," Scott said.

Scott went back to the computer and typed in an override to lock the doors.

"How long do we need?" Scott asked.

"Not long at all, Scott," Carl said. "I need to ask you a question, and I'm going to need you to answer me honestly, and in terms I can understand."

"Okay," Scott said. "I can do that."

"Nothing that's said between us will come out of your mouth, or we'll have another conversation that's not so pleasant. You get me?" Carl asked, pointing again to his gun.

"I understand, Carl, loud and clear," Scott said. "Loud and clear."

"I know you do, Scott. I have no doubts at all that you understand," Carl said, as he began to ask Scott about what he needed to know.

Once Carl was finished, it was a little before eight. He couldn't believe he had been talking to Scott for almost an hour. He made his way back to his car and to the Bellagio to pick up Dalton. When he arrived at the casino, Carl made his way into the lobby and saw Dalton across the way getting off the elevator. He met Dalton halfway and shook his hand.

"Today's the day," Dalton said, shaking Carl's hand. "You look different."

"Big day, figured I'd shave," Carl said. "How are you holding up, buddy? How's Katie?"

"I've been better, but I'll make it," Dalton said. "Katie seems fine. Still sleeping. I was careful to be quiet and not wake her."

"Good," Carl said. "Let her rest. We'll bring her with us this evening once we get all the details."

"Sounds good," Dalton said.

Carl put his hand on Dalton's shoulder. He knew Dalton was suffering in silence.

"We're going to make this right, brother," Carl said.

Dalton nodded.

"You ready to do this?" Carl asked.

"Ready as I'll ever be," Dalton said.

Carl and Dalton walked to the car. Before they got in, Carl stopped and motioned for Dalton to come closer to him.

"I figured we would speak before we got in the car. Who knows if it's been bugged again? Remember, we mention nothing now. We hear him out. You explain your reasoning and get what you need to get done to go back," Carl said quietly.

"I'm good to go, it's you I'm worried about," Dalton said.

"Me?" Carl asked.

"You're the one that needs answers. Are you going to be able to sit there and not say anything to that guy?" Dalton asked.

"I'll do my best to keep my tongue bitten," Carl said. "Can't ruin this for Katie, either. She needs answers, too."

"I know you will," Dalton said.

"Dalton, I need to tell you something," Carl said. "Walk over to the fountains with me."

"Okay," Dalton said, following Carl to the fountains in front of the Bellagio. "What's up?"

"I actually went to the office earlier this morning," Carl said.

"Earlier? Why?" Dalton asked.

"I needed to talk to Scott. We had a nice conversation," Carl said.

"Scott knows!" Dalton said. "What the hell, Carl? He's going to tell someone!"

"I'm pretty damn sure he isn't," Carl said. "I need to tell you about our conversation. I thought about keeping it from you, but I think it's important we're on the same page. There's another part to the plan. One I failed to mention last night. We can tell Katie later, because we'll need her help, too."

"Another part of the plan? Jesus Christ! I thought we were just getting answers. What now?" Dalton asked.

Carl spent the next fifteen minutes explaining the final part of his plan to Dalton.

"Carl, I believe this could work," Dalton said. "You sure about this?"

"It will work, and I'm for damn sure," Carl said.

When they were finished discussing all the ins and outs, they walked back to the car and made their way to the final meeting with Jeffrey Riker before the Escapement.

CHAPTER
THIRTY-TWO

AFTER KNOCKING ON his office door, Dalton and Carl were invited in by Mr. Riker, who had a huge grin on his face. They sat down in front of his desk and Mr. Riker took his seat behind it.

"Today is the day, Mr. Mallet," Mr. Riker said. "Today is the day!"

"Yeah, I suppose it is," Dalton said, trying to smile.

"Carl explained your situation to me. I'm sorry beyond measure for your loss," Mr. Riker said.

Dalton simply nodded, trying to hide the hurt on his face. He wasn't doing a good job of it. Carl patted him on his back, letting him know, without words, he was there for him.

"Dalton," Mr. Riker said. "I spoke with Carl last night and he informed me of your decision to go backward in time. Is this still the case?"

"Yes. Yes, sir, it is," Dalton responded.

"In the rhetorical question that I posed, you said you'd like to see the future, but you were split. I'm assuming the deciding factor was the loss of a loved one. You wish to change the past. I am correct in this assumption?" Mr. Riker asked.

"I would say you're absolutely correct in your assumption," Dalton said. "Do you think it can be done?"

"As I said before, I believe in alternate timelines," Mr. Riker said. "I truly believe you can go change a past without changing the present. I do believe you will just change the future of the timeline you find yourself in."

"Is there a chance I won't make it?" Dalton asked. "Be straight up with me here."

Mr. Riker paused, taken aback by his question, and answered as best he could.

"Dalton, we take a chance at everything we do in life," Mr. Riker said. "There's always a possibility with anything we do that something could go wrong. I know we've done everything on our end to make sure there won't be any mistakes."

"Well, either I make it and go save her, or die and be with her," Dalton said. "I can live with my choice."

Dalton stared right into Mr. Riker's eyes and seemed very determined. Carl just sat there, listening.

"Very well," Mr. Riker said. "The next thing we're going to need to know how is far back to send you. We don't need to know right now, but at least an hour before we commence. The only thing we need to do now is get you to the lab and get all your measurements. Height, weight, blood sample, DNA, all of the things that Scott will need to make this process a success."

"Okay," Dalton said. "Can I ask another question?"

"Absolutely," Mr. Riker responded.

"When I go back, will there be two of me? Do I need to avoid my past self, like the movies? How does that work?" Dalton asked.

"Do you want there to be two of you?" Mr. Riker asked.

"Does he have a choice in the matter?" Carl responded.

"From previous trials with animals, we found that you can go back and coexist with your former self. However, if that is not to your liking, we can incorporate a program during the loading stage that allows you to take the place of your former self, so to speak. When you arrive, your other self dissipates into thin air, leaving only you to take over the timeline," Mr. Riker explained. "I think that information is on the files located in your computer, Carl."

"They would have to be," Carl said. "They sure aren't in the briefcase, not from what I've seen, anyway."

"When I go back, I only want one of me around," Dalton said.

"Consider it done," Mr. Riker said. "We'll process that information into the machine right away and when you know how far back in time you want to go; we can get that taken care of as well."

"What about the where?" Carl asked.

"Where?" Dalton asked.

"Ah, yes. The where!" Mr. Riker said. "We need to know exactly where you want to go in time, as well. We know you're from North Carolina, but you can go anywhere. We only need a year, a month, a time, and a location. We learned this and modified our machine after our third subject ended up on the news. The one that appeared out of nowhere on the strip. Remember?"

"I remember you telling me about that yesterday," Dalton said. "I just want to be where Britney is. Not overseas, but before she left. I'll need some time to think of exactly when."

"Hopefully, you'll have it figured out before this afternoon," Mr. Riker said. "For now, let's get down to the lab and get your specifics."

The three of them left Mr. Riker's office and made their way to the lab. When they walked in, it looked almost the exact same as the day before. Everyone was checking and rechecking all the equipment. They all seemed very busy.

"Scott," Mr. Riker said. "Mr. Mallet is here to get his specifics. Let's not keep him here all day, shall we?"

"Yes, sir," Scott said. "Come with me, Mr. Mallet. Right this way." Scott led Dalton through the doorway behind the lab and proceeded to get everything he needed to make the trip a success. This left Carl and Mr. Riker in the lab together.

"This is going to change everything," Mr. Riker said.

"It sure is going to be something," Carl said.

"So, you've had a chance to look over everything in the briefcase, Carl," Mr. Riker said.

"For the most part, yes, I have, sir," Carl said. "I'd like to look over the rest of the files on my computer, though, being it's obvious I missed the entire part with the animals. I started yesterday before Dalton called and I'd love to be up to date on everything before we continue our little time-division out here."

"Let me show you something," Mr. Riker said, leading Carl through the same door Dalton had disappeared behind. Through this door was a hallway. Mr. Riker acted as Carl's guide. The hallway contained several doors before ultimately leading to a dead end.

"There is more than a lab down here," Mr. Riker said. "These five doors here on the left are the sleeping quarters and rooms for the staff housed here. We have an automated cleaning crew as well, totally robotic and revolutionary. They take care of all that stuff down here. Leave it to the engineering division to come up with such a thing."

He opened one of the doors and Carl saw it looked like a hotel room on the inside. There was a living room, bathroom, kitchen and bedroom. It was fully furnished and one of the so-called tiny robots was in full cleaning mode.

"They're all like this. We've had no complaints at all. It's like a home away from home down here," Mr. Riker said.

"I see," Carl said. "This is very nice. The robots themselves would make us a fortune."

"They're already in the process of being produced and marketed, my good man," Mr. Riker said.

"Of course, they are," Carl responded.

"Now, these four doors on the right are a bit different," Mr. Riker said. "The first door there is where subjects go to get ready. That's where Dalton is now. The second door is another small lab. The last door is my office down here. The third door, well, that's your time-lab office."

"No way," Carl said.

"Come on, let me show you," Mr. Riker said.

They walked to the third door and Mr. Riker opened it. It was almost an exact replica of Carl's office upstairs, minus the view.

"I'm at a loss for words," Carl said.

"Everything should be the same as it is upstairs," Mr. Riker said. "Duplicates of your files. Computers are linked. And we're still side by side. How about that?"

"Mr. Riker, this is more than I could have hoped for. Thank you so much," Carl said.

"Again, Carl, thank you," Mr. Riker said. "If you would like to look over the files in your office while Dalton is finishing up, please, don't let me stop you. I'll have Scott come and get you when Dalton is good to go. If you need me, I'll be in the lab, helping out with the last-minute prep work."

"Thank you, sir," Carl said.

Mr. Riker stepped into the room Scott was in to let him know Carl's whereabouts. Carl sat behind his desk and turned on the computer. He entered the same access code and password as his upstairs computer and was led back to his files. He combed through everything until he got to what he wanted to see. Carl didn't have a code like he did yesterday, so he had to maneuver through the multiple files and information until he got to the file on Subject #4.

The file was set up like Katie's brother, a couple of documents and a video. He wanted the video. He moved the mouse over the file and double-clicked.

'Access Denied'

He tried again.

'Access Denied'

He looked for Subject #1 and found it. When he clicked the video, it worked. Same for Subject #3. He had already seen Katie's brother's video. He tried the Subject #4 video one last time.

'Access Denied'

So, the son of bitch not only doesn't tell me about Vanessa, he makes the video unable to be seen.

Carl closed all the files. He was shutting down his computer when Scott and Dalton came through his doorway.

"He's all set," Scott said. "I guess we'll see you two later on?"

"What time do we need to be back, Scott?" Carl asked.

"Check with Mr. Riker before you leave," Scott said. "I'm thinking around three or four, but he'll know for sure."

"Scott," Carl said, "thank you for everything. I truly mean it."

"Thank you, Carl," Scott said as he nodded and walked off.

"How bad was it?" Carl asked Dalton.

"Not too bad. They even gave me a Ninja Turtle band-aid," Dalton said, lifting up his shirt sleeve to show Carl.

"You're a damn child; do you know that?" Carl said, smiling.

"Did you find what you wanted to find?" Dalton asked.

Carl shook his head no but answered just the opposite.

"I looked over what files I could. I'll do some more searching when we come back. Let's get you back to the room so you figure out exactly when you want to go back," Carl said.

Dalton and Carl walked down the hallway and back to the lab. Mr. Riker was waiting.

"Gentleman, it's ten on the dot right now. Let's be back by two, shall we? We will commence the Escapement at three. I can't wait!" Mr. Riker said.

Dalton and Carl thanked Mr. Riker and made their way back to the car. Before they got in, Carl pulled Dalton to the side.

"I don't have access to her files. I can see the rest, but nothing with her," Carl said.

"We figured as much, didn't we?" Dalton asked.

"Yeah, we did, but I was hoping we'd get lucky. I just wanted to make sure," Carl said before they got into the car and drove away.

Once Dalton and Carl were gone, Mr. Riker dialed an extension from the phone next to the computer he was working at. It rang twice and was answered.

"Did he try to access the file?" Mr. Riker asked.

"I told you he would, and he did," a voice on the other end answered.

Mr. Riker hung up the phone and continued to get ready for the Escapement.

CHAPTER
THIRTY-THREE

CARL AND DALTON drove back to the Bellagio. When they exited the car, Dalton explained to Carl how there were multiple bugs inside his room.

"Guess we'll have to talk somewhere else then," Carl said. "We also need to make sure we put them all back before you check out."

They made their way up to Dalton's room and walked in. Dalton's bedroom door was closed shut. He assumed Katie was still sleeping. When they walked in, he pointed to the tape Katie had placed the night before, showing the location of where the bugs should be placed.

"Make yourself a drink if you'd like," Dalton said.

"Don't mind if I do," Carl said.

Carl walked to the bar and grabbed two glasses. He filled them both with water. As he was doing this, Dalton peeked into the bedroom and saw that Katie wasn't there. Instead, there was an index card on top of the box that was on his dresser. He picked it up and read it.

'Went home to shower and change. Come to my place when y'all are ready. No bugs there. We need to talk about this box. Make sure you bring it with you. Katie.'

Below those words were her address. Dalton brought the note to the counter where Carl was standing with the water and laid it down in front of him.

"Smart girl," he mouthed to Dalton, pointing to his temple.

They drank their water.

"Well, Dalton," Carl began. "You have another decision to make.

You've got to decide when and where you want to go. Sky's the limit, my friend."

"Yeah," Dalton said. "What if I screw this up?"

"Screw it up?" Carl asked. "Who do you know that has ever had a way to go back and fix mistakes they made in their lives? You have the ultimate reset button in the form of a time machine. What you do with it is entirely in your hands!"

"That's why I don't want to mess it up," Dalton said. "First man to travel back in time wastes his chance. Not a good headline."

"Who reads the newspaper anymore?" Carl asked. "Forget the headlines. You're going back to change things. Rarest opportunity ever. I'm envious and happy for you at the same time. You, Dalton, you are going to make Mr. Riker, me, hell, our whole department, more famous than we already are. This is a game-changer! No matter what you decide to do, you will be our success story!"

"Thanks, Carl," Dalton said. "When you put it like that, it sounds, well, too good to be true."

"But it's true," Carl said.

"You want to go out for a while, Carl?" Dalton asked. "It's my last day in Las Vegas. Hell, it's my last day here in this timeline, apparently. I'm pretty sure I'll be going back home to North Carolina and changing things while we were both there, so would you like to take me on a proper tour of this town? Make some stops along the way. I at least owe you a proper drink."

"Truer words have never been spoken," Carl said. "Especially if you're buying. I know just the place."

Dalton and Carl put the glasses of water down. Dalton put the index card Katie had left in his pocket and walked back in the bedroom to grab the box. He placed it in his carry-on bag and threw it over his shoulder. They both left the room. It wasn't until they got on the elevator that Dalton spoke again.

"Think whoever was listening bought it, if they even heard it?" Dalton asked.

"Without a doubt," Carl said. "Let's go find Katie and see what she's up to."

"And see what she knows about this damn box," Dalton added.

When Dalton and Carl got into the car, they put Katie's address into his GPS. The car navigated the entire ride there. It was easy to get to, right off the strip. Dalton saw Katie's car in the driveway and they pulled right in behind it. They walked up to the door and rang the doorbell. After a few moments, the door opened and Katie met them with a smile. She had her hair wrapped in a towel. She was wearing a hoodie and some jogging pants, along with a pair of tennis shoes.

"Hey guys, don't judge," Katie said. "I'm going for comfort, not winks and whistles. Come on in."

"Kids these days," Carl said, and walked in. Dalton followed.

Katie's place was small but inviting. She had candles lit and the entire house smelled of apples. Music was playing, and it was loud. She danced her way to the stereo and turned the volume down.

"I like to sing in the shower," Katie said. "Music makes me happy. I had just gotten out and threw on some clothes when I heard your doors shut. I was hoping it was you two. Didn't want to bring out the gun show again."

"Katie," Dalton said. "Why do you always feel the need to break out the armory?"

Katie rolled up the sleeves to her hoodie and flexed an old Hulk Hogan pose in front of Dalton.

"Because I have the right to bear arms, bitch!" Katie said.

Carl began to laugh and Dalton followed. Katie rolled her sleeves back down and snorted. This made her laugh even harder.

"This girl is crazy," Carl said. "But I like her style."

"Thanks, Carl," Katie said, calming down from her laughing fit.

"How'd it go this morning?" she asked.

"Went great," Carl said. "We're all set I believe."

"I need to figure out when and where I am going," Dalton said. "They got all my specs and they're processing them as we speak. We have to be back at two."

"I can do two," Katie said.

"Did you sleep okay last night?" Dalton asked. "We were still expecting you to be there when we got back."

"I slept pretty good," Katie said. "I heard you when you shut the door. I didn't have a change of clothes or else I would've been there. I'm sure the water pressure in your shower is hella better than what I've got here. I got all my stuff and just drove back. I figured you guys would find the note and be here soon enough. Have you two had breakfast?"

"I have, actually," Carl said.

"Well, thanks for bringing me some," Dalton said. "I could eat."

"I could too," Katie said. "I'm in the mood for pancakes."

"I could eat a couple of pancakes," Dalton said.

"Well, shit, kids," Carl said. "Why don't you both hop in the car and daddy will take you out for pancakes. Maybe they'll give you a menu to color on, too!"

Katie smiled and gave Carl the finger. Dalton shook his head.

"Give me five minutes and I'll be all set. We can take my car. I'll drive. I know this great little place down the road. Chris used to take me there when I was little. I'll be right back," Katie said.

She disappeared down the hall and they both heard a hairdryer come on.

"Guess we'll wait for the kid," Carl said.

"She's a good kid," Dalton said.

"That she is, Dalton," Carl said. "She reminds me a lot of Vanessa."

"Really?" Dalton asked.

"Yeah," Carl said, chuckling. "Not afraid of shit. Quick comebacks. Cute smile. Overall good person."

"She seems like she is," Dalton said. "I'm glad we could help her. I'm glad she could help you."

"Me too," Carl said.

"You two aren't waiting on me," Katie said, walking by them. She stopped and looked at them talking to one another. "I'm sorry. Did I ruin a tender moment? Let's go, I'm driving."

Carl put his hand on her head and pushed her to the door. She laughed as she walked out. Dalton followed the both of them, closing the door behind him.

"Katie," Dalton said. "I brought the box with me. You said you wanted to talk about it?"

"Yeah," Katie asked. "How exactly did you and Carl open the drawer?"

"I pressed one of the buttons on the front and he pressed the other one," Dalton answered.

"That's what I thought," Katie said, getting into her car.

They made their way to a little diner down the road. It wasn't even ten minutes from Katie's house.

"That's the place, over to the right. All-day and all-night breakfast," Katie said. "Dalton, bring the box inside and we'll look at it after we eat."

Katie parked the car in the lot and the three of them got out and made their way into the diner. They picked a small booth near the back corner of the place. They seemed to be the only ones there, besides the staff. Dalton sat with Carl and Katie sat across from them. Katie and Dalton both ordered pancakes and juice. Carl just wanted coffee. As they waited on the food, Katie brought up the subject of the box.

"Dalton, do you remember me asking you about the box last night?" Katie asked.

"Not really," Dalton said. "I was pretty much out of sorts."

"And you had every right to be," Carl said as their drinks arrived.

"Well, I asked to mess with it and saw that the drawer was open," Katie said. "I looked inside and saw wires attached to the buttons. This thing was made by someone pretty damn smart. The buttons are actually finger-print sensors. So, if it took you and Carl to open it, someone had to have your prints."

Carl looked at Dalton.

"Who would have our prints?" Carl asked. "Dalton, you don't remember anything from the plane? Nothing at all?"

"I wish I did, Carl," Dalton responded.

"Have you noticed the top? The glass pieces?" Katie asked.

"I saw those when I first looked at it, but I didn't really dive into it," Carl said.

"Do you know what they are?" Dalton asked.

"I have an idea," Katie said, right as the food arrived.

"Why don't you kids eat first. We can talk business later," Carl said.

Not much was said as they ate. Katie and Dalton must have been hungry because they ate it as quickly as they got it. Carl sipped his coffee, enjoying the company.

"Those pancakes were freaking amaze-balls!" Katie said.

"It was all pretty good. Your coffee looked tasty," Dalton said, looking at Carl.

"I told you I'd already eaten breakfast. Coffee is fine. I don't even know how you two tasted it, you ate it so fast." Carl said.

"Breakfast food is the best," Katie said. "No matter what time of day."

"I ate fast because I want to know about this damn box," Dalton said, pulling the box from his bag and placing it on the table.

"Those glass pieces on top, beside the LED's, I think those are fingerprint coded, too," Katie said.

"You sure?" Carl asked.

"Kinda," Katie said. "The weird thing is, it's from a design I made."

"A design you made!" Dalton said. "What in the hell are you talking about, Katie?"

"I'm not just a pretty face, Dalton," Katie said. "I went to school for a few semesters at UNLV. Studied electrical engineering. Really got into the communications part before the money dried up. I didn't want to take out any loans. Learned what I could while I was there. I enjoyed it.

I always experimented with different things, that's how I made the RF device we've been using to find the bugs."

"Well look at you, kid," Carl said. "You should go back. That device worked great. You have a knack for stuff like that it seems."

"If you have an extra eight grand lying around you aren't using, I'd love to," Katie said.

"Eight grand?" Dalton asked.

"Yep," Katie said. "And that's in-state. The out-of-state is ridiculous. I was a few credits short of graduating, but the money ran out, and I needed to go to work. I help out at a mom and pops repair shop. We repair all kinds of electronics. Cell phones mostly. Every now and then a TV or something big, but I like that kind of stuff. I like to figure things out. I'm still saving to go back to school and get my degree, it'll just take a bit longer."

"What about community college?" Carl asked.

"I went after high school," Katie said. "Stayed two years then transferred. No degree acquired, but enough credits to transfer. I fell in love with UNLV. I'm saving up to finish there, and that's where I was working on a project where I came up with this."

Katie took a piece of paper from her back pocket and slid it across the table to Carl. When he opened it, he saw what looked like the actual box sitting in front of them. His and Dalton's mouth dropped open.

"That's the same reaction I had last night," Katie said.

"Katie, this IS your design," Carl said.

"What?" Dalton asked. "Katie, you made that box?"

"No, but I may have designed it," Katie said. "Thing is, I haven't shown anyone this paper. Not until now, at least. Dalton, put your thumb on one of the glass pieces on top. If it doesn't light up, try another."

Dalton placed his thumb on the piece to the top right. Nothing. He tried the top left. Still no luck. When he placed his thumb on the middle piece near the bottom, the light beside it lit up a green color.

"Holy shit," Dalton said. "She's right."

"Carl, your turn," Katie said. "It worked with you helping before, why not try again?"

Carl put his thumb on the top right piece of glass and it lit up green.

"There's one more piece," Carl said.

"Here goes nothing," Katie said.

Katie placed her thumb on the remaining piece of glass and watched it light up green as well. They heard something inside the box start to move, a mechanism of some sort, and the lid to the box cracked open, followed by an array of chimes.

"Son of a bitch," Carl said.

"What the hell is going on?" Dalton asked.

"I don't know," Katie said. "I'm just as freaked out as you are. What's inside?"

Dalton opened the lid to the box. Inside was a vial of liquid and a folded, clasp envelope that had his name written on the outside. Dalton took out the envelope and opened it, finding a letter and pocket watch on the inside. He placed the letter on the table for all of them to read.

Dalton,

You've come so far. Only a little more to go.

Drink the liquid inside the vial and remember me.

Take the pocket watch to the meeting. It belongs to someone else.

When you hear the alarm, save me.

Let Carl know everything will work out.

Tell Katie she can keep the box.

A friend

"Well, that's not weird at all," Katie said.

"Dalton, are you gonna drink that?" Carl asked.

Dalton already had the vial in his hand and was unscrewing the top.

"Bottom's up," Dalton said.

The moment Dalton swallowed, every memory from the plane ride to Las Vegas came flooding back. He remembered Susan. He remembered her giving him the box and telling him she was repaying the favor, whatever that meant. Dalton also remembered Susan vanishing in front of him.

"A woman named Susan gave me this box. She called it an EmGee box, then she disappeared. Vanished into thin air. Told me only people I trusted would be able to help open the box with me. Do you two know anyone named Susan?"

Carl and Katie both shook their heads no.

"Well, she knew of us. Somehow. And I think she's trying to help," Dalton said. "But what does 'when you hear the alarm, save me' mean? She's gone."

"I don't know, man, but we'll take any help we can get," Carl said.

"What do you mean she disappeared?" Katie asked.

"She just vanished," Dalton said. "We drank to knowing each other, and that's when she gave me the stuff that made me forget. I just remember her vanishing. Disappearing, like her body turned clear and she was gone."

"Okay, let's try to sort this shit out back at Katie's place," Carl said.

"Sounds like a plan," Dalton said.

They all three sat in silence for a few moments waiting for the check to arrive. Dalton slid the box to Katie for her to keep. He put the pocket watch in his front pants pocket.

When the bill came, Carl paid their tab in cash and they returned to Katie's car. She drove them back to her place. When they got out, they stood around the car and talked.

"Okay, you two need to get back to the Bellagio and get Dalton squared away. I'm going to stay here and mess with this box. Want to meet back here before we go? Maybe talk about this thing some more?" Katie asked.

"Katie," Carl said. "We want you to come with us, but the plan for today has changed a bit."

"What do you mean, it's changed?" Katie asked.

"There's another part to the plan," Carl said. "We're going to need your help."

"Let's go inside," Katie said. "You can tell me all about it."

Dalton and Carl followed Katie back into her house. They all sat in the living room as Carl explained the final parts of their plan to her. Dalton chimed in when he could, filling in the gaps of anything Carl may have overlooked. When they were finished, they asked Katie how she felt about it.

"Honestly, two o'clock can't get here soon enough!" Katie said.

THIRTY-FOUR

CARL DROVE DALTON back to the Bellagio and Katie followed them in her car. Dalton wanted to pack up his things and get all he needed before the meeting at two.

"I won't be coming back, so I may as well get everything," Dalton said.

They arrived and went inside.

"It's probably best if I stay down here, being there are bugs and all," Katie said. "Don't forget to remove the tape and put them back."

"We won't," Dalton said.

"We'll make sure it's all good, kid," Carl said. "Why don't you stay down here and try to win us some money?"

"With what? My exceptional looks," Katie said, motioning her hand from her head down to her torso like she was bowing.

"You dumbass," Carl said. "Here."

Carl gave Katie two hundred dollars.

"I can't take this," Katie said.

"Keep yourself busy," Carl said. "Have some fun, but don't lose it all."

"I'll just play some nickel slots. I'm not going to lose your money. Well, I'm not going to lose all of it," Katie said. "If you take too long, I'm going to go back to the car inspect that box some more."

"We're going up to the room to get his things. It shouldn't take long. We'll be right back," Carl said.

"Aye, captain," Katie said, saluting Carl.

Carl turned from Katie and walked with Dalton to the elevators.

"Damn kids," Carl said with a smile.

They got in the elevator and made their way to Dalton's room. Carl grabbed the bugs from the bathroom and placed each one back where he saw tape. Once he finished, he removed the tape from the bug locations while Dalton continued to pack his things and straighten the room up a bit. They both knew what they could and couldn't say, so they kept their conversation to a minimum.

"You got everything?" Carl asked.

"Yep. Wanted to look around one last time," Dalton said. "Hell of a place to stay."

"Las Vegas is a hell of a place to be," Carl said.

Dalton walked to the window and looked out over the strip.

"Never in a million years did I think I'd be in this kind of room, not to mention this type of situation," Dalton said.

"No one does," Carl said. "You're lucky, Dalton. You get to go back. You get a do-over. You can right whatever wrongs you feel have been done. No one gets that opportunity. No one. And to be honest, for this to be a shadowing gig, you're a good person. It's been an honor and pleasure getting to know you."

"Likewise, Carl," Dalton said. "Thank you for everything. How 'bout you take me on a tour showing me the rest of this city? Then I can make like a tree, and get out of here."

"It's make like a tree and leave, butt-head," Carl said, laughing.

Dalton grabbed his room key and walked out the door. Carl followed behind him. They took the elevator down to the lobby and went to the desk to checkout.

"Sir," the man behind the counter said. "You're paid up through Friday. Are you sure you'll be checking out?"

"I'll be traveling out of town later today," Dalton said. "My time here is officially up."

"Riker Industries has covered the cost of everything," Carl said. "Do we need to do anything else?"

"No, sir," the man said. "We hope you enjoyed your stay."

"I did," Dalton said. "This place is amazing."

"Thank you, sir," the man said.

Dalton and Carl moved away from the desk and walked toward the casino.

"Now where is that little spitfire with my money?" Carl said.

"Over there," Dalton said. "Sitting at the slots with some big ass sunglasses on."

They walked over to Katie.

"How's it going, slick?" Carl asked.

"It's going," Katie said. "I bought these cute sunglasses after you left and got an Icee. Now I'm sitting here pissing away the rest of your cash."

"Well, how much do I have left? Or should I even ask?" Carl said.

"How dare you doubt me, old man!" Katie said, handing him back a wad of cash.

Carl counted it.

"Katie, this is over four hundred dollars! Did you rob someone?" Carl asked.

"Did I rob someone? Dammit, Carl! No, I didn't rob anyone. I sat down at the machine over there and won eighty dollars right after you two went upstairs. Then I went to the next slot and won over a hundred. I walked to a shop and got these cute sunglasses next, then I saw an Icee machine. I haven't had an Icee in forever, so I bought one. I just put a twenty in this one, but it hasn't paid out yet," Katie said.

"Damn, kid," Carl said. "I need to let you gamble for me from now on."

"Just lucky," Katie said. "I usually lose it all."

"Well, you didn't today. You ready, spark plug?" Carl asked.

"Where are we going? It's only twelve," Katie said.

"Dalton wants to see a little bit of the town, but not on foot. Promised him I'd show him around," Carl said. "Plus, you can play with that box while we go. I'll bring you back here to get your car."

"Sounds good to me! Let's ride, Clyde. Shotgun!" Katie said, bouncing up and following them out.

Carl drove them down the strip. Dalton took in all the sites while he sat in the back seat. Katie kept turning the radio stations, singing, and turning the box every which way. Carl continued to drive. When they made it to the 'Welcome to Fabulous Las Vegas Nevada' sign, Katie told Carl to pull over. Carl did and they got out.

"I want a picture!" Katie said.

"A picture?" Carl asked. "I don't like pictures."

"I don't care what you like!" Katie said. "Sir! Sir! Could you take our picture?"

A random guy in the crowd around the sign smiled and let Katie know he would. She handed him her phone. Katie grabbed their shirts and pulled Carl and Dalton with her in front of the sign.

"Now, act like you're happy and smile," Katie said.

"Okay," the guy with Katie's phone said. "Say cheese!"

"Bitch tits!" Katie said.

Carl and Dalton both laughed and the guy took the picture. Katie started laughing and ran to get her phone from the guy.

"Walgreens, now!" Katie said, running back to the car.

"I guess we're going to Walgreens," Dalton said. "Do you even know where a Walgreens is?"

"Yeah," Carl said, shaking his head. "Come on."

When they arrived at Walgreens, Katie quickly jumped out and ran inside. Carl looked in the backseat at Dalton.

"Guess when you got to go, you got to go," Carl said.

Dalton laughed and they exited the car. When they walked into Walgreens, they saw Katie sitting at the photo counter.

"Whatcha' doing, kid?" Carl asked.

"Give me five minutes and I'll show you," Katie said.

"We'll be in the car. Hurry up," Carl said.

Carl and Dalton walked back to the car and got in. Dalton sat up front. He placed the box in the backseat.

"You think she can handle this?" Dalton asked.

"I have no doubts about her at all," Carl said.

Katie skipped out of Walgreens and up to the passenger side door. She saw Dalton sitting there and pointed at him with a mean look on her face. She quickly started laughing and jumped in the back.

"This is for you," Katie said, handing Dalton a picture. "To remember me when you go back. If you have time, come show me the picture. I'll freak out at first, but hopefully, I'll warm up to you."

Dalton looked at the picture she handed him. It was them at the 'Welcome to Las Vegas' sign. He smiled and put it in his coat pocket.

"Thank you, Katie," Dalton said.

"Got one for you too, Carl," Katie said, handing him a picture. "Thank you again. For everything."

"Thank you, kid," Carl said. "Traffic is picking up. Let's go back to the Bellagio. We can go over everything again before the meeting. One more time at the fountains."

Carl drove them back to the Bellagio. They exited the car and discussed the plan again while looking at the fountains. Katie made sure to bring the box with her.

"I'm going to miss this place," Dalton said.

"You ready?" Carl asked. "It's about that time."

"Guys, wait!" Katie said.

"What is it, Katie?" Carl asked.

"I'm a little freaked out right now. Look!" Katie said, pointing to the box.

The box was upside down and Katie had removed a plate from the bottom of it, revealing three handwritten letters.

"K-S-W. Is that supposed to mean something?" Dalton asked.

"Everything I work on, hell, everything I do, I always leave an imprint. Something small. Something hard to find. I always handwrite my initials and cover them up. Those are my initials, Dalton," Katie said.

"What's your full name, Katie?" Carl asked.

"Kaitlyn Suzanne Williams," Katie said. "Guys...why are my initials on this box?"

THIRTY-FIVE

C ARL SLAPPED DALTON on the arm.

"Suzanne. Susan. What if they are one in the same?" Carl asked.

"But she was much older, Carl," Dalton said.

"I'm Katie," Katie stated. "I've never liked my middle name and I damn sure wouldn't go by Susan, unless..."

"Unless what?" Dalton asked.

"When I was little, I used the name Susan to prank call people," Katie said. "Still me, but not me. But how is this possible?"

"How's any of this possible?" Dalton asked.

"Okay, let's not get ahead of ourselves," Carl said. "A lot is happening all at once."

"Guys, I can't be Susan, can I?" Katie asked. "I didn't win the contest."

"Susan used a different thing to travel, Katie," Dalton said. "Maybe you come up with it later, who the hell knows?"

"This is wild," Katie said. "Let's state facts. I made this box, there's no doubt about that. Someone gave it to you. Could be me, might not be. No real way of knowing. How do we find out for sure?"

"We don't," Carl said.

"We don't?" Dalton asked.

"Nope, we don't," Carl answered. "We now have to trust what was in the box. If Katie made it, and I believe she did, it was for us. Everything in it was meant to help us in some way. The watch. The pocket watch. The letter. All of it. All in due time. Time is closing in on us right now, and all we can do is trust it and move forward with what we've got."

"He's right," Katie said. "I don't complete custom work for just anyone. I know that about myself. It was either for me or someone I trusted."

"The letter said when I hear the alarm, save me," Dalton said. "Am I supposed to save Katie?"

"I don't know if you are or not, but I'm staying close to you, just in case," Katie said.

"It's getting close to time. Are we ready?" Carl asked.

Dalton and Katie nodded their heads.

"Time for answers," Carl said.

Carl and Dalton walked back to the car. Katie got in her car and followed them to Riker Industries. There was no turning back now. As they approached the security gate, Carl lowered his window.

"Well, look who it is," Carl said. "How's it going, Larry?"

"Same ol', same ol'," Larry said.

"Larry, the woman in the car behind me is actually going to be my intern," Carl said.

"Intern? Are we doing that shit again? No one tells me anything!" Larry said.

"Hell, I just found out about it myself. UNLV is doing something with their engineering department. Got the email this morning after I left and was told she was coming today. Met her for lunch and told her to follow me here," Carl said.

"Well," Larry said. "I guess as long as she has her student ID with her, we'll be good to go."

"You're all about some damn badges," Carl said.

Dalton shot Katie a quick text informing her to have her student ID from UNLV ready. He looked in the side-view mirror and saw her shuffling around her car. Carl looked in the rear-view and saw her give him a thumbs up.

"Do I need to pull over to the side and wait for her?" Carl asked.

"Yeah, probably so," Larry said. "I'm going to issue her a temporary pass for today until you can get me all the paperwork."

"Sounds good, Larry. Thanks." Carl said, pulling off.

He saw Katie pull up to Larry smiling. She showed him her old student ID and Larry started filling out a temporary pass for her.

"We're lucky she had that ID," Dalton said.

"I figured she would've had it in there somewhere. If not, we would've gone back and got it. I'll take it as a win," Carl said.

Larry waved her on and Carl got back on the road. Katie followed them to the parking lot. They all got out and stood around their cars.

"Are we ready?" Carl asked.

"I am, no turning back now," Katie said, tapping her purse.

"Here goes nothing," Dalton said.

They walked into the building and got in the elevator. Carl used his key and they proceeded to the lab underneath.

"What do we do if Riker's in the lab?" Katie asked.

"We handle it," Carl said.

The doors opened to the set of bigger doors. Carl used the password and the doors opened. They walked through them. Scott met Carl as he came through. Carl held up a note asking Scott to turn the bugs off if there were any. Scott obliged.

"Where is he?" Carl asked.

"He's in his office," Scott said. "Who's that?"

"She's a friend," Carl said. "He up top or down the hall?"

Scott pointed up.

"Scott, I can't thank you enough for this morning," Carl said.

"I feel like I owe you more than that, considering the circumstances," Scott said.

"Okay," Carl said. "Well, call him down here and we'll be even."

"Will do. Want us to wait in our rooms?" Scott asked.

"Yeah, that may be for the best. I'll tell him I asked you all to go research something while we spoke. I'm sure if we need you, you'll know," Carl said, pointing at the camera.

"I already programmed the cameras to come through the monitors in my room, just in case," Scott said.

Scott walked to a monitor behind the machine and grabbed the phone he used to communicate with Mr. Riker.

"Mr. Riker."

"Yes, Scott."

"Dalton and Carl are here."

"Time has gotten the better of me, Scott. I'll be right down."

"I'll be in my room. I need to finish up some last-minute tests. The others are resting until go time."

"Sounds good, Scott. Headed that way."

"Ten-four."

"He's on the way," Scott said. "Good luck."

"Thanks, Scott," Carl said.

Scott walked through the door in the lab and went in his room.

"Is that the machine?" Katie asked.

"Yep," Dalton said. "That's it."

"And this is where you want me to hide?" Katie asked.

"For now," Carl said. "Don't worry, it's not ready yet. We'll leave the door open. You can fit behind it."

Katie went inside and squeezed behind the door. Carl and Dalton stood in front and let her know when they couldn't see her. They heard the elevator ding on the outside.

"He's here," Dalton said.

"Yeah, the son of a bitch is here," Carl said. "Time for answers."

The doors opened and Mr. Riker walked through.

"Gentleman!" Mr. Riker said, clapping his hands together. "The time is finally here! I'm excited, Mr. Mallet, how about you?"

"Yes, sir," Dalton said. "I just want to thank you for the opportunity."

"I want to thank you for making us more famous than we already are," Mr. Riker said. "After this is over, everything changes."

"Yes," Dalton said. "Everything will change."

"Scott got you all squared away this morning, so let's attend to the formalities. We'll attach the beacon to your wrist. It's like a watch. Actually, it serves as a watch as well as allowing us to see if you make it there okay. We can then track you from there if we need to. It will be used to show our success once the media gets wind of this. Also, make sure your eyes stay closed. We can blindfold you if need be," Mr. Riker said.

"Okay, those sound doable," Dalton said.

"Of course, they are," Mr. Riker said. "Now, where, and when, are we going?"

"About that," Dalton said. "I think we may need to sit down for this."

Carl rolled two chairs over. Mr. Riker took one and Dalton took the other. Carl went back and got himself a chair.

"Well, now that we're comfy, where and when are we headed?" Mr. Riker asked.

"I don't know yet," Dalton said.

"We need to know that information in order for this to work, Mr. Mallet," Mr. Riker said.

"Well, I feel certain I'll know once this conversation is over," Dalton said. "Carl?"

"Mr. Riker, can I ask you a question?" Carl asked.

"Absolutely, Carl," Mr. Riker said. "What's going on?"

"Mr. Riker," Carl began. "I was going through some of the footage in my research and I found I don't have any access to the files, folders and movies from Subject #4. Why is this?"

Mr. Riker sat back in his chair. His entire expression changed.

"I think you're already aware as to why," Mr. Riker said.

"She's been gone for three months," Carl said. "Three fucking months. And you knew. YOU SON OF A BITCH, YOU KNEW!"

"Yes, Carl, I did," Mr. Riker said.

"Why did you hide this from me? Why all the secrecy? Why did you let her do this?" Carl asked.

"Do you really want to know?" Mr. Riker asked. "Once we go down this road, there is no return trip."

"I think it would be best if I knew," Carl said. "You owe me that much."

"So be it," Mr. Riker said. "Vanessa appeared one night three months ago, visibly upset. We've always been close, all of us. You know this. She came to me, Carl. She told me about the fighting. She told me about the drinking. She wanted to try again, you know, for a child, but you didn't."

"We tried so hard, for so long," Carl said. "When she almost died, I didn't want a repeat of that shit. I'd rather have her than nothing at all!"

"You two just couldn't agree. You both wanted kids, and unfortunately, after so long of trying and finally getting pregnant, the scare happened and you all of sudden didn't anymore. She still did. She couldn't take the fights. She wanted to find the old Carl. The one that understood her. The one that she remembered wanting the same things. I gave her that opportunity. I explained the risk. It's what she wanted," Mr. Riker said.

"And you let me go on believing she just left?" Carl asked.

"That's what she wanted. She wanted you to get over it and move on. She still loved you, Carl. But she loved the old you. Not the one torn down by life and all its shit. She just wanted you back. So, she went to find you," Mr. Riker said.

"Where did she go? When?" Carl asked.

"Not too far. One year into the past, Carl. Right before she got pregnant. Do you remember those days? You came to work so excited. You thought it would never happen. Neither did the doctors, especially after trying for so long. Then she did. You were so happy," Mr. Riker said.

"I remember the exact day. I remember it well. I also remember when she went into labor too early and our kid was born and died on the same damned day. I almost lost her. I remember that day pretty goddamn well too!" Carl said.

"We all do. Something like that changes people, Carl. It changed you. And you know it did. Vanessa did too. She had all she could take. The decision for her was easy. She didn't want anyone else. She just wanted the old you. Like you, Mr. Mallet, she decided that her former self would dissipate as she arrived, so there wouldn't be two of her fighting over ol' Carl here," Mr. Riker said.

"What about Chris Williams?" Katie said, coming out from behind the door. "I was never told about Chris or compensated, even though you told them the families were. Why?"

Mr. Riker spun around in his chair.

"Hello, Katie," Mr. Riker said. "Nice of you to join us as well."

"How do you know who I am?" Katie asked.

"You'll find out soon enough," Mr. Riker said. "Chris received all the money upfront. He got drunk and lost it in one night at the casino. He wanted to go back and stop himself from blowing all the money. He wanted you to have it. An accident happened that he signed a waiver for. I'm sure he wouldn't have wanted you to know what happened to him or the money."

"That wasn't your decision to make!" Katie said.

"Hindsight is always 20/20, and I've made many mistakes. I live with them just like we all do," Mr. Riker said. "Is there anything else, from the whole of the group?"

"How do you know who I am?" Katie asked.

"I was getting to that," Mr. Riker said. "Carl? Dalton? Anything else?"

Dalton and Carl looked at each other. Carl had tears in his eyes. They both shook their heads no.

"Well, then, I shall attempt to answer your question, Ms. Williams," Mr. Riker said. "But first, may I ask all three of you a question?"

"Why not?" Carl asked.

"Do you know what happens to me in a year?" Mr. Riker asked.

The three of them looked at each other confused.

"How does this even remotely relate to how you know me?" Katie asked.

"You know, a year from now I'll disappear. I'm not sure if the time project or anything I do keeps going. I vanish out of thin air one hot, summer day, never to be seen again," Mr. Riker said as the door that led to the hall-way opened.

They all three turned to the sound of the door opening and saw a figure walk through.

"No way!" Katie said. "Absolutely no fucking way! Are you guys seeing this shit?"

"Seeing, yes. Believing, not so much," Dalton said, standing up and covering his mouth with his hand.

Carl stood up in shock.

"How is this happening? What is this? It can't be!" Carl said.

"Of course, it can, Carl," the figure said, coming into view. "I built the damn thing, why couldn't I use it?"

An older, sneering Jeffrey Riker walked right past the three of them and pulled up a chair next to his younger self.

"Now sit down, let's talk," the older Riker said.

Dalton, Carl, and Katie looked at each other in horror as they sat back down, waiting to hear what he had to say.

CHAPTER
THIRTY-SIX

"**B**EFORE I START, does this photo look familiar to any of you?" the older Riker asked, handing Carl a photograph.

Carl took the photograph, still in disbelief of what he was witnessing.

"No way!" Carl said. "No. Damn. Way!"

He showed the photo to Dalton and Katie, each of whom couldn't believe their eyes. The photo they were holding was the exact one they had taken earlier, except this picture was older, creased, and had stains that looked like blood spatter on it.

"How?" was the only word Carl could get out.

"Let me try to explain. You see, ten years ago I was sitting right here in front of you three. Alone. You asked the same exact questions you just finished asking and I answered them the same way. Apparently, the young lady to your left, Katie, decided she didn't like my answers and drew a gun on me, which I will be taking now," the older Riker said.

The older Jeffrey Riker extended his hand. Katie pulled the gun out of her purse and gave it to him. He then unbuttoned his shirt enough to show her a bullet wound scar on his left shoulder.

"This was a token of your appreciation, young lady," the older Riker said. "Once I was shot, Dalton and Katie, you decided to destroy the machine. Carl disagreed. He wanted his wife back. You tried to talk him out of it, but he drew his gun on both of you, which I'll be taking now also, Mr. Gilbert."

Carl took out his gun and placed it on the floor. He kicked it over to the other side of the room. The older Mr. Riker continued.

"Once you drew your gun, they backed off. When you got into the machine, something went wrong. I'm not sure what happened, but I have a theory it was something with the DNA not matching. Nevertheless, it was tragic. You died in the machine. I was still lying down, bleeding from my wound, but Dalton and Katie vowed no one would be traveling through time again and proceeded to destroy my machine. All the blood, sweat, tears, and work we had put into it, was destroyed in a matter of minutes. You two pulled Carl out and went to town on my equipment and this lab. You tore up everything and left me for dead here on this very floor. Scott finally came out of his room and helped me. You see, Katie actually hid in Carl's office last time and found a way to lock all the doors so my technicians couldn't get out. Scott found a way out and saved my life. He stopped the bleeding and got me the medical attention I so desperately needed. We buried your body, Carl, and I saved this picture, knowing I would go back to avert this travesty. My lifelong dream, gone. We were able to piece what was left of the machine back together in order to use it one last time. It took about a year. The time circuits were badly damaged and locked on traveling ten years to the past. The day I disappeared from my reality, I ended up here. I immediately went to my former self, because I knew I could be beneficial to the building of the time machine. This time, there would be no mistakes. I allowed time to work like it always had, with only a few changes, no course correction. Just let it play out like it had before, but I would be ready this time. And I do believe we were."

"I wasn't going to shoot you!" Katie said.

"Then why bring the gun?" the younger Riker asked.

"I caused the course of time to change by being here. Nothing that happened before will happen again. I know this is a parallel reality, which is why I told my younger self to explain that to you this time. Some events have happened that didn't happen on my original timeline, so you may not have shot me this time, Katie. But I couldn't take that chance. I also didn't have the option to remove my former self, so here we are, the both of us," the older Riker said.

"So, what now?" Carl asked.

"The original plan," the younger Riker said.

"Wait, what original plan?" Dalton asked, reaching in his pocket.

"What I wanted to happen in the first place," the older Riker said. "Mr. Mallet, you will be traveling to the past to save your girlfriend, since she is dead this time."

"This time?" Dalton asked.

"Previously, before you destroyed my machine, you wanted to go to the future," the older Riker said. "We just couldn't take that chance this time, so we made sure you would want to go back."

"What are you saying?" Dalton said, his face turning red and fists balling up.

"You know damn well what I'm saying," the older Riker said. "We have connections all over the world. Getting to her was easier than we thought."

Dalton went to jump out of his seat and Carl caught him. It was everything Carl could do to hold him back. The older Jeffrey Riker held up Katie's gun at him.

"Sit down or get shot, Mr. Mallet," the older Riker said. "Your choice!"

"You son of a bitch, I'll kill you!" Dalton said. "I'll kill you!"

"Not today, you won't," the older Riker said.

Carl wrestled Dalton back to the seat in the middle of him and Katie. Katie had her hand over her mouth and began to tear up. In the middle of the fiasco, the pocket watch that Dalton had fallen to the floor.

"Where did that come from?" the older Riker asked. "Where did you get that?"

"What's it to you?" Dalton asked, fists clenched. Carl still had an arm over him.

The older Jeffrey Riker bent down to pick up the pocket watch and stared at it in disbelief.

"This is mine," the older Riker said. "This is my old pocket watch that went missing shortly after she shot me. Where did you get this from?"

"He pulled it out of his ass," Carl said. "Why does it fucking matter, you've got it back. I hope the hell you're happy. Now, what about this plan of yours?"

"As I was saying before I was so rudely interrupted, Mr. Mallet will be traveling to the past. Carl, you will run the time division with us and we will bring Vanessa back. Katie, well, you're what they call a loose end."

"A loose end?" Katie asked.

"Now, wait a minute," Carl said.

"No more waiting," the younger Riker said. "He said what he said. She's a loose end and was shown confidential information that could potentially ruin our company."

The older Riker lifted up the gun and pointed it at Katie. When he did, the watch Dalton was wearing from the EmGee box let out a loud ringing noise. *The alarm!* Dalton thought. He immediately jumped from his chair to shield Katie.

When the older Riker pulled the trigger, the pocket watch emitted an electric shock that brought him to his knees and botched his aim.

Katie fell out of her chair and onto the floor, face down, with Dalton on top of her. Blood came flowing from under her body. Carl yelled.

"You son of a bitch!" Carl said. He went to charge at the older Mr. Riker, but he turned his gun to Carl.

"You really don't want to do that! Whose idea was this?" the older Riker said, reaching in his pocket and grabbing the pocket watch, throwing it across the room, shattering it.

Carl's fists were balled up tight. Tears came to his eyes but did not fall. Anger and hate coursed through his veins. He stood there, knowing if he moved, he would be shot next.

"She was a loose end, Carl. She shouldn't have been here. Her blood is on your hands, not mine," the younger Riker said.

"Why?" Dalton asked. He stood up and walked over towards Carl with his hands up. "Carl, she's..."

"I know, Dalton," Carl said.

Dalton put his arm on Carl's shoulder and leaned into him. He grabbed the back of Carl's neck and pulled him closer to his head.

"She's alive," he whispered.

Two loud gun blasts rang out. Dalton jumped away from Carl and they both saw the older Riker on his knees, bleeding from a bullet hole in the chest and another in the head. The younger Riker screamed.

"NOOOOOOOOOOO!"

"When you pull a gun on someone, you better shoot to kill, you son of a bitch!" Katie said.

When Dalton had gone to the floor to check on Katie, she whispered to him about the other gun in her purse. Dalton moved her purse closer to her before getting up to let Carl know she was alive. While the Riker's attention was turned to Dalton and Carl, Katie took her shot and made it count.

Dalton jumped back over to Katie. Carl grabbed the gun that the older Riker dropped on the floor upon being shot.

"Are you okay?" Dalton said.

"He shot me in the arm. Grazed my shoulder. You jumped just in time. I'm fine. He's not," Katie said.

The younger Riker was kneeling in front of the older Riker.

"What have you done?" the younger Riker asked.

"Apparently, what I should have done in my other timeline," Katie said.

Dalton helped Katie to her feet and she gave Carl her gun. Carl pulled her to him and hugged her.

"Glad you are okay, kid," Carl said. "Guess that was you that gave Dalt that box with all the timepieces."

"Is everyone okay," Scott said, running into the room. "Everyone else is still in their rooms because they heard gunshots. Is everyone okay?"

"Do I look okay?" Katie asked.

"Oh, my heavens, you've been shot. She's been shot!" Scott said. "We'll get that taken care of as soon as possible."

"I can't believe this. I've done everything for both of you!" Mr. Riker said.

"You have," Carl said. "Including making my wife disappear. I should shoot you right now, just for that. But the killing is over."

He continued to hold the gun on Mr. Riker.

"I'll be going back with Dalton to get my wife," Carl said.

"You can't," Mr. Riker said. "That machine will not work with two people. We don't even have everything you need to go with him."

"Yeah, we do. Scott took care of that early this morning. After we're gone, go public. Do what you want, I really don't give a shit. I want you to know that the files you gave me will be sent to every major news outlet this side of Las Vegas, and all those people that died, that blood is on your hands," Carl said. "Unless..."

"Are you blackmailing me now?" Mr. Riker asked.

"Katie needs some cash. I think about a hundred thousand should do it. She needs to finish school. You're also going to cover her medical expenses for life," Carl said.

"I didn't shoot her!" Mr. Riker said.

"The older you did!" Carl said. "One in the same to me, asshole. Either this is all revealed or you can keep it quiet by paying her out, your choice."

Carl led Mr. Riker to his office, still holding the gun on him, and watched as he opened a safe behind the desk. Mr. Riker took out a large sum of cash and placed it on top of the desk.

"That should do it," Carl said. "You're doing the right thing."

Mr. Riker closed his safe, not saying a word. Carl placed the money in a small duffel bag, led Mr. Riker back to the main lab, and gave Katie the bag. Katie opened the bag and began to cry.

"Carl, this is way too much," Katie said. "I can't accept this."

"Go finish school, make something of yourself in this world," Carl said. "Take this zip drive with you. All the files that were on my computer were copied to it this morning. If anything happens while we're gone, anything at all, make this shit go public. Get out of here and don't look back kiddo."

"Carl, I don't even know what to say," Katie said. "I am going to miss both of you so much."

Katie hugged Carl first.

"Thank you for being honest with me about my brother," Katie said. "Thank you for all of this. I can never repay you, not in a million years. I love you, Carl."

"I love you too, kid. Now get out of here," Carl said. "Dalton and I have somewhere to be."

Katie picked up the bag and walked over to Dalton. She hugged him tightly.

"You're like the brother I never wanted," Katie said, smiling. "Thank you for everything. Thank you for saving my life back there. I love you, Dalton."

"You saved our lives, Katie," Dalton said. "Just not yet. Go back to school and get smarter so you can tell me how the hell you did it. Love you too, Katie. Susan. Whoever the hell you are."

Katie laughed and wiped the tears from her eyes.

"Scott, can someone escort her out and get her some medical attention?" Carl asked.

"I'll handle it, Carl," Scott said. "I'll make sure she's well taken care of. I promise."

Scott went back down the hallway and came back with a technician. He explained the situation to her and she walked over toward Katie, checking on her. Carl extended his hand and shook Scott's, thanking him one last time. Katie picked up her bag and walked toward the elevator with the technician, making sure she turned around and flipped the bird to Mr. Riker on the way out. Once Carl heard the elevator move, he looked toward Dalton.

"You ready to go?" Carl asked.

"Yeah," Dalton said. "I'm ready."

"Scott, you remember what to do when we leave, right?" Carl asked.

"Yes, sir, but I really don't want to," Scott said. "We spent so much time on this."

"You promised me this last thing," Carl said.

"I know I did, Carl, and I'm a man of my word. Once you two are gone, this machine will not exist anymore," Scott said.

"You can't do that!" Mr. Riker said.

"He can," Carl said, pointing the gun at Mr. Riker, "And dammit, he will."

THIRTY-SEVEN

D ALTON WALKED INTO the machine first. He stood over to the side as the technicians checked everything out. Once he was good to go, they asked if he wanted a blindfold and he said yes. Carl confirmed with Scott when and where they were going.

"Are you sure, Carl?" Scott asked.

"I want to be there when she arrives. Dalton is okay with it. Get us there so I can be with my wife. Once she's safe, we'll be working on Dalton's situation," Carl said.

"You got it, Carl," Scott said.

Carl tried to give his gun to Scott.

"Make sure he doesn't do anything stupid," Carl said, pointing at Mr. Riker, who was sitting on the floor, hands tied.

"I don't like guns," Scott said.

Carl laid the gun on the table beside him.

"Hopefully, you won't have to use it," Carl said.

Carl walked to the machine with Dalton. One of the technicians performed their last-minute checks and gave Dalton and Carl their beacons. They placed them on their wrists and gave the technicians the thumbs up. Dalton put his blindfold on. Carl decided to keep his eyes open until he had to shut them.

"Here we go, buddy," Carl said as the doors closed.

The countdown started at 60 seconds and counted backward. Several technicians hit some switches and pushed some buttons before walking back behind the door. The countdown reached 50. Carl was staring at the screen letting Dalton know what was going on for as long as he could.

Once the countdown reached 40, Scott led Mr. Riker out of the room. He then turned to close the door behind them.

30 seconds.

Inside the machine, the warning came for their eyes to be closed. Carl told Dalton they were thirty seconds away and he closed his eyes. All the lights in the lab and in the machine began to blink. Slow at first, then faster every five seconds.

20 seconds.

"Hold on tight Dalton. Getting close now," Carl said.

10 seconds.

5 seconds.

A computer voice said, "Countdown complete. Escapement successful."

Scott opened the door and walked back to the computer. He looked at the screen and saw two beacons blinking.

"It worked!" Scott said. "Mr. Riker it…"

Scott was stopped from speaking by a lead pipe across the face. The gun on the desk dropped to the floor. Mr. Riker grabbed Scott by the collar and pulled him up.

"I will not let you destroy my creation!" Mr. Riker said. He took the gun from the floor and pointed it towards the door.

"All of you better get in your rooms, or I'll make you disappear too!" Mr. Riker said.

The technicians ran to their rooms as fast as they could and Mr. Riker used the computer to lock them in. He squatted beside Scott.

"Now where, oh where, did you send Katie off to?" he asked.

Scott did the best he could to get some words out to Mr. Riker.

"Oh, it doesn't matter. Thank you anyway, Scott. You've been a model employee, but you sure can't tie a knot worth a shit. Before I leave, I just want to let you know that I played with the time circuits today as a last resort fail-safe on my end. You didn't send them where you think you did. Let's hope they're still alive by the time I get to them," Mr. Riker said, grabbing the gun and shooting Scott in the head.

"Your turn, for now, Ms. Katie Williams," Mr. Riker said aloud, looking at the blinking signal from the beacons on the monitor. "And after I find you, I'll go find Carl and Mr. Mallet. Enjoy the trip while you can, gentleman. I'll be seeing you soon."

Mr. Riker walked to the elevator and made his way up and out of the lab.

EPILOGUE

CARL OPENED HIS eyes. He had heard the countdown go to one and then nothing. It was as if he had an out-of-body experience. He was laying down on the ground in some tall grass. Dalton was on the ground next to him, still blindfolded, in the fetal position. He looked around and saw nothing but trees.

"Dalton, you awake?" Carl asked.

"Yeah. Did we do it?" Dalton asked. "Did it work?"

"Well," Carl said. "We're not in the lab anymore and you're lying next to a giant pile of shit. I'd say it worked."

Dalton took off his blindfold and looked around.

"Does any of this look familiar?" Dalton asked.

"Not at all," Carl said. "Something isn't right."

"What do you mean, something isn't right?" Dalton asked.

"We're supposed to be in my neighborhood. We're supposed to arrive at the same time as Vanessa in the same location. Scott said she went to our neighborhood," Carl said.

"Where are we, Carl?" Dalton asked.

"I have no idea," Carl said. "What's that noise?"

"Sounds like water?" Dalton said.

Carl helped Dalton to his feet and they walked as far as they could. They stared out over the vast amount of water in front of them. They were surrounded by nothing but water. Waves were crashing hard upon the shore. The sun was beginning to go down.

"Carl," Dalton said. "Did you happen to see any houses as we were walking?"

"Not a one," Carl said. "And that's a shitload of water."

"Carl," Dalton said. "Where are we?"

"I don't know, kid," Carl said. "But we're damn sure going to find out."

TO BE CONTINUED...

ACKNOWLEDGEMENTS

W RITING A BOOK is hard, especially when you are a number's person. To me, numbers have always made sense, but words, not so much. However, I've always loved good stories and crazy ideas, so why not give it a shot? If anyone decides to read it, I hope you enjoy reading it as much as I did writing it. This sure wouldn't have been possible without the help of some really good people.

Big thanks go to my Pops! We've been through quite a bit together and I can't thank you enough for everything. I know this book's not your style, but I promise to write a western at some point! Love ya, Pops!

Thank you to Kasey and Kyle, my sister...and brother from another mother.

From my sister's initial shock when she found out I wrote something to her support for the finished product, I couldn't be more appreciative. I love you, Seester!

Kyle. AKA Brochacho. AKA BIL. Thank you for being the brother I never had. Love ya, big homie!

Molly Grace and Klint, my favorite two people in the world!

MG, thank you for asking questions, playing games and kicking my butt at Uno to get my mind off the book. You are my little buddy for life. Love you, Monkey Butt!

Klint, you madman! Thank you for keeping me on my toes not hurting me too bad in your dojo. Love you, Ninja!

Skull, Cousin Nikki, Sherrill, and Lockard—Thank you all so much for taking the time to read and offer me feedback on this thing. I appreciate all of you and hope you like the final version as much as you did the initial one. Skull, we have some sequels to work on!

P.J. Hoover—Thank you for the developmental edit, the time you spent with my work and the suggestions you offered to help make my book that much better! You are awesome and I appreciate all of your ideas and questions that made me go back and change things for the better. Live Long and Prosper!

Thea Magerand—Thank you for a kick ass book cover! You took the idea in my head and brought it to life. You are extremely talented and have the monopoly on all of my covers from here out.

Phillip Gessert—The man with the plan. You took something that gave me a headache and made it work with no issues. Thank you for making my text look like a book. You are a Righteous Dude!

Last, but never least, I want to thank my Mom. I miss you every day. You were with me every step of the way while I was figuring this thing out. I hope you liked how it turned out. This book was for you. I love you, mama...always.